Taken

Alex pressed a hand to his stomach, and blood flowed over
it. Black spots swam before his eyes as the battle raged
around his home.

Lindsay. Where was Lindsay? He called out her name,
feet splayed for balance, one hand pressed to his belly in a
futile attempt to stop the bleeding.

Then, as suddenly as they had assaulted, the *Tuatha Dé
Danann* knights turned and made their retreat, leaving the
mangled MacNeil knights behind. A few of Alex's men
followed, but they were not mounted and were discouraged
when the trailing enemy knights turned to address them.
Finally, the faeries made their retreat and disappeared into
the forest beyond.

For Alex, the world tilted and darkened, and he went to
one knee. A roaring filled his head. Once again he called
Lindsay's name and had no reply. Then there was nothing
at all.

Ace titles by Julianne Lee

KNIGHT TENEBRAE
KNIGHT'S BLOOD
KNIGHT'S LADY

Knight's Lady

JULIANNE LEE

ACE BOOKS, NEW YORK

THE BERKLEY PUBLISHING GROUP
Published by the Penguin Group
Penguin Group (USA) Inc.
375 Hudson Street, New York, New York 10014, USA

Penguin Group (Canada), 90 Eglinton Avenue East, Suite 700, Toronto, Ontario M4P 2Y3, Canada
(a division of Pearson Penguin Canada Inc.)
Penguin Books Ltd., 80 Strand, London WC2R 0RL, England
Penguin Group Ireland, 25 St. Stephen's Green, Dublin 2, Ireland (a division of Penguin Books Ltd.)
Penguin Group (Australia), 250 Camberwell Road, Camberwell, Victoria 3124, Australia
(a division of Pearson Australia Group Pty. Ltd.)
Penguin Books India Pvt. Ltd., 11 Community Centre, Panchsheel Park, New Delhi—110 017, India
Penguin Group (NZ), 67 Apollo Drive, Rosedale, North Shore 0632, New Zealand
(a division of Pearson New Zealand Ltd.)
Penguin Books (South Africa) (Pty.) Ltd., 24 Sturdee Avenue, Rosebank, Johannesburg 2196,
South Africa

Penguin Books Ltd., Registered Offices: 80 Strand, London WC2R 0RL, England

This is a work of fiction. Names, characters, places, and incidents either are the product of the author's imagination or are used fictitiously, and any resemblance to actual persons, living or dead, business establishments, events, or locales is entirely coincidental. The publisher does not have any control over and does not assume any responsibility for author or third-party websites or their content.

KNIGHT'S LADY

An Ace Book / published by arrangement with the author

PRINTING HISTORY
Ace mass-market edition / February 2008

Copyright © 2008 by Julianne Lee.
Cover art by Judy York.
Cover design by Annette Fiore.

ISBN: 978-0-441-01573-3

ACE
Ace Books are published by The Berkley Publishing Group,
a division of Penguin Group (USA) Inc.,
375 Hudson Street, New York, New York 10014.
ACE and the "A" design are trademarks belonging to Penguin Group (USA) Inc.

PRINTED IN THE UNITED STATES OF AMERICA

10 9 8 7 6 5 4 3 2 1

For my fabulous new agent,
Ginger Clark

Contact Julianne Lee at
www.julianneardianlee.com

CHAPTER 1

Lady Lindsay MacNeil bolted awake at the landing trumpet and her heart surged to pounding. A sleepy smile touched her lips, and it spread across her face as the thin, tinny notes reporting the arrival repeated, wafted from above by the sea wind. He'd come. Alasdair an Dubhar MacNeil, Earl of Cruachan and Laird of Eilean Aonarach, had returned, recognized by the castle watch who saw the arms painted on his sails. How had she missed the first sighting? She should have heard the trumpet long before now. She sat up in the enormous silk-dressed bed and peered toward the window at the far end of the room, a rectangle of small panes made bluish by the predawn light. Early yet; perhaps there had been no sighting in the darkness, or there had been fog. Perhaps the sentry had been asleep and not sounded the sighting call. Or maybe she herself had slept through the announcement of an approaching boat, and that shamed her.

In any case, she slipped from beneath the heavy bedcovers, hurried to poke the fire to life and feed it a log, then

plucked a small, yellow spring wildflower from the arrangement of purple, white, and yellow sitting on the table near
the window. She leaned into the deep stone sill and pulled
open the glass to look out. It was a far reach across the
thickness of wall in the slanted sill, the rough stone cold on
her bare belly, and she shivered. But her heart lifted at the
view of the barbican and quay below, and when she shivered again it was a thrill of joy.

Her husband's ships stood at the quay, already unloading men and horses. Two large black dogs, lanky young animals that resembled what would one day be called a
Scottish wolfhound, bounded up the steps to the keep at a
gangly, playful lope. They were littermates, born the summer before, and had attached themselves to Alex. The earl
had named them after his brothers back home: Carl and
Pete. They went everywhere with him, had accompanied
him to Cruachan, and now announced his presence with
their barking and wrestling. His voice called to them, but in
spite of their size they were still puppies at heart and they
ignored him.

Alex's figure below, familiar by his build and the way
he moved hurrying up the steps to the keep, caught Lindsay's eye, and she let the flower drop at just the right moment. She made it in time, and it floated gently downward,
to land only a few feet ahead of Alex trotting up the steps.
He slowed to pick it up, pushed his mail coif back from
his head so it lay about his neck in a collar of metal, grinned
at her, and put the tiny blossom to his nose. His hair was
awry from the coif, and his chin bristled with dark stubble
of several days, but his cheeks glowed pink with health. No
sickness, no wounds while he'd been gone. Her heart lifted
with joy for that. Then he resumed his hurry into the keep,
surcoat flapping, spurs and chain mail jingling. Lindsay withdrew to the room, closed the window, and turned to wait for
him. He was but a moment.

Alex came straight to the chamber, followed by the dogs, who bounded into the room and settled themselves in their accustomed spot atop sheepskins near the hearth. Pete sniffed and snuffled at the air, and Carl curled up immediately to sleep. Alex bolted the door behind him, a little breathless from the steep climb but his grin bright and steadfast. His eyes shone with the pleasure of seeing her, and she guessed it was because she wore not a stitch and it had been two months since he'd left for his other island, Cruachan. For a moment he regarded her, then said in modern English for the sake of privacy from the servants in the anteroom, "Saucy wench." Lindsay thought his American accent mellifluous. Exotic, and she treasured it the more because she was the only one to whom he spoke in it, for she was the only one in the household—and nearly the only human in this century—who could understand it.

She resisted a grin and went wide-eyed with feigned innocence. "O bold knight, you have misjudged me terribly. I am but a poor girl without proper attire—"

"Nor attire of any sort, it would seem."

"Indeed." She lowered her head as if ashamed of her situation, then peeked at him from under her eyelashes and continued, "I place myself at your mercy and pray you to be gentle." Her hands went to the small of her back, and she shook her shoulders so her breasts would sway. His gaze went to them, and his grin widened. He licked his lips, then bit his lower one as he stared. She stepped closer to him. "Please do not ravish me too harshly. You are so large and strong, and I am but weak and mild."

That brought a snort of amusement, for they both knew she was stronger than most men and might even beat him in a fair fight. She held in laughter of her own, and her chest jiggled with it. With a theatrical swagger Alex unbuckled his sword belt, set the weapon against the side of the stone hearth, discarded his iron-plated leather gauntlets to the floor, then began untying the opening of his surcoat. It went straight to the floor in a mound of red and black silk. Lindsay closed the distance between them and slipped her arms around his neck for a kiss. The mail was cold and bumpy against her skin, a hardness that excited her. Alex was warm and breathing inside the hauberk, flesh and blood and bone protected by the mesh of iron rings. He held her tightly, and the rings pinched a little. It gave her goose bumps. She murmured into his ear, "Take care, bold knight."

"Beware, tender maiden. I cannot make promises, for my lust is too great." His breaths came heavily with that genuine lust, and he pressed his mouth to her neck.

"Would you take me unfairly?"

"Would you offer yourself, then break your promise?" His eyelids drooped and his lips touched her forehead as she helped him remove his coif and hauberk, then let them slip to the floor. Off came his spurs and boots, and when the belt that held up his trews was unbuckled, they and his drawers also went to the floor, leaving him in nothing but his knee-length linen shirt. He took her in his arms and pressed himself against her, and she slipped her arms around his neck again. Warm and breathing. And whole. Each time he left the island, each time he donned his sword belt, each time she fought alongside him, she feared for him and prayed for his safety. Today he'd returned to her whole and not bleeding, and that was cause for thanks. Even celebration. She brought her leg up around his waist and gave a hop, and he lifted her to his hips. He was enormous and hard against her as he carried her to the bed.

She lay back, and he climbed onto the bed with her to kiss her hard. Her knees parted and he settled between them. She wanted him inside her, but he dallied, teasing, as he sometimes did to make her beg. His face was at her chest, all bristly stubble and nibbling teeth. The roughness made her gasp. Her voice went thin, but she found it and said, "O . . ." It gave out for a moment, then she gathered her wits and continued, "O bold knight, I promised myself to you and I am yours. But I tremble at your touch." She pressed her hips to his belly in a smooth, rocking rhythm. "I quake under your gaze." A moan escaped her. "I fear you will overwhelm me." Her fingers raked through his hair. "Despoil me." Her breaths became panting. "Ruin me for any other man." She captured his mouth with hers and her knees lay back on the feather mattress, spread in desperate invitation.

Alex broke away and lifted his head, looked into her face, and said, "I will have you, and no argument. I say to you, fair, gentle . . . *demure* maiden, lie back, close your eyes"—he grinned and uttered a snort that was nearly a giggle—"and think of England." Then with one hand he guided himself into her and was home.

England was quite the furthest thing from her mind.

Trefor MacNeil stared at the hole in the root-riddled earth ceiling above. It was a tiny circle of light amid the shadows cast by the fires in this chamber, dripping with what Trefor could only surmise was rain from the world above. He'd been down here an awful long while, it seemed. Without the sun to inform him, he only knew time as cycles of tiredness and rest, hunger and satisfaction. And, of course, longing for Morag and getting no satisfaction. If she was around, she was keeping away from him. Or the faeries were keeping her from him. But she was one of them. Sort of. Enough to be in cahoots with them, in any case, and he was coming to learn that might not be such a good thing.

And now he looked at the hole, visible in the ceiling for the first time since he'd fallen through it however many months—or years—or centuries—ago. He knew enough about these guys to know that time had no meaning for them and if he managed to find a way through that hole, there was no telling whether he might find dinosaurs or spaceships. That knowledge made him not so eager to leave. Nevertheless he stood, staring upward, unable to take his eyes off the circle of light. It had appeared a moment ago—what he perceived to be a moment, in any case—and now seemed to mock him, as if it had always been there and there must be something wrong with him that he'd not seen it before. Though he'd looked. Oh, how he'd looked. Searched. Prowled the caverns in this faerie hole, looking for a way out. There it was, and there were enough twisted, winding tree roots along the walls and ceiling for him to climb out.

If he dared.

Brochan came into the chamber, climbing over and around gnarled columns and rises of root and earth, cocky as ever, and cried out, "Are ye praying, then, lad?" Hair askew and tunic raggedy and poor, he made a bad impression as king of his realm. Trefor gathered he was pretty much standard for an Irish petty king, though, and knew Brochan and his people hearkened back to prehistoric times.

Trefor looked at him and asked for the thousandth—or maybe millionth—time, "Where's Morag?" Though he was conversant in a dozen or so languages, including medieval Gaelic and Middle English, he spoke modern English because he knew it irritated the little faerie.

"She'll come when you're ready." He always said that. "And when she's ready as well." He always said that, too.

Trefor scratched an itch on his thigh and tugged at the

tunic they'd given him to wear. It was too short, and there were no trews, so he was forever struggling to keep himself covered. Like wearing a hospital gown. A dirty one made of rough, poorly spun linen that itched. "So, when will I be ready?"

"You are now. I dinnae ken where your lady is off to. She should be here." He glanced around in a show of looking for her. "I'm guessing you'll be wanting to leave without her, though."

It took a moment for what the faerie king had said to sink in, and when it did Trefor felt a moment of dizziness. This was too good to be true. "Ready? I'm done here?"

"Prince Trefor of the Bhrochan is ready to greet the world. If he cares to venture out."

"No more training? No more conjuring the *maucht* and memorizing the foliage?"

"Are ye disappointed?"

Hardly. That stuff bored him to distraction. But he'd learned it for the sake of one day being released. He had little regard for any of the wee folk except Morag, who was more human than not, in any case. He cared nothing for the magic, for it had always come at a high price for him. Though his pointed ears proved him to be part faerie, and his mother was distantly descended from the *Tuatha Dé Danann*, the blood was thin in him, and he'd been raised in twenty-first-century Tennessee, far from these small Bhrochan folk who now called him "prince." Whatever that meant to them. What it meant to him was that the things he'd learned here seemed to make it all easier. Magic wasn't such a mystery as it had been, and there were fewer surprises from these psychotic leprechauns. So it wasn't as if his time here had been a waste. The headaches had stopped as well, and he no longer had to weigh so much pain against working the craft. "I would move on with my life if you don't need me anymore."

"I never needed you. 'Twas Morag who wanted ye here."

"Then where is she? What's going on here?"

"Do ye care? Does it matter to you at all what her purpose is in you?"

Trefor hesitated in his reply. He'd become accustomed
to Brochan's riddle-me-this sort of talk and knew there
was always more to it than craziness. The faerie was trying
to tell him something, and he would probably do well to
know what it was. He admitted, "I care." Morag had lured
him here. Had led him from as far away as twenty-first-
century Tennessee and then left him to the mercy of this
crazy faerie who was a distant relative of hers. He'd once
thought himself in love with her, but these past months
had put a question to that. She would be here if she gave a
damn.

Brochan stuffed his thumbs into his belt and sat on a
handy bulge of tree root, polished by the bottoms of many
faeries before him. "Have ye thought much about where
she's been?"

Trefor muttered, "Yeah."

"Not here, aye?"

"No, not here."

"Do ye think she's forsaken you?"

"I wonder."

"Do ye think she had a purpose in bringing you here?"

"You keep saying she did. You've been saying for
months that I'm meant to be the prince of this place." He
looked around and knew he wanted nothing more to do
with this dank hole in the ground. "I'm supposed to use
what I've learned here and fulfill a mission of some sort. Is
all that nonsense her idea?"

"All that *nonsense* is your fate. You're meant to do certain things, and we've given you the means to do them. For
it would hardly be sporting for us to send you out to the

fray without the knowledge required to accomplish your destiny."

"Fray?"

"Aye. The struggle's the thing, don't ye know. I see the spark of concern in your eye; are ye afraid?"

Trefor blinked, then shut his eyes against intrusion from this guy, who always seemed to know too much. "No. I fear nothing." Not in a long time, anyway. It was as a child he'd lost his sense of safety, and with nothing else to lose there was little anymore that truly frightened him. Losing Morag had once come close, but even that was waning. He looked Brochan in the eye. "So tell me what lies ahead. What's my destiny?"

The little man laughed, a high, munchkinlike giggle. "Were I to tell you, it couldnae happen. Destiny requires you to learn for yourself what will be."

"Free will."

"Nae so free."

"But that doesn't make sense."

"It will."

Frustration made Trefor snort, and he looked around the room and shifted his weight with impatience. "Okay, how about a hint? If I climb out that hole, where will I find myself? Which way should I go? Is my father still out there, or has he died of old age? Turned to dust, maybe?"

Brochan gave another laugh. "No, the time hasnae flown for you as it might have, for not only are you Danann but you ken the ways of the folk. Alasdair an Dubhar is still there"—he raised a finger of warning—"but not so close as you imagine."

"He's not aged any?" More important, had his mother not aged? Last time he'd seen his parents, after being raised apart from them, they'd been less than five years older than himself and his mother had rejected him for it.

The hurt smoldered in his gut, and some nights he lay awake with the pain. He had faeries to thank for that, too, for the Bhrochan had left him with the Tennessee foster system, then brought him to the fourteenth century and deposited him in it three decades too early for comfort. Too much to ask that they consider how they screwed him up with his parents, he supposed.

"They've aged no more than you have, young Trefor."

That was a disappointment. "And what is expected of me when I leave? I don't imagine you taught me your magic tricks for the fun of it."

"Och, but it was for fun! If ye think I ever do anything for aught but the fun of it, ye cannae know me very well!"

"But you have an agenda. You're a man with a plan, and don't tell me there isn't something ulterior in everything you do."

Another giggle, and Brochan said, "Were ye my son, I couldnae be more proud of ye, lad, Danann though ye are! Aye, I must confess I have a wish. And the only thing I'll tell you of it is to seek out the king, Dagda Mór of the *Tuatha Dé Danann*."

"And then what?"

"That's for you to learn, lad."

"No hint?"

"I've already told ye too much."

"You've told me nothing."

"Find the king, and all will come clear."

"And if I choose not to look?"

The bright light of a bird's eye came to Brochan's grinning face, and he said, "There is no free will, Trefor MacNeil. Not truly. You cannae *not* go looking. 'Tis not in you to not look."

"Watch me."

"Och, aye, I will. I live for it."

Trefor's lips pressed together. "All right. Be my guest."

He looked up at the hole again and figured it was time to go. The sooner the better. He reached for a handhold on one of the tree roots. "See ya later."

Brochan waved to him. "Hasta la vista, baby."

Trefor paused and frowned at the crazy faerie, surprised once again at the lack of time-sense in the creature, though he shouldn't have been. It had been this way since his arrival. Then he began the climb out of the faerie realm and back to the world Brochan had promised would be little changed from when he'd left.

Right, like he could trust what that nutcase would tell him.

Alex lay beside Lindsay and knew well why he'd always found it easy to resist the temptation of other women. Okay, maybe not so easy, but worth the effort at least. Whenever he was honest with himself the word "besotted" occurred to him, and even after two years of marriage he took teasing from James Douglas and Hector MacNeil for allowing his wife to own his heart. Certainly neither of them had ever let a woman in where she could do damage.

But he cared little about what they thought on that subject. Those guys didn't know Lindsay. They'd never understood the power and passion a strong woman could bring a man. And he guessed, by the medieval culture that prized social status over love, neither had ever been with a woman who loved him. Alex thought that fairly pathetic. Those guys didn't know what they were missing.

In spite of the high fire in the hearth, chill air moved him to draw the corner of the down comforter over himself and his wife. The room had warmed up from the revived fire, but the castle was drafty and the early spring morning played over his skin. Exhausted though he was from his voyage—not to mention the greeting he'd received—he didn't sleep, but instead lay with Lindsay in his arms to feel her breathe. Each rise and fall of her chest against him eased his soul. He'd missed it these past weeks. Normally she would have gone with him, to be by his side and fight there if necessary, but this trip to Cruachan had been only administrative and short, and she'd been needed at the keep to oversee those household knights who had been left behind for security. It was her first time ramrodding the troops without Sir Henry as her proxy, and Alex was curious to find out how it had gone. But the warmth of her and the soothing rhythm of her breaths lulled him.

Just as he dozed, Lindsay disengaged herself from him and slipped from under the comforter, donned her dressing gown, and went to the anteroom door to ask after breakfast. Alex heard as if distant the murmuring voice of her maid, who informed her the meat was nearly ready and the household would gather soon in the Great Hall above. The master could be served there, or in his chamber if he preferred.

Lindsay raised her voice to ask him, "Which do you fancy, Alex? Do you think your courtiers will require their earl's presence right away?"

Alex replied, sleepy, low, and dull, "No. Bring me my breakfast here and tell them I'm chasing my wife around the bedchamber. That'll amuse them more than watching me eat would."

Lindsay chuckled, ordered breakfast in, then returned to the chamber and stoked the fire again. Maintaining such things within the lord's sanctum was a chore, but the alternative was to give up privacy and allow the servants free access to the chamber. Their modern sensibilities balked even more at that than at doing for themselves. The locals, particularly those living on these islands so far removed from the mainland and the Scottish upper classes, didn't seem to care for the attitude, as they disliked anything that was unfamiliar. It raised commentary that the earl and countess required their servants to sleep in the anteroom, to knock before entering the bedchamber, and to perform cleaning duties only while the room was unoccupied. "Strange ways," they said in whispers sometimes overheard. "They're Hungarian; I think I would dislike to live in the eastern mountains, for it would be too lonely."

Alex knew they would be even more horrified if they were aware of the truth of his origins: that he and Lindsay had come from the twenty-first century. As a U.S. Navy fighter pilot he'd once routinely commanded enough firepower to lay waste to every farmhouse on this island in minutes, and the closest he'd ever come to the "eastern mountains" was flying air patrols over Kosovo in search of surface-to-air missile sites.

He rolled over in the bed to watch Lindsay poke the fire. Her movements were smooth, lithe, and he knew her to be as deadly to her enemies as the large cat she resembled. That excited him in ways he'd once thought impossible. Not long ago Lindsay had killed a man in a fair fight, then cut off his balls before he was quite dead. Appalling in its cold-bloodedness, but in the final analysis Alex knew this was a woman he wanted on his side, and he was proud to be the one she called "husband." He lusted for her even now, though he was unable to do anything more about it. Nevertheless he enjoyed feasting his eyes. "Why did you bother getting dressed?"

"You know why."

He cast his glance toward the anteroom. "The servants wouldn't care."

"I would. Besides, it's cold."

"Come here and warm up, then." He held up the covers in invitation, but she only came to sit by him on the mattress and he laid them back down.

She asked, "Do you reckon we'll be needed in the Borderlands this summer?"

"I think we can count on a summons, either to the Marches with Douglas or Ireland with King Robert. Given a choice, I'd rather go to Ireland. It's been too long since Robert has laid eyes on me. Don't want him to forget why he made me an earl."

"He made you an earl because James Douglas likes you. God knows why; you treat him like a disease."

Alex gave her a sideways glance. She knew why he didn't like Douglas. The man was a rake, and entirely too friendly with Lindsay. Even before she'd been outed as a woman, he'd liked her way too much, and Alex didn't want him around. Better to ride with Robert, who was as horny as Douglas, but had prospects among noblewomen of far higher status and greater conventional beauty than Lindsay. Robert certainly had no interest in Alex's Hungarian commoner wife.

She waited for him to reply, but he wasn't about to. They'd been over this before; further discussion was unnecessary. She changed the subject. "How did the trip go?"

"Henry Ellot has a handle on things now. I hate to lose him as my X.O., but I need a tacksman on Cruachan and he's all I've got I can trust."

There was a silence, and Alex knew they were both thinking the same thing. Trefor should have been that tacksman. Finally, Alex said, "Any word from the kid?"

"He's hardly a kid."

"He should be." A note of bitterness crept into his voice, and he tried to cough it away, but it was no good. "By my reckoning, he should be about six or seven months old. He should be nursing, drooling, and crapping in diapers."

"In that case he would hardly be much good administrating your lands on Cruachan, would he?" Lindsay smoothed the hair away from his forehead. Her voice was soothing, as if she were talking to a child. "We can't help what was done. He grew up in a different century. Without us. There's no changing the . . . past."

Alex lay back on his pillow and grunted. Then he glanced sharply up at her, the monthly question in his eyes, but she shook her head.

"No. Not yet." No baby, though they'd been trying since last summer, when they'd learned their newborn was a grown man.

He grunted again and looked past her to the fire. "Well, I thought he wanted to be part of things here. He was all hot to plant himself in my household, call himself cousin, and be my tacksman. Where is he?"

"His men are all wondering the same thing."

"Have any of them left for greener pastures and a less impulsive master?"

"He might be dead. We can't know for certain what has happened to him."

Somehow that thought struck Alex's heart as sharply as if he'd known Trefor the entire twenty-seven years of his life and raised him as he would have if Trefor had not been stolen from his crib. "He's not dead."

Lindsay didn't reply to that, and Alex wondered whether she cared one way or the other. She said, "In any case, Henry will serve well on Cruachan and you'll find another second in command. Myself, perhaps."

"You know that can't happen."

"I know no such thing."

"The men barely tolerate your presence on the field as it is. They'd be mortified to take orders from you during a battle."

Her face set to the hard anger he knew meant she was no longer listening to him. Arguing further would be pointless, but she pressed. "They took orders from me this past month."

"Was the castle ever under attack?"

"I told you it wasn't."

"Then you're still untried. Nothing matters to these guys except battle."

"They know I was giving orders to Ellot during the MacLeod-Breton rising, and they respect that."

He sat up and rested an elbow on one knee. "They accepted it because no mistakes were made. Furthermore, they assume no mistakes were made because Ellot was here. Unless you plan on being pure D perfect all the time, you'll need a mouthpiece for dealing with the men. I can't have you for my second. You can fight, but you can't lead because they won't follow. Not gonna happen."

"It's humiliating to ride behind the squires."

That made him chuckle, for she sounded exactly like the other knights, who wouldn't be caught dead at the rear of any battle. She was one of the guys in more ways than anyone thought. "It's the way it's got to be. I can't help it."

"Would you if you could?"

That made him blink, and he cast about for what she could have meant by that. "What, you think I'm afraid of you? That I'm holding you back? That I would *bother* holding you back?"

Her expression was a firm scowl, and he took that as a "yes."

"Think about this, Lindsay." He bent his head to look her in the eye. "Just for a moment, think hard about the reality here. In this time—this culture—your status hangs entirely on mine. As long as I'm alive, you can't take my place. There would be no point in holding you back."

Her eyes hardened further, for she disliked the fact of her position, and he wished she would just accept it and move on. There was nothing either of them could do about the times in which they lived. Not anymore. "You don't take me any more seriously than they do."

"I still don't know why you want to fight."

"We've been over this before, and you do, too, know why. I want it for the same reasons you do."

"It's my job, and I'm good at it."

"I'm good at it also."

"But it's not your job. Yours is to keep the castle from going to hell." He glanced at her belly, then away, but it was too late to pretend he hadn't almost said her job was also to have children. Harder to accomplish here than it had been in the twenty-first century where Trefor had been born, and the image that often came of Lindsay on horseback, wielding a sword, with a hauberk bulging at the front with pregnancy, appalled him. Even more frightening, if she were to conceive in these circumstances she might lose the baby before ever knowing about it.

The anger rose from Lindsay in palpable waves, and she rose to go sit in a chair by the hearth. "Stop treating me the way An Reubair did."

Now it was his turn to be angry. "Don't you say his name in this house." *Castle*. This was his castle.

She peered sideways at him. "He wanted me to marry him and make babies for him, just like you."

"I said I don't want to hear it."

"Of course you don't. You don't want to hear anything that annoys you, or reflects badly on you. All you want is to have everyone around the fire carrying on about what a great warrior is Alasdair an Dubhar MacNeil. God forbid there should ever be a murmur of criticism."

In an effort to appear insouciant, he resisted the urge to leave the bed. He swallowed his rage. The hand draped over his knee wadded into a fist, and he dug his nails into his palm. He said, "I just don't want to hear about that Danann ass." His voice gave him away, he was sure. Even he could hear the temper in it.

She fell silent, and he trusted it was because she had

nothing more to say about the faerie knight. She was part
Danann, but more human than faerie, and she'd not even
known of her fey ancestry until six months ago. He counted
on her loyalty. An Reubair was an arrogant pig, a border
raider like Douglas. Alex had to have faith that Lindsay saw
Reubair for what he was. He struggled to keep it, but faith in
anything came hard these days.

CHAPTER 2

It was March and the weather had mellowed from winter. Work on a bathhouse had begun shortly before Alex's trip, and today he spent the day observing its progress. Privately, he didn't think the convenience worth the expense, particularly since there were servants to fill and empty the small iron tub he and Lindsay had been using in the bedchamber, but he did like the idea of a tub large enough to hold them both at once. Small as it was, the little tub had been astonishingly expensive just for the iron, and never mind the trouble it had taken to get the village blacksmith to construct it. A larger one was out of the question. This new wooden construction would be the next best thing to a Jacuzzi back in the States. Alex appropriated a corner of the Great Hall for it and had workmen begin chipping space from the living rock that formed that wall.

This seemed quiet, restful work to Alex, for whom construction had always meant loud machinery and sawdust. Here there was only the *tink-tink* of chisel and stone as workmen excavated at a pace Alex thought criminally

slow. Every so often someone would cart away a bucket of
stone to the village outside the castle gate, to be broken
further for use as gravel. Nothing was ever wasted among
Alex's vassals. There was barely a dent in the wall. This
was going to take forever.

The tub wouldn't be large, but it needed to be built beneath cisterns on the roof of the Hall. Knowing how to pipe
water and heat it was one thing, but having the tools and
materials necessary for it was another entirely. Royalty had
running water these days; he was only an earl who lived in
the sticks. The sewage pipe he'd laid through the lower barbican last fall had been incredibly expensive. Well worth it
for the sake of not having a steaming pool of raw human
waste directly beneath his bedroom window, but the pipe,
which had to be shipped in from Glasgow, and the labor
had nearly tapped him out. This bathhouse would do the
same, and for a lesser need. But he did it to make Lindsay
happy.

As he supervised the work, other castle residents and
some servants also watched. They paused in a cluster near
the stair, or slowed in their progress through the room, lingering as long as they thought they wouldn't be noticed by
their master. Most were puzzled by the project, curious to
see what a bathhouse might look like. If Alex noticed anyone loitering too long, he turned to them with a bland gaze
until they would realize they had better things to do than
gawk, and would move along like rubberneckers at a car
accident.

Father Patrick, however, lounged freely in a cushioned
chair he'd moved from the high table and sat back with his
hands folded over his belly and his outstretched legs crossed
at the ankles. His filthy, bare toes flexed and pointed, flexed
and pointed, in a tick of barely contained energy. He was a
young man, barely out of his teens, and Alex marveled that
such a kid could dedicate himself to the church so fully as to

become a priest. And a good one, near as Alex could tell. For some it was a case of having nowhere else to go, but with Patrick it was a personality quirk Alex hadn't yet figured out. He was a skilled and enthusiastic fighter, and it remained a mystery to Alex how the priest had become as deft with a sword as himself. Perhaps even better, for Alex had never wielded one until three years ago. Patrick had proven himself competent in his religious vocation—more so than most priests north of the channel—otherwise Alex might have thought him a knight masquerading as a man of the cloth.

Alex said to him, "Ever see one of these before?"

"A hole in the side of a rock face? Aye, I've seen my share." The priest grinned a bit of mischief at his joke.

Alex snorted. "A bathhouse. Ever seen a bathhouse?"

"Nae. I heard tell of one once, in France during my studies. I might have gone for a look, but it would have been an expense beyond my means." His tone suggested he thought this project also a frivolous expense. "I'm not that sort of priest."

Alex guessed that had fed Patrick's curiosity about the construction. His chapel priest wanted to know why so much money was being spent on something so unnecessary, and explanation would be difficult. The only Middle English Alex knew that came close to "hygiene" translated as more like "cleanliness," but he tried to make himself clear. "It's healthful to be clean."

"I keep clean enough with my ewer and bowl, I think. A simple and affordable habit, and not so grandiose as immersion. God gave us streams and ponds good for that, in any case."

Alex said, "The water here will be heated."

Patrick's eyes went wide. "Warm water, you say? Even more wasteful. And enervating. It weakens a man to wash in hot water. God will certainly take you to task for it."

There was no humor in his voice. He sounded absolutely sincere in his belief, and annoyed in the bargain.

"Waste not, want not?"

"Indeed." Patrick was a straightforward man. Less so than the island vassals, who were no more than simple Scottish farmers and never minced words with each other or with their laird, but more plainspoken than the knights in Alex's household who were cagey nobles of mostly Norman descent. The earl took the priest's meaning for what it was worth and let the subject go. Patrick was a spiritual shepherd, not Alex's financial advisor.

But the priest continued in that vein. "Waste is a terrible thing, and you should be alert to a certain temptation you've created among your vassals, who are stealing it."

Alex frowned, puzzled. "Stealing . . . what? Waste?"

"From your new pipes that move the dung from your garderobe to the sea, through the barbican. You don't attend to the collecting of it yourself, and that leaves it for the common folk to steal."

At first Alex wanted to know why anyone would steal sewage, but instead he asked, "Father, you haven't just passed along someone's confession, have you?"

Patrick was shocked, and even blustered a little at the offense. "Certainly not, and shame on you for suggesting it! The theft is common knowledge in the village, and fights break out among a number of farmers who from time to time dig away the mounds of dung beneath the pipe outlet on the rocks by the quay. An argument arose over the practice of putting a large bucket under it while the garderobe is being flushed out. Some distinguish that as stealing—as opposed to picking up the waste from the ground—where others do not. It's become a source of great debate amongst your villagers. You would do well to put an end to the bickering over your castle dung so nobody is hurt over it."

Alex's nose wrinkled. Fertilizer. He knew farmers used human waste to fertilize their fields, but it had never occurred to him they might fight over it, or consider it stealing to take it. "I'll have to arrange with Donnchadh for equitable distribution of the stuff on cleaning days."

"And charge them for it."

"No. No charge."

"They'll nae respect you for that. Nor themselves, and you should know that your people are too prideful to take alms."

Alex considered that for a moment, but shook his head. He disliked the idea of charging people to cart away the shit from his toilets, no matter how valuable it seemed to them. "No. It'll be a boon. A favor for my beloved vassals who have proven their loyalty to me this past year, against the MacDonalds of Cruachan and the traitorous Bretons before that."

Patrick nodded, seeing his point and agreeing with him. "A wise laird you are, and a kind one for your concern over the spiritual lives of your inferiors, for though you've made it plain you don't value the dung, they nevertheless understand their actions as stealing and suffer their souls to the sin."

"Castle crap too tempting for them?"

"Would you tether a sheep in the meadow outside the castle curtain, leave it to the elements, and not expect someone to come along and take it home? Or gold? Would you drop a bag of gold in the track that runs through the village and not expect someone to pick it up?"

"Most would leave it, or bring it here, knowing it was mine." And also knowing that anyone who saw a person with such a large amount of cash would blab it around in a heartbeat. Privacy couldn't exist on an island inhabited by only a few hundred people.

"But there would be some to take it. And fight over it."

"Is that my responsibility?"

"Aye, it is, for you are their leader. Their example. They put their trust in you."

Alex grunted. He'd once known that, and wondered why he'd forgotten it. "Point taken, Father."

After a strung-out silence underscored by the chink and clink of the workmen carving rock, the priest said, "Would there be news of progress in Ireland?"

For a moment Alex was puzzled as to what progress he meant, but then he remembered. "Robert, you mean."

"Aye. Has he won the hearts and minds of those Irish chiefs whose allegiances are to Edward II?"

"I've not heard since July." Neither had Alex been paying much attention even then. His mind had been on Lindsay at the time, and he'd been in the Borderlands, away from Robert's campaign in Ireland, in any case. It occurred to Alex that he knew very little about what was going on with Robert in Ireland. Lindsay, whose grasp of history was stronger than his, had told him Robert's brother would die there soon, and the campaign would ultimately fail, but she remembered none of the details of that failure.

"Do you think he'll succeed?"

Alex looked over at the young priest who lounged in his chair and who seemed uncaring. The demeanor was a lie. Patrick was one of the most caring men Alex knew.

In reply, Alex only shrugged and said, "I'll find out if and when His Majesty gives me a summons to join the fight." He didn't look forward to being part of the failure in Ireland, but knew he needed to join Robert or his brother Edward Bruce in order to protect his standing as a royal vassal. His yearly duty to his liege was forty days of military service—a pretty good deal in return for the lordship of two islands, the wealth that came with them, and the privilege of membership in parliament. By comparison, it made the pay he used to draw from the U.S. Navy for signing over his life look like slavery.

There was also that too much time away from the king might cause Alex to be forgotten. Or worse, undermined by a rival. He needed to keep his toe in the door.

L indsay stood atop the roof of the Great Hall, staring out to sea. It was a calm day, though a bit chilly, and visibility was good. The spring sunshine warmed her face though she huddled into her cloak against the breeze, and she considered her future. Each month brought a new question of whether or not she would have another child, and each month she wondered what she hoped for. Never mind choosing between career and family; there would be no real career for her, only the privilege of fighting beside her husband if the occasion arose.

Was it worth the medical risk? She'd talked Alex into making Nemed return them to the future for the safety of their baby, but it had been a brief stay in the twenty-first century. Trefor had been stolen from her only days after his birth.

Then there was the emotional risk. She'd given herself over to him, only to have that part of her ripped away by those evil faeries. He'd been raised in America, taught by hired help, and named by strangers. She hadn't even been able to name her own son. Now he was an adult and beyond her reach. She doubted the value of trying again, for the vulnerability was too much to bear.

A dot appeared on the horizon, and her gaze went to it. A boat. At first it was too distant to see much, but as it drew closer she saw a hint of gold in the sail. Red and gold, the colors of the king's arms. Her pulse skipped and picked up pace. A king's boat. Only one, so it wouldn't be the king himself. Just a messenger. She turned to alert the watch, but he'd already seen the sail and raised the trumpet to his mouth to sound the approach. Lindsay went back to watching the ship sail in.

Momentarily there was a footfall behind her, and Alex passed her on his way to the crenellated battlement to look out across the water. She watched him there, standing nearly at attention, intent on the king's messenger. The breeze picked up locks of his hair and blew them around his forehead. He sighed. "I wanted to finish the work on the bathhouse before they summoned me."

"We won't need it until we return."

He turned and threw her a look. "We?"

"You know I'm going with you."

He grunted and returned his attention to the boat out at sea. Not that he needed to watch the slow progress of the vessel, but she guessed he simply didn't want to have to stare her down. He could protest all he wanted, but he couldn't keep her from going with him.

"Look at it this way. You'll be more likely to get an heir if we're not separated. For instance, we both know Robert won't have a son until just before his death, because his queen has been locked away in England."

"I should lock you away."

"Fat lot of good that would do."

"If I thought I could keep you here—"

"You can't. There are some things I feel vulnerable over, and being cut down by a sword is just not one of them." He was ignoring her, so she added, "Having another child is." He turned to look at her, listening now, and she elaborated. "You would have me give you children, but you don't realize how truly frightening that is to me. It's like opening a wound that will never, ever close. Having met Trefor at his age, I know that no matter how old he gets there will always be that

terror. I can't imagine what it might be like for a child I actually raised myself."

"I'd like to imagine it. I want to experience it."

"You want an heir."

He shrugged and nodded. "That, too. Is there a reason
I shouldn't? We have a legacy to pass—"

"You have a legacy. What I have is a uterus."

"Stop that!"

She pressed her lips together, then said, "I know you
can't help it. It's not your fault the system is what it is. It is,
nevertheless, true."

"Yeah. Nothing we can do about it." He turned his attention back to the approaching messenger. "You are coming
with me. I know I can't talk you out of that."

"And we'll try to have another child. I can't talk you out
of that."

He sighed and shook his head.

She went to him and took his hand. It was a strong, large
hand, callused by sword, reins, and pen. A knight's hand. A
nobleman's. The palm was hard and dry, the fingers thick
and knuckles wide. She wrapped it around her own hand,
and his squeezed hers.

A lex leaned down to kiss Lindsay lightly on the mouth as
reconciliation. They disagreed often, but he loved her
anyway and only wished she could be happy. That he could
make her happy. Riding around killing people wasn't going
to do it. He knew, because it wasn't all that fulfilling for
him, either. He gazed at the oncoming ship and wondered
whether it might carry the king. It was a thrilling thought.

The thrill passed, however, when he saw for a certainty
there was only one ship, and that a small one. Even if Robert
were inclined to come to this backwater unannounced, he

would certainly not have come with so small an entourage. There was a twinge of disappointment as Alex realized it must only be a messenger. It seemed Robert was eager to have Alex's forty days' service for the year, accompanied by fifty men. Alex drew a deep breath and let it out slowly.

Rats.

Alex went to clean up and change his clothes before the ship would land. This visitor might be only a messenger, but he was the king's messenger and would be a man of rank. Probably better rank than Alex, and he needed to be presentable. Unfortunately there was nothing to be done about the Great Hall; it was a mess and would stay that way for a while. He could receive in the smaller meeting room downstairs.

With his half-grown puppies at his heel by the hearth in the meeting room some called a "presence chamber," he greeted his visitor with proper protocol. John Rothbury of Morpeth, an earl from the Lowlands Alex knew only by reputation. After formalities, they sat casually at a corner of the large table downstairs to talk, two of Morpeth's squires hovering behind him, alert for a hint of whatever he might need. Alex had only his page, eight-year-old Gregor, who stood ready near the stairs.

Lindsay strode into the room from the laird's quarters, dressed as the lady of the household and looking like a million bucks. Literally. She wore one of her best gowns and sported the necklace Alex had given her when they'd married. Rubies set in gold, it was a treasure he'd saved out from booty awarded to him after one of his first raids, though he could ill afford it. In modern times it might be worth several million dollars, and in the current economy it would have supported his household for more than a year. Lindsay wore it to impress Morpeth, and Alex could see it was having the desired effect. Morpeth watched her cross the room with a basket of sewing tucked in the crook of one arm.

She sat near the hearth in a small but comfortable chair. Near enough to the table to hear everything, but far enough not to be obtrusive, and angled away from the table. It was an overstuffed upholstered chair made especially for her, with a fluffy, down-stuffed seat cushion that had the entire island in awe of luxury, and it was where she sat whenever there was something she needed to overhear without intruding. "Don't mind me," she said softly, "I have some embroidery I'd like to finish, and I enjoy the sound of men's voices." Then she began picking at the work in her hands and made as if she weren't listening, but Alex knew better. He'd heard her joke once that she enjoyed the sound of men's voices because it lulled her to sleep, but he knew she was hanging on every word. He gave her a warning glance. Morpeth returned his attention to Alex and ignored her entirely.

Over a light repast of green cheese, fresh bread, and smoked fish, Alex received his formal orders from Robert, in writing on parchment folded into a leather wallet. No surprises there; the obligation was ongoing and Alex was well aware of the strings attached to his title. Then conversation continued in a social vein as the king's representative felt out the newest member of the peerage. Alex knew he was being examined. Though his visitor put on a casual and friendly air meant to disarm, there was no mistaking the pointed questions that attempted to shine light into areas of Alex's life he usually didn't care to discuss. Especially his past, a subject that put him at a disadvantage because even his cover story had him a foreigner. Everyone knew he wasn't native to Scotland, but the more he talked the more he risked tangling himself in a web of lies. But to avoid answering questions might invite distrust, so he spoke casually of his past as if it had happened in Hungary and he'd been raised by his mother's cousin in lieu of his ostensible Scottish father, the recently deceased MacNeil of Barra. All lies. But none of it was Alex's invention. The story was made up of conclusions assumed by Robert, and who was Alex to gainsay the king? He invented as little as possible and stuck to what had already been said.

Morpeth seemed well pleased with the new peer, but one could never tell for certain what went on in the mind of a courtier. Hooded eyes and a constant gentleman's smile hid well a man's true feelings, and Alex was certain he wasn't the only accomplished liar in the room. He did his best to bring the subject around to his reputation as a Scot, made at the battle of Bannockburn since his arrival in this century, where what he told was mostly truthful. He emphasized his relationships with James Douglas, Earl of Douglas, and Hector MacNeil, Laird of Barra. He made an especially big deal over the story of how he'd been knighted and given his nickname of "An Dubhar" by Robert himself. That the name was Gaelic and meant "Shadow of Death" seemed to impress the visitor, who said Alex seemed more Scottish than foreign, which Alex knew was a hard-won compliment.

Once the grilling was done, Alex invited his guest to spend the night in his own quarters. The earl accepted it as due, which it was, for the lord's chambers were the only accommodations in the keep that came even close to being adequate for the visitor and his servants. After as elaborate a supper as the castle could produce this early in the year, Alex and Lindsay would spend the night in the windowless room off the meeting room below the Great Hall.

Immediately, word of the summons to Ireland was sent by crier to the village near the castle, and to the farms across the island, and from there by fishing boat it would go to Cruachan the next day. Vassals or their sons would be needed to fill in the ranks of men required of their laird by the king. Alex knew it would take no effort to convince the men to fight; there were plenty of young men among the MacNeils, MacConnells, and few MacDonalds under his

authority who had missed the Breton uprising and the Cruachan fracas, and would leap at the chance to sail off to Ireland and throw themselves upon a worthy enemy, to test
themselves in battle.

But, eager as the men were to fight, the chance came
sooner than anyone thought. Or even wished for.

That very evening at dusk, while the island elite sat at
table in the Great Hall and servants gathered here and there
about the castle for their dinner, a trumpet sounded at the
inland curtain wall. Alex and Lindsay, seated at the high
table with their wealthy, highborn, and well-connected
guest, looked up, but paid little attention otherwise. Nobody thought it amiss, for it was probably just someone
from the village wanting an audience with their laird.
Everyone in the Great Hall continued eating and anticipated the approach of a MacConnell or MacNeil. More
than likely it was Donnchadh MacConnell with yet another
complaint from the villagers, and Alex braced himself for
an argument with his most contentious vassal. Donnchadh
was a good, loyal man, but he could sometimes be a pain in
the ass if he wanted something Alex couldn't give.

All heads came up at a second trumpet, this time of
warning and accompanied by a mass war cry that sounded
close enough to be inside the bailey. Alex's next thought
was another rising, possibly of the Cruachan MacDonalds,
but this cry was unfamiliar. The voices weren't MacDonalds of any stripe. Trefor? The horror of that sent a shiver
through Alex as he leapt to his feet and shouted to Gregor
for his sword. The hollering came nearer, definitely inside
the bailey below, and alarm turned to outrage.

Not enough time to don his armor; he received his
weapons and shield and ran from the Hall into the bailey.
His guest was forgotten as he looked down the hill toward
the inland curtain.

There, off down the wending slope of the bailey, he found

a mass of knights swarming through the entry, beneath a fully raised gate. Mounted and armed, they rode up the winding path between the castle outbuildings as if in slow motion, hacking and slashing all who came to meet them.

"Who are those guys?" They didn't appear to be anyone he'd seen before, nor even heard of. Their armor was odd, even more strange than the full suits that would come from the Continent later in the century. Their chain mail gleamed with a brightness that suggested it was not only made of silver but had been polished moments before the attack, both of which were impossible for ordinary knights. Their horses also shone with health and hard polishing, with fresh, brightly colored silken bards flapping and flowing with each stride and leap up the stone path.

At the top of the bailey slope, Alex's gathered men-at-arms filed at a run from the Great Hall with their swords raised. Rothbury as well, he and his entourage ready to fight in self-defense. Lindsay ran past Alex and into the bailey, her sword also in hand, her other fist grappling with her skirts, and death in her eye. Alex quit wondering who these guys were, gave a great roar, raised his weapon, and joined the fray.

On foot Alex and his men were at a disadvantage, except when they could use obstacles to protect themselves. The close quarters made it difficult to dodge the attackers, and so the horses became targets. As quickly as he could make his sword move, Alex hamstrung two mounts. Then he fell upon one of the riders, who defended with a brightly flashing blade. Rage surged in Alex, the more because he was fighting inside his home. This breach was unthinkable. He battered with his shield, and his opponent fell backward down the slope. Alex finished him off with a kick to the head and his sword point through the throat. Then he turned in search of another invader while the dying man choked on his own blood.

He found another opponent, hauled back his sword to strike, and caught a glimpse of pointed ear. Trefor? Alex held his attack to know, and found himself facing a faerie, but not Trefor. Stunned and vulnerable, Alex dodged and parried, knocked to the side by his opponent. One quick glance around, and he saw all the enemy knights were faeries. *What the hell?* Danann. They were all *Tuatha Dé Danann.*

The faerie attacked, and Alex defended but was caught off guard and fell backward. He tripped over a protruding stone and slammed onto his back in the path. His opponent hauled back in almost a leisurely manner, and though Alex tried to roll he was too slow. The glinting faerie sword caught his belly and the point slipped through his hauberk. The stab was like a sock in the gut, and Alex let out a howl of pain. Metallic agony. The enemy yanked out his sword, gazed at him a moment, then moved on with a look on his narrow-eyed face that said he was satisfied Alex would die soon.

Alex retrieved his sword from the stone pathway beneath his hand and struggled to roll over and follow, but the paralyzing pain made him woozy. One hand pressed to hold in his entrails, for he was certain they would spill onto the ground, and blood flowed over it, red and sticky. Black spots swam before his eyes, and the battle raging around him slowed in his perception. He watched the enemy swarm to each corner of his castle, slaughtering his knights and murdering the servants. He figured he was about to die, and he found himself surprised it had finally happened to him.

Lindsay. Where was Lindsay? He struggled to his feet and searched the melee but didn't see her. He called out, "Lindsay!" But there was no reply other than the clanging of swords and the dull clank of weapons on armor. Feet splayed for balance, one hand pressed hard to his belly in a futile attempt to stop the bleeding.

Then, as suddenly as they had assaulted, the invaders turned and made their retreat. Leaving the mangled Mac-Neil knights behind, the faerie knights stood down and hurried from the bailey and back out to the island interior. A few of Alex's men followed, but they were not mounted and were discouraged when the trailing enemy knights turned to address them. Finally, the faeries made their retreat and disappeared into the forest beyond.

For Alex, the world tilted and darkened, and he went to one knee. A roaring filled his head. Once again he called Lindsay's name and had no reply. Then there was nothing at all.

CHAPTER 3

Trefor emerged from the hole in the ground with some difficulty. He was a mite larger than the Bhrochan, and he guessed this breach had not been made for him. He wriggled and squirmed his way through, until the earth squeezed him like a glob of toothpaste onto the grass in the clearing from which he'd come six months before. Then he lay there to rest a moment after the hard climb. He was out of shape; he'd had too much lounging around in laziness with the wee folk and needed to get back to real life. As soon as his breathing returned to normal, he sat up and looked around. Well, no better way to solve that problem than to get walking back to the castle. He climbed to his feet and set out, tugging his tunic at the back when the breeze annoyed too much.

Along the way, he sensed presence. Not just one, but many, and the track he trod evidenced the passing of a number of large horses. Chargers, not the tiny garrons of the local farmers. An armed party had passed through here, headed for the western shore. Back the way he'd come. Alex's knights

on patrol? Training exercises, perhaps? That was the logical
assumption, but the sense he had was not peaceful. There
was violence here. Anguish. Blood was in the air, though
there was none on the ground to be seen. Something bad had
just happened, and he shuddered with evil energy.

In a hurry to get away from it, he ran part of the way to
his father's castle and arrived at the inland curtain in short
order. It was only a few miles. Relieved to be back, he
jogged across the pasture before the inland curtain, toward
the portcullis where he would call to the sentry for admit-
tance.

But instead of leaving the evil behind, he found he'd run
toward it. A rain of crossbow bolts thudded around him,
and he skidded to a halt. "Hey!" He held up his hands to
show he was unarmed and went very still. A dark line of
men-at-arms stood along the battlement, most of them re-
loading their weapons, but enough of them had not yet
fired and held a bead on him so he didn't dare move. "Hey,
you men! It's me! Sir Trefor Pawlowski! What is the reason
for this?"

The knights above lowered their weapons, and one spoke.
"Trefor Pawlowski? You dress strangely for a knight."

"Let me in. You know it's me." If any of these guys were
his own men he was going to tear some new orifices.

The speaker did know him, for it was one of his men,
and the gate opened for him immediately. But nobody
seemed interested in where he'd been, nor were they concerned about this irritation, and as Trefor went up the path
and looked around, all thoughts of kicking ass over being
shot at dissipated. The castle was in an uproar over a recent
attack. Blood still stood in puddles and rivulets on paving
stones underfoot, so that Trefor's bare feet slipped in it.
Some bloodied bodies were laid out near the stables, and a
couple of them had the pointed ears and unnaturally shiny
armor of the *Tuatha Dé Danann*. Out of old habit, he

touched his hair to make sure it covered his own faerie ears. Something really weird had just happened here. But before he could stop to find out what, he needed to procure some proper clothing. He tried to refrain from tugging at his tunic as he made his way up the winding path through the bailey to the keep, and wondered whether his stuff was still there.

The Great Hall was empty of people. Everyone seemed busy elsewhere. He saw nobody in the presence chamber downstairs, either, and went to the room off of it he'd occupied when he was here. The place was larger than most of the bedchambers he'd seen, but windowless, and it felt like a cave, much like the burrows he'd lived in for the past few months. A feeling of chronic claustrophobia set in.

He found his belongings there, stacked at the far end of the quarters he'd occupied six months before. It looked like someone else was about to use the room, for there were fresh linens on the beds and a ewer of clean water on the table. No dust anywhere. He threw off his filthy tunic and poured water into the bowl to wash.

His mother's waiting maid, a coarse village woman who didn't like him much, burst into the room and stood regarding him with surprise. Mary's face was smeared with tears and blood. "What do you want?"

He ignored her as he continued to wash. She waited for a reply, but he declined to speak.

Finally she said as if desperate for something to say, "This room has been prepared for Himself."

"What happened out there?"

"Your people attacked us, that's what."

His people? "My people are here. What are you talking about?"

She glowered at him, and her lips pressed together in a stubbornness he recognized. He would learn nothing from her, and it was only because he looked like a faerie and therefore a stranger. So he said, "Why is the earl, *my cousin*, sleeping here?" He took a towel to wipe his face dry. "What's wrong with the lord's own quarters?"

"They're for a visitor tonight. An *important* guest." By which, of course, he was to understand he himself was not important. He ignored that, too.

"And where is our fearless leader?"

Mary blinked and stammered a bit, then said, "He's indisposed."

Trefor looked around. "Where?"

"In his own bed. He's wounded, and wondering where you've been these past months."

"Around. I've been around." Trefor squelched his concern over the report his father had been wounded, but couldn't help asking, "What happened to him? What's going on here?"

"Not that I believe you would concern yourself at all, but the earl was wounded defending the castle."

Trefor figured that was a "duh." He asked with strained patience, "Against whom?"

"Nobody kens who the attackers were. But they've taken our dear Lady Cruachan. She's gone missing since the battle, and nobody can find even a body."

A heavy thud of alarm hit Trefor's gut, and it was all he could do to pretend it hadn't knocked him sideways. His mother had never known him as a son. She'd never liked him any better than Mary did, and during the short time between her return from the Borderlands last summer and his departure to the Bhrochan domain he'd been barred by Alex from even speaking to her. But even so, just by the day or two he'd been with her after his birth, she was still more of a mother than he'd had in the Tennessee foster care system. Though he tried to keep his voice uncaring, he could hear the hard edge to it when he responded, "What happened?"

Mary's eyes were wide with tears now. "Nobody can say. The faeries broke through the portcullis and swarmed the bailey. The earl defended us with his life, and now he may be finished."

Without another word, Trefor turned to yank a shirt, a pair of trews, and a belt from the pile of clothing atop some of his other things against the wall and threw them on. Then he hurried to Alex's quarters, where he found his father sitting on the edge of the bed.

Alex looked up as Trefor blew into the room and came to a stuttering halt at sight of Alex and the people surrounding him. Trefor's father was white of face and blood soaked. A bandage purple with blood wrapped his midsection, and his face and hands were smeared red. A few servants stood by with linen cloth, water, and sewing tools for suturing, and there was a well-turned-out stranger who plainly was the "important" guest Mary had mentioned. The stranger was also blood spattered but didn't appear to have been wounded. He and Alex were the only ones in the room who didn't seem frightened; everyone else was teary eyed and moving about their business with surreptitious clumsiness.

Alex looked up at Trefor and said, "Good of you to join us." Sarcastic as ever, that Alasdair. "Where have you been?" He panted a little from the pain but otherwise was holding himself together.

Trefor's lips pressed together, and he refrained from replying, for anything he might have said just then would have been unproductive. Alex knew who the Bhrochan were, but Trefor didn't care to speak of them in front of this fancy-dressed guy he didn't know. Even in this century, where belief in faeries was more acceptable than in the modern era, he kept his ears covered for a reason, and in fact checked once more to be certain they weren't giving away his heritage to a stranger.

"What happened?"

"I was stabbed."

Trefor waited for an actual response, and the visitor

replied for Alex, "The castle was attacked. We don't know who it may have been, and the countess has gone missing. She must have been what the enemy sought, for they broke off of a sudden and left us, and there is no body to be found."

"You've searched the entire castle? Every corner of the bailey?" Trefor knew his mother was a fighter and could have ended up anywhere, wounded and perhaps dying. Or already dead.

Anguish. Blood. He'd sensed it on the trail.

"There's no sign of her. All others are accounted for."

Alex, breathless from his pain, interrupted. "Trefor Pawlowski, this man is John Rothbury, Earl of Morpeth, messenger from the king."

Trefor and Morpeth nodded greeting to each other, and Trefor's nod dipped low enough to almost be a bow. He'd been in this century long enough to recognize pecking order, and obeyed the protocol.

Trefor then turned to Alex and took on a condescending tone meant to piss him off. "Don't tell me you've lost her *again*."

Alex threw him an evil look, and Trefor tossed it right back. Wounded and bleeding, Alex drew some deep breaths, then began to struggle to his feet. Mary went to him, protesting he should lie down for he was in no condition to stand, but Cruachan growled at her so she stepped back. Then he pulled himself upright. Everyone in the room tensed, ready to catch him if he should fall. But, though he trembled with the effort, he held himself steady and didn't sway.

Morpeth said, "You won't be of much service to the king now, I'm afraid." His tone of regret suggested he thought Alex was about to die.

Alarm rattled Trefor again, and his jaw clenched.

Alex said, "Nonsense. Return to Robert and tell him my men and I will meet him in Ireland as requested." Sweat ran from his brow and past one eye, and he paled even more.

"I cannot tell him that." The king's representative spoke gently, but his conviction was clear. He had no faith Alex would live to fulfill his promise.

Trefor thought he might be right but saw an opportunity and leapt upon it in an instant. "I'll go."

All in the room turned to him, and he resented their surprise. They thought of him as a distant cousin, and further that, his loyalty was in question. Nobody but Alex and Lindsay knew he was Alex's son. They never gave him credit for being a MacNeil, and that angered him nearly as much as the rejection from his parents.

"No, I'll be fine," said Alex.

"Of course you will, cousin. But you have other business to attend to, more important than the war in Ireland."

Alex gave a quick glance at Morpeth, whose eyebrows went up at the suggestion Robert's summons might not be the most important consideration here. Then Alex said for his benefit, "There is nothing more important than the defense of Scotland, Trefor, and I'm shocked you could say there was."

"Your wife. If you live, she will need you."

"She is lost," said Morpeth.

Trefor guessed this guy didn't know the Earl of Cruachan very well if he thought Alex would let his wife go so easily. If there was any possibility Lindsay was still alive, Alex would find her and bring her back. The one thing Trefor had been able to figure out about his father was that. He used that knowledge now.

"Surely, Morpeth, you can't expect Cruachan to let his wife languish in the hands of his enemy," he said.

"No more than Robert 'lets' his wife be captive of the English king."

Trefor blinked, puzzled to learn this. He glanced at Alex, who nodded affirmation that the Queen of Scotland was currently imprisoned in England. Nevertheless, Trefor

pressed Alex. "The attacker was Danann. You know it had
to be An Reubair."

The blow landed like a right hook. Alex actually
flinched. He looked long and hard at Trefor, and the slightly
younger man gazed blandly back. They both knew it must
be the truth. The dead faeries sprawled in the bailey outside
were testimony to it. Who else of the Danann would have
done such a thing? An Reubair—*The Robber*. The faerie
knight who had once employed Lindsay as a hired sword.
Alex's eyes flared bright with anger, and a warm satisfaction filled Trefor. He was as good as on his way to Ireland,
where he would be within notice of the king and in Alex's
place. Almost as good a deal as the inheritance he would
never get. He turned to Morpeth for his acceptance of the
offer.

Morpeth was no fool, and it was plain he didn't care
who came to fight for Robert, so long as there were suffi-
cient men to fill the tribute. He nodded to Trefor and said,
"The king will be pleased to see you and the men of Eilean
Aonarach in Ireland within a fortnight." Then he said to
Alex, with what appeared heartfelt sorrow for the loss of
a peer, "God be with you, Cruachan." Everyone present
knew Morpeth figured Alex would die soon, and most of
them thought the same thing. With that, the king's messenger left the room, his business concluded.

The instant Morpeth was out of earshot, Alex sank to sit
on the edge of his bed again and hissed at Trefor in modern
English, "You little shit."

"Whatever do you mean, dear father?" Irritation rose,
for he was nearly the same age as Alex, and Alex knew
Trefor hated being called "little." Never mind the other.

"You know exactly what I mean. If you undermine me
with Robert I'll have your head on a platter."

"If I undermine you with Robert, you'll be in no position to ask for my head."

"Take care."

"Have faith."

Alex fell silent at that, and some of the anger left his eyes. Like he was thinking. Considering the possibility Trefor wouldn't betray him. But he said nothing. Instead he continued his descent to the bed and lay back, his arm across his bandaged gut. Then his eyes closed and he went still, and Trefor thought for a moment he might have died. But Alex breathed again, and Trefor found the relief of it disconcerting. It would all be so much simpler if Alex would just go ahead and croak, and have done with it. Then Lindsay would be lost to her faerie buddy and Trefor might be able to maneuver himself into the empty spot in Robert's good graces. But Alex was still breathing, and Trefor felt like a monster for wishing he weren't.

A lex slept. When he awoke, the room was dark and seemed empty. He called for Father Patrick, and the pain of raising his voice above a whisper sliced through his gut, sharp and metallic and terrifying. A murmur of people he couldn't see went up in the bedchamber, and he summoned the strength to insist he wasn't dying. Nobody was convinced, and the priest stepped in from the anteroom where it was apparent he'd been waiting. Bent over Alex in his bed, he gripped his beads and began to murmur a prayer, but Alex held the fist and rosary with a hand flaky with dried blood and whispered low enough that only Patrick would hear, "Stop. I don't need that right now; I need to get out of here."

"Out?" The priest also whispered, possibly in collusion but probably more in astonishment.

"Put me on a fishing boat and get me to wherever An Reubair is."

"If you travel, then you will die."

"I won't. There's no smell of bowel in this wound, and I haven't bled out yet so I'm not likely to."

"But if you travel—"

"I'm going to heal." Never mind peritonitis; if the bowel wasn't cut he figured he would beat infection just by pure will. He couldn't die now. Lindsay needed him. There was no choice but to go. "Get me out of here, and I'll heal on the way there. Pick five men, including yourself. Just the men, not their squires. Nobody but knights on this trip. I'm taking us to the Borderlands, where An Reubair is making raids. He's a . . . a man—"

"A faerie."

Alex fell silent. He'd known Patrick believed faeries existed but hadn't realized the priest knew anything else about them.

Patrick said in response to Alex's surprise, "None of the enemy dead in the bailey are human. It doesn't take a sharp intelligence to understand their leader is also one of them."

Alex grunted, then continued, "Reubair is a faerie lord, vassal to the elfin king Nemed, and he leads a band of mercenaries making raids in the Borderlands. We've got to go there to get Lindsay back. Neither Morpeth nor Trefor can know we've gone until we're away. Tonight."

Patrick nodded, but his expression was still grim. "The travel will kill you."

"No, it won't. No more than lying here would."

"It could."

"Get the men, Patrick. The four best swordsmen, and a fisherman to take us." Alex was tired of arguing.

The young priest thought for a moment, nodded again, and left the chamber. Alex lay back with his eyes closed to rest as long as he could, and Mary came to clean and redress his wound.

He called for his page, and when Gregor came he gestured for the boy to come close. Gregor's eyes were wide and glistening, holding tears that spilled the next time he blinked. The blond eight-year-old bent to hear his foster father, and Alex told him, "You'll stay here. Care for the dogs, and if I don't return they will be yours."

The seriousness of the situation was dark concern in the boy's eyes. Alex was continually surprised by the gravity of children in this time. Gregor often struck him as more man than boy. "You're leaving without the puppies?" He hesitated, then added, "And me?"

"I can only take a few men with me. It'll be weapons and bedrolls for us on this adventure, moving too fast for wagons and servants. And no unruly puppies. You're big enough to understand that."

"Aye, my lord."

"Good boy. And tell no one where we've gone tonight. Go to your bed, and when they discover we've gone you tell them you were ordered to bed and never saw us leave. Which will be the truth."

"Aye, my lord." With that, his eyes wide with apprehension, Gregor bowed and left the room.

The fire was dying and night outside the window was pitch-black when Patrick came to help Alex from his bed. His wound was agony, and every movement sharpened it until he could barely breathe. He struggled not to lean on the priest, but his legs wouldn't hold him up. The stairs to the Great Hall loomed like Everest. It was going to be a long climb.

He made it to the landing, then stopped to catch his breath before turning to face the long ascent. There, at the top of the steps beneath a large, flickering torch in a sconce, sat Trefor, elbows on knees and gazing down at Alex and Patrick.

"Going somewhere?"

Alex didn't reply. Patrick only watched Alex for a cue.

Trefor said, "You shouldn't kill yourself just to prove something to me."

"I don't care what you think."

The look on Trefor's face told him how transparent the lie was. "You won't be much good to her if you're dead."

"I'm no good at all to her here."

"There is that, I suppose." Trefor shrugged as if he didn't care what Alex did, but it was also a lie Alex could see through. Trefor continued, "Don't worry about being backstabbed. I'll look out for your interests with Robert as well as your men."

Alex couldn't help giving away his skepticism with a tilt of his head. The more Trefor insisted, the less Alex believed. But all he said was, "Good."

"Really."

"Try anything, and I'll come after you with a crossbow."

"Alex—"

"I mean it."

Trefor went silent, his mouth pressed closed. Then he said, "Aye, my lord." He rose and left the stairs. Alex and Patrick proceeded on their way, up the stairs, and out to the barbican where they joined the four other men who would go with them to the mainland to find Lindsay.

Lindsay fought her captors the entire way to wherever it was these men were taking her. At first they tried to keep her by binding only her hands, but as soon as she gained her feet she ran and they had to chase her down in the western forest of Eilean Aonarach. Though she shouted for help, no farm was near enough for anyone to hear her. The knights bound her feet, but once she was thrown over a horse she wriggled free. They wound ropes around her skirts, and she struggled all the same, cursing and shouting for help. Finally she was gagged, silenced, and held immobile, and when they reached the beach she was thrown into the bottom of a boat like a sack of rocks. For their irritation, they were a bit more rough about it than they might have been. They muttered to each other in their faerie old tongue as they cast off, and their tone made it clear they thought she was being unreasonable in her resistance.

It was a trip of two days, and on the second day they let her sit up on a plank bench, bound to it and gagged. God knew who would hear her this far out on the sea, but they kept the filthy rag tied inside her mouth day and night, except when they fed her. She looked around at the faerie knights who didn't bother to hide their pointed ears. Brazen men, they were, wearing enchanted armor that never oxidized or bore dirt, letting their Danann ears show like badges. They spoke always in the old tongue, casually and with no heed to her beyond that she not leap from the boat and drown herself.

They certainly had no regard for her. They ignored her as if she were baggage and only spoke to her in Middle English to direct her to do something. They fed her sufficiently but gave her the impression it was grudging. As if they were under orders to guard her health and deliver her in one piece. She ate, slept, and abided until there might be an opportunity to escape. When they removed her gag, she knew they must be far from habitation and her hope waned.

A chance to escape never came. When the boat landed on a rocky shore, the group set off in a westerly direction. The land was green. Everywhere Lindsay looked, varying shades of green met her eye, brighter than the islands of Scotland and less rocky. Every so often, off in the distance, she would see a wisp of mist, and as they traveled those foggy spots came closer. Soon they thickened and joined each other, and then Lindsay found herself peering around in it. Hills became shadows, and outcrops of gray granite were ghosts that appeared and disappeared as the horses wended their way along the path. Trees loomed, then were erased behind them as if they'd never been there.

Then, far more suddenly than when they'd entered it, the cluster of knights emerged from the mist to sunlight. As if escaping from a solid thing, Lindsay looked behind to find a perfectly even bank of gray fog that ran like the Great Wall of China from horizon to horizon. A chill skittered up her spine, for this was not natural. It smacked so loudly of magic—very powerful magic—that she now feared what might happen to her. None of the faeries she knew who were this powerful were creatures she wanted dealings with. She didn't think even Danu herself—the queen of the *Tuatha Dé Danann*—was this powerful anymore. The expedition plunged into forest. She shivered as she rode and anticipated meeting the magical being who was her captor.

CHAPTER 4

Another day of travel, and Lindsay figured she wasn't getting away easily even if she were to break free of her bonds. By now her wrists were raw and bleeding, and every muscle in her body was stiff from the awkward position of her shoulders. Riding like this was a nightmare of struggling to not fall off, and if she did it was certain these faeries would simply throw her across the horse's back again and move on. So she held her seat as best she could, and hoped there would be relief soon.

It came when they arrived at a castle. An enormous, rambling construction of stone that shone like fanciful depictions she'd seen of Camelot. Not metallic, exactly, but gray stone with glints of shiny bits that picked up the sun and threw rays even in this overcast day.

"Where are we?"

The faerie knights didn't reply. Didn't even look at her. She sighed and watched the castle grow nearer. Its size was astonishing, compared to her own home where the keep was only a few rooms. This complex seemed to sprawl across the dale, and several towers rose from its center. It was in pristine condition and appeared new. She thought it might very well be, and wondered if they could be in Wales, where Edward I had been busy constructing fortresses in recent decades. An intact castle built by Edward would mean they were in English territory, for most of the garrisons captured by Robert had been torn down over the past couple of years. Even Edinburgh and Stirling had not been spared, for Robert was loath to risk having them recovered by the English king and used against him.

But this castle didn't seem very English. It was too smooth. Too perfect. Too . . . shiny. It was in keeping with the glinting armor of the knights who held her. Edward hadn't built this. Nobody human could have. Not in this century.

Then it came to her: the conversation she'd had with Reubair when he'd proposed marriage to her and told her of lands he held in Ireland. Hidden places no human could find. He'd said Ireland was much larger than any map would ever show, for there was a domain in which the so-called "wee folk" ruled. Where he ruled. A sick, sinking feeling stole over her, and she guessed who she was going to find behind this raid.

The riders passed through the gate and into the streets of the town where the common folk lived. Some folks gathered to greet the newcomers, with a familiarity that suggested they were friends and relatives. Others hung back but watched as the cluster made its way toward the keep that towered over the closely built shops and houses. Shortly the knights and their prisoner arrived in the bailey outside the keep.

Lindsay was hauled from her horse and shoved in the direction of a small door. She stumbled over her skirt and was shoved again. When she fell, nobody helped her to her feet, and she struggled to recover herself and move on.

They waited in silence and didn't shove her again. Too inconvenient to wait again, she supposed.

Through the door into the keep they went, down some steps into a tiny chamber more dank than one might have imagined by the structure above. Apparently the Danann love of shine and cleanliness didn't extend to their dungeons. They went through a labyrinth of equally filthy chambers, through this door and that door, until Lindsay was quite lost. The chambers were empty of people, but in some of them stood tables scattered with tools. Lindsay was afraid to look too closely at the implements, for she guessed they were not kitchen utensils. Then finally they came to a chamber barely the size of a London water closet. A cell, with no opening except the door, in which was a ragged peephole barred with iron that did not shine.

One of the men grabbed her and cut the ropes binding her hands to her waist. Without ceremony or preamble of any kind her dress was also cut from her, ripped and yanked off by those who had brought her there.

"Hey!" She tried to twist away, but her guard held her firm and didn't seem to care whether his knife sliced fabric or skin. The dress, shift, and drawers all were taken from her, her headdress pulled off, and her jewelry taken, including her wedding ring and the ruby necklace she'd worn to impress the king's messenger. Finally, as naked as the day she was born, she was shoved into a corner of the small chamber, and her kidnappers left. The door thudded shut, and there was a loud clank of a key lock from the outside.

She held a palm to her throat, where the necklace had been, knowing the thing was gone forever. It had been a special gift from Alex, a holdout from an early reward from Robert, given to her at a time when he could hardly have afforded such a costly thing. Even now it was beyond their means, but he'd never sold it and had insisted she keep it. Now it was gone. With the wedding ring. Her fingers absently rubbed the spot where the ring had been, for it felt more naked than the rest of her. She never took that off, even when alone with Alex. Especially when alone with Alex. Now it was gone.

This place was all darkness, for there was no torch in the preceding chamber and the peephole was as dark as the solid walls. And cold, for there was no straw, nor even dirt on the floor. A cubicle of stone, as bare as herself. She felt around, to be sure there was no breach in the walls, then sat on the floor to wait. The thought struck her she might be left there to die, and a skittering of terror danced over her spine, but she tamped it down with a deep breath. They'd brought her here for a reason, otherwise they wouldn't have bothered and would have killed her back on Eilean Aonarach. Instead, they'd fed her and made certain she would be in more or less good condition on her arrival here. They intended something for her, and they would make sure she stayed alive for it. So she dabbed tenderly at the sores on her wrists and waited. Eventually she dozed.

There was no telling how long she waited, except by the growling of her stomach. Long enough for her to be very hungry, but not long enough for that hunger to pass into starvation. Hours but not days. The cold had gained inroads on her, and the shivering was constant by the time she heard the rattle of a key.

The door opened, and Lindsay pulled in her legs to hug her knees in an attempt to cover herself. She squinted at the torchlight outside, shading her eyes against it to see a tall silhouette over her. The man reached behind for the torch, brought it into the room, and Lindsay finally saw who her captor was. As she had guessed.

"An Reubair."

"Sir Lindsay." His voice was flat. Expressionless. "Welcome to Castle Finias."

She leaned her head back against the wall behind her, gazed up at him, and didn't bother to stand. A welter of questions flurried through her mind, but she asked none of them, for she was certain she wouldn't like any of the answers. A long silence spun out.

Finally he said, "Did they treat you properly on your journey?"

"Properly, as in, did they take me away from my home and my husband, chase me down, tie me up so I bled, then rip my clothing from me and leave me here to grow cold and hungry? Why, yes, you wanker, it's been a most enjoyable holiday."

"They didn't feed you?"

For a moment she debated not replying but decided that would get her nowhere with him. "I'm not starved."

"You're not dangerously injured?"

"No."

"Then you were treated properly." He said it with the bland, aristocratic conviction of someone who didn't care much what anyone else thought about anything.

"All right, Reubair, why? Why am I here?"

"Because I want you here."

"I've gathered that. What is it you want from me? I mean, besides children."

"Nothing. 'Tis the children I desire."

"So now it's rape. You'll recall, the last man to rape me ended up with his genitalia dropped into a cook fire."

"Jenkins was an idiot. You and I will be married, for the children must be legitimate."

There was a bit of cognitive dissonance, then Lindsay remembered Reubair was a Christian. He wore a gold cross around his neck, hung from a heavy gold chain. A little weird, to her mind, but she figured a faerie could believe whatever a human could and it was his own business.

But, even weirder, Reubair knew about Alex and knew

she was not free to marry. "We've been over this; I've already got a husband."

"An Dubhar is dead."

The room suddenly became too cold to bear. Shivering took her, and she began to struggle for air. "No. He's not dead." Not possible. Unthinkable.

"He surely is. And once I have confirmation of it, you and I will be married."

Lindsay's eyes narrowed at him. He sounded utterly certain she would heave over and marry him, and that Alex was the only thing keeping her from it. "You can forget that. I won't marry you, Reubair."

"You will."

"No, I won't. So bring me some clothing, give me a horse, and I'll be on my way. There's no chance I'll agree to marry you."

He snorted. "Oh, I realize you'll never agree. I can't expect that, and don't know that it matters. My priest will marry us, and once we're wed you will be my wife." He explained no further, and Lindsay was puzzled that he seemed to think no further explanation was necessary.

"Not without my consent."

Now it was his turn to appear puzzled. "Consent has naught to do with it."

"Such a marriage would not be valid."

"Indeed, it would. And will. You'll be my wife and will be obligated to bear my children. My heir."

Lindsay was gobsmacked. A memory of something Alex had said some time ago wriggled its way to the surface of her mind. He'd once told her he could force her to marry him. Back before she'd agreed to it, he'd said Hector had urged him to force her into marriage. She'd not believed it possible—had thought Alex was having her on—but now Reubair was saying the same thing. "Marriage by force?"

"Aye. As 'valid,' as you say, as any in the eyes of God." Which, of course, in these days where secular life was little differentiated from the religious, meant it was the law.

The walls of this close cell closed in even more. Lindsay's mind boggled. A long scream rose, but she swallowed it in silence and shivered harder than ever. It was a struggle to control her breathing. She wanted to leap up and scratch Reubair's eyes from his face, but only dug her nails into her palms. Her mind raced for an out, and she brightened when she found one.

"Robert won't stand for it. If Alex is dead . . ." Her eyes shut for a moment to blot out the image. ". . . If he's dead, then my guardianship reverts to the king along with all of Alex's property. He decides who or whether I can marry."

"He'll agree to it, particularly since it will be already accomplished by the time he hears. No question. You're neither rich enough nor well enough connected for His Majesty to care much what happens to you now that Alasdair an Dubhar is gone. So long as I ask for no dowry, he'll be happy to have me take you off his hands. Particularly since his coffers have never been full and his military campaigns are expensive."

Lindsay's heart sank, for she knew it was true. She had no family in this century other than Alex. Her cover story about being from Hungary had her as being without parents, dowry, or influence. She just wasn't important enough for Robert to fuss about, and Reubair was certainly wealthy enough to buy off the needy king. All she could do was stare at her captor and hug her knees.

Reubair gave her a good, long look, as if appraising her body for future reference, and a little smile turned up the corners of his mouth. "Once the marriage is consummated, I believe your heart will soften toward me."

"Unlikely."

"We shall see." He handed back the torch to the dungeon

guard, then retreated from the cell. The guard shut the door with a dull clank of iron lock and turned the key in it. Footsteps, another clank, and Lindsay was left in the darkness to turn over and over in her mind the horror of what she'd just been told.

For a time a sudden cold snap in the weather sent her huddling into a corner, clenched in a fetal curl with her arms wrapped tightly around her knees. She occupied herself in miserable shivering. For the first time she thought she might succeed in dying, and knew she would welcome it. She avoided thinking about Alex, for whenever she did her chest tightened with grief until she could barely breathe. The ache in her heart was too much to bear in this place, so she removed her thoughts from home and husband and focused on the situation at hand. Probably the time since her arrival had added up to a number of days. The exact number was unknowable, for meals seemed irregular and she slept often out of boredom. The cold was a constant. From time to time she stood to stretch and walked circles within her cell, her fingers lightly skipping over the stones in the wall so she wouldn't bump into them. It was a short walk around, and so dark that at first she could only orient herself by feeling the door as she passed. After a few days, however, she realized she'd learned the topography of the rough-hewn stones at shoulder height. On the left wall was a spot where the mortar was very thin and the stones close together, and the back wall boasted one very large stone that bulged at the far end. The corner of the room was exactly one pace beyond it. Soon that stone became like a friendly face one might encounter every day at a bus stop year after year.

The food was plain, and though it was a bit stale she figured it was better fare than other prisoners might get. Reubair definitely wanted her whole and well.

So she stopped eating.

The peephole in the door was small, but the spaces between the bars were just wide enough for her to push through the bits of bread and meat brought to her. When her jailer began bringing stew and soup, difficult to funnel out the hole, she simply poured the food into the slop bucket into which she peed. Water was all she consumed. For how many days, she couldn't tell. No sunrise, no sunset, and the hunger was constant. Eventually it became a hardness in her gut. She sat on the floor of her cell in a stupor, dozing lightly off and on. It crossed her mind they might let her die, and after a while she began to think that wouldn't be such a bad thing.

The loneliness invaded as relentlessly as the cold, and when food came she tried to talk to the guard who brought it. That was an exercise in futility, but any exercise was good. Every attempt to pry words from Reubair's underlings failed, and she might as well have been talking to the walls. Which she did a bit of, in a murmur that was nearly prayer. Sometimes it segued into prayer, but in the end she remained cold, lonely, and hungry.

The darkness became eternal. Her mind became convinced it had always been there, and would ever remain. Seamless. Infinite. Lindsay accepted it, for there was no choice. Sometimes she hummed to herself to banish the silence, but she could do nothing about the darkness. When Reubair came again, his presence seemed nearly surreal, for her reality had become cold and loneliness, and did not include him.

The door clanked open, and she looked up to shade her eyes against the torch carried by the jailer. A dry comment about how good it was for him to drop by stuck in her throat. By the time the thought was formed, it seemed pointless.

Reubair said, "You must ask for a divorce."

"Very well, I divorce you." She giggled at that. Not

terribly witty, but intensely entertaining relative to all else that had held her attention lately.

"I have a letter for you to sign, asking the pope for a judgment of annulment. Your marriage to Cruachan is invalid."

"It's not."

"It is. The banns were not said three times, but only two."

"Not true. And what would you know about it, in any case? You weren't there. I didn't even know you then."

Then realization struck her, and her heart lifted in sweet relief. "Alex is still alive. You've had word, and he's still alive."

Silence. Reubair declined to reply, and that was as good as a "yes."

Tears sprang to her eyes. Alex was still alive. She murmured a quick prayer of thanks.

Reubair said, "You will sign this paper."

"I will not."

"You will sign it, or you will rot here."

"Very well." A look of triumph slipped onto his face, but she added, "I'll get on with my rotting, then. If you would be so kind as to shut the door when you leave, that's a good fellow."

Triumph turned to a scowl.

She asked, "Why do you want me to sign your silly paper? Most men in your position would simply forge my name and have done with it."

"That would be against the law and invalidate the annulment."

"No one would know."

"God would know."

Lindsay opened her mouth to ask why he thought God would be okay with a letter signed under duress but realized it would be pointless. Along with the obvious technology shortages of this time, she'd spent the past few years coping with the culture shock of a legal system that conflated canon and secular law to the point that the two were often indistinguishable. Reubair didn't want the annulment so the pope would be happy with the forced marriage; he wanted it so God would be happy with it. Somewhere along the line, the legal technicalities of priest and ceremony became all that mattered, and apparently there was no law against forced marriage or forcing someone to sign a letter. The spiritual aspect of those things never occurred to anyone.

Instead, Lindsay said, "Get out. I'll not sign your letter. I'll die first."

"You could very well." There was no dire note of threat in his voice, but only reflection of regret. "But first there are other things I might do to convince you to obey. Are you certain you won't reconsider?"

"If you want me attractive and healthy enough to bear children, you won't want to let your torturer at me."

"There is torture, and then *torture*. We Danann can be creative, and we know our humans."

A shiver ran through her, and she hoped it was too dark for him to see it. "Bring it on."

Reubair didn't reply to that, but only gazed at her for a moment and then left. The cell door clanked shut behind him.

The darkness enveloped her once again.

But only a few minutes later the guard returned. "Get up," he said. A shackle chain dangled from his hands.

She climbed to her feet. He knelt and attached the shackle to her ankle, locked it with a key, then handed her the other end of the chain. "Come with me."

Curiosity made her forget to be afraid. What in the world was he up to? She followed him out of the cell, up several flights of stairs, and through more chambers and more stairs. Lindsay would have been quite unable to find

her way back to the cell even if she'd wanted to. The
warmth of these upper rooms where fires burned merrily in
each hearth thawed the worst of her cold extremities. Then
they arrived at what appeared to be the Great Hall. Almost
too warm now, her fingers and toes burned as circulation
returned.

It wasn't mealtime, so there was only a scattering of extremely well-dressed people here and there in the huge room.
When she and the guard entered, they all looked up, fell
silent, and watched her make her progress across the floor.
She became suddenly and acutely conscious of her state of
undress, and a hot flush rose to her skin. All the more humiliating, everyone in the room could see her break out in dark,
splotchy red all up and down her body. She crossed her arms
in front of her, one forearm over her breasts and one angled
across her crotch.

Aside from that, she struggled not to show her discomfort. It was difficult, but she managed to stare as openly as
the onlookers and noted they were all faeries. Aside from
her one brief meeting with Danu some years before, these
were the first she'd ever seen who appeared to be nobility.
But then she recognized one of them as a raider named Iain,
one who'd helped Jenkins rape her. He was dressed more
stylishly, in more distinct faerie fashion, than he'd been
when he was her comrade making raids on English villages
in the Borderlands the year before. Her eyes narrowed at
sight of him, and his only reaction was to look away.

She was led from the Great Hall to the bailey outside, to
an outcrop of rock that rose from the ground near a high
garden wall. There the guard retrieved the end of the chain
from her hands and knelt once again. He slipped a spike
through the end link, set it against the rock, drew a hammer
from his belt, and pounded the spike into the rock.

Lindsay looked around at where she was and realized
what was happening. She was tethered to this rock, in the

middle of the bailey where people were coming and going as on a busy street.

The guard finished his work, stood, and walked away.

"Wait! Why are you leaving me here? How long . . ."

He wasn't responding, and she realized how long she'd be left here. Until she signed that blasted letter. She looked up at the high windows of the upper stories of the keep. Reubair thought he could embarrass her into surrender. *Fool.* She'd show him just how easily embarrassed she was not.

At least, she'd bluff it and hope he would give up soon. Once more acceptance was the key. She was naked and chained to a rock, and all the protests and yanking on her shackle wouldn't change that. So she investigated the limits of her restraints. The rise of rock to which she was chained was only about knee-high, and the chain allowed her to climb just to the other side. There was a flat space between the rock and the garden wall, and if she stretched out her leg and an arm she could barely touch the rough, glittering stone. She looked around at where she was and sighed. "Rock and hard place, indeed."

On the bailey side of the rock, the chain would almost reach the center between keep and stable. Except for the outcrop of granite, the area within her range was flat earth and a few patches of paving stones. She sat on her rock, huddled with her knees pressed to her chest, and watched people stare at her as they walked past.

She wanted to crawl into a hole, and had there been any sort of tool handy she would have dug one. She was expressionless as she stared back at passersby, who sometimes continued to gawk, but more often than not looked away and hurried on.

Food came as usual, but as soon as it was delivered she threw it as far as she could. Dogs ate it. If Reubair thought she would forget to not eat in her humiliation, he was mad. She drank the water but refused food.

After a while, she needed to pee. She didn't want to do it here and put it off, though she knew she wasn't likely to be brought a slop bucket. She was right. By sunset her bladder was so painfully full she thought she might have damaged it. She had to go, or it would dribble down her leg and that would be infinitely worse. So she went to the farthest reach of the chain, between the rock and the garden wall, and squatted on her heels. The stream puddled and ran, and to her dismay touched her foot. It occurred to her to be glad there was no clothing for it to soil. Her foot would wipe more or less clean in the dirt. After a good, long drip dry, she stood, kicked dirt over the spot, and went to the opposite quarter of her area. There she huddled into herself again and shivered as the sun went down.

It went like that for days. The hunger strike continued, and she weakened. The weaker she became, the more she slept, the less she cared who gawked at her in the bailey. The corner she used for peeing began to stink like a garderobe, but she cared even less about that. Whenever the horror of her predicament crowded into her mind, she turned her thoughts to Alex. Her husband was still alive, and that was all that mattered.

When the guard came and threw some clothing onto her where she slept, she picked it up and stared dully at it. A heavy silken overdress with extraordinarily long sleeves, underclothes of equally silken but less weighty fabric, and slippers with points that curled back over her toes in the faerie fashion that was now coming in vogue among humans. The guard retreated immediately, before she could ask what was going on.

Lindsay rose, and a wave of dizziness sent her sideways. She staggered a couple of steps, then righted herself and held up the dress. She felt of the clothing. Something to wear, after so long without so much as a blanket to wrap around herself, seemed an unthinkable luxury. Never mind modesty, the warmth of it would be heaven. Quickly she sorted out the pieces and put them on as best she could without someone to help her with buttons and ties. No drawers, though. She couldn't have pulled them on over the shackle anyway. Just as she was noting the sleeves that covered almost to the tips of her fingers, the guard returned and unlocked the shackle on her leg.

"That way," he said and gestured toward the keep. Back through the Great Hall they went, the guard indicating at each juncture which way to go. She went up a circular stairwell, straightening her clothing and struggling to arrange her hair with her fingers. Beneath the fine silk she was as filthy as ever, and there were wee beasties crawling around on her scalp. A bath would certainly have been too much to ask for, but she would have given a lot for some private time at a fireside in order to pick herself clean of parasites. She scratched her head and wondered where the guard was taking her.

Through another door, into yet another chamber, then another, and finally Lindsay found herself in a chamber that had no further exit. A bedchamber, containing a large bed hung with heavy curtains and one much smaller closet bed with carved wooden doors. Opposite the hearth hung a rich, colorful tapestry depicting a swarm of winged fey hunting a dragon, and at one end of the room stood a heavy table large enough for an elaborate setting for four people. Just then it was set for only two, but groaned under many platters of food. Enough for a good company of men, it seemed. The smell of it wafted through the room, and Lindsay's mouth watered terribly for it. Her gut turned and heart pounded, and it was all she could do to not leap upon the food and cram fistfuls of it into her mouth. Dizziness nearly sent her to her knees. Even the dinners at Eilean Aonarach were never this tempting, and hunger sharpened unbearably the sublime pleasure of the smell.

Sitting in a chair at one of the set places was An Reubair. He lounged against the back and leaned heavily on one arm, long, blond hair loose around his shoulders and head tilted a bit as he regarded her with an air of appraisal. She was suddenly so conscious of her unkempt state she could hardly look at him, but she forced herself to stare back. Also in appraisal. Her body gave a hard shiver, then was still, finally warm enough to stop shaking. Like Iain, Reubair was dressed in überclean tunic and trews without spot, smudge, or unnecessary wrinkle. Rings graced his fingers and a heavy collar lay about his shoulders. The good-sized links in it were of gold, some of them enameled, crosses alternating with roses. She'd once been told he was extremely wealthy, but she'd not believed it at the time. In retrospect, she should have believed the ancient stories of faerie treasure might have been true.

"You smell," he said in a flat, matter-of-fact tone.

"You're an asshole. I can take a bath, but I'm afraid there's no hope for you."

He smiled at that, and the amusement showed in his eyes. God save her from men who thought she was cute and funny. "Have a seat. Help yourself to supper." An insouciant hand waved toward the dishes on the table, of slabs of beef and poultry, of crockery filled to brimming with baked fruits stuffed with nuts and covered with sauces, of delicate confections made of spun sugar so perfect she knew there must have been magic of some sort involved in their construction. When she didn't respond, but stared dully at the floor, he urged her, "Go ahead. There's nothing to be afraid of."

She glanced sideways at him. If he said it, it couldn't be so. She moved not a muscle, for if she did she would lose all control over herself.

"Oh, come now," he said, his voice thick with impatience and frustration. "You've won. I've taken you off your chain. You should be happy now."

"I want to go home. And I want my wedding ring back."

"Be grateful for this."

"This"—she glanced around the room—"is captivity."

"Killing yourself will get you nowhere but dead."

"Then I'll be with Alex." She cut her eyes toward him. "Or not."

That silenced Reubair for a moment. After some deep thought he said, "Let us talk. If you would be reasonable, perhaps you could show me my error. Surely your mental faculties are impaired by this starvation tactic, so eat first."

Just how impaired it had made her was clear, by the fact that she considered seriously his words. She glanced at the food on the table and had to swallow hard the saliva that filled her mouth, betraying her weakened resolve.

"Please. Eat. Then if you insist I will return you to your cell and you can continue your protest until you die."

That did it. Instinct for survival overcame higher conviction, and her body moved without orders from her brain.

She sat in the chair to Reubair's left and helped herself to a piece of beef. It was the most delicious thing she'd ever eaten. To say she wolfed it would have been a denigration of actual wolves, for the meat was tender and hot and it slipped down her throat without chewing to speak of. Grease ran down her chin and dripped from it, and since there was no napkin she wiped it with the tail of the tablecloth. As she ate, Reubair also picked up a large chunk of the meat, took a bite, and chewed slowly, gazing at her. She looked away from him. Then he took a stoneware pitcher and poured something that looked like spiced mead into the silver goblet set at her place. His goblet had already been filled, and he took a sip. It was ordinary grape wine, and she wondered why he'd not offered her that. But then, he knew she disliked

English wine as much as she did mead, so it was no matter. She began to slow some in her eating, chewed, swallowed as quickly as possible, and took another bite. Then, with a wad of meat in her cheek, she said, "I won't marry you." She sucked some grease from her fingers and chewed some more.

"You will. Furthermore, by the time it happens I think you'll want it. And it will happen whether you do or not."

"I'll die first."

"Don't be that way. I'm wealthy and can give you everything you've ever wanted; why not make the best of it?"

"You can't give me anything I've ever wanted. You don't love me; you don't respect me. I have a son, so you're too late to make me a mother." Reubair already knew that, but he didn't know Trefor had grown to adulthood in another century, just as he didn't know she herself was not of this time. She figured all that was best left unsaid. She continued, "I'm not impressed by great wealth; you're not so good with a sword as to make me swoon at your prowess; and whatever magic abilities you have would leave me cold even if I ever saw them. In short, you have nothing to offer me."

"Then I must take you by force."

"And, as I've already pointed out, that's far easier said than done. I will not only fight you every moment, but I will make every effort to ensure that any child you foist on me will not come to term."

"Also easier said than done, short of killing yourself."

She gave a slight nod in acknowledgment of the truth of that, which brought raised eyebrows and, she thought, a bit of apprehension to his eyes. "You can be restrained," he pointed out.

"I recommend it."

"Be reasonable." He leaned forward and stared into her face, his voice almost pleading.

A blurt of laughter bubbled from her, and she glanced

around to indicate her surroundings. "This is hardly a reasonable situation!" She took a sip of the spiced mead and continued, "The idea that I could ever want to forsake a husband who loves me and willingly spend the rest of my life with someone who wants to use me for an incubator is utterly ridiculous. Absurd. *Impossible.* Come to your senses, Reubair. Reason has no place here."

He sat back and sighed. "Perhaps you're right. I'm the one who has been less than realistic."

His sudden capitulation gave her pause. She looked at him and wondered what was afoot.

But he continued, "I hope you'll consider my words. Once I have received confirmation of An Dubhar's death, I think your feelings might change. A woman alone can be terribly vulnerable."

"I'm not like most women, and you know that."

"You're enough like other women, where it matters, that you must see the advantage of being my wife rather than Cruachan's widow."

"Dowager Countess."

"Only until Robert marries you off."

"Better to anyone but you."

Now he sighed in frustration. "Well, Sir Lindsay, you see that's where I would convince you you're wrong. 'Tis better I should be your husband, for another husband might be fool enough to beat you."

"Only once."

"Then you would be a widow again, but not for long, for you would be hung. Or burned. You wouldn't want to be burned."

"Of course not. No more than I would want to be married to you. In fact, it's rather a toss-up to determine which would be worse."

There was no reply to that, and Reubair's eyes narrowed at her.

She looked around the room, then at her empty plate. Unfortunately her shrunken stomach couldn't hold any more and now ached with fullness. She contemplated the remaining food on the table, then said, "I'm finished here. Is there any chance of having a wash before you return me to the bailey and take back these clothes?"

Reubair's lips pressed together in disgust, and he reached for a bell sitting on the table. It gave a tiny, musical tinkle, and a servant entered the room immediately. Lindsay noted the valet was human. It occurred to her that humans might be the second-class citizenry in Reubair's domain, and she wondered if his fixation on her constituted a form of slumming.

Without a moment of hesitation, Reubair gave orders for a bath to be set up before the hearth, and Lindsay's heart couldn't help but soften. *A bath.* Not just a ewer and bowl, but actual immersion in hot water. Reubair owned a tub, apparently, and he was going to let her use it. She reached over to break off a rose made of sugar from the arrangement before her and sucked on it thoughtfully. For a hot bath, she wouldn't even care that she was going to have to strip in front of him.

The tub was heaven after so many days in dirt, cold, and darkness. Hot water soaked into her corners. She picked fleas from her head and flicked them lazily into the fire and hoped Reubair would let her stay until she turned entirely into a prune. He sat at the table and kicked back in the chair, lounging and gazing at her and saying nothing. No bubbles in this bath, and he was getting an eyeful, but she ignored him and began picking the dirt from under her nails. Even if he was going to send her back to the dungeon or the bailey, she would have these moments of comfort and he could look all he wanted. There was no fear of him. If he tried to touch her she would damage him, and he knew it.

There was a knock at the door, and at Reubair's bidding a faerie knight entered, breathless and unhappy. Pale, even for a Danann; his cheeks held no roses, and he'd even broken a sweat. "I've bad news, sir."

Reubair pursed his mouth, then said, "Let's have it, then."

The knight gawked at Lindsay in the tub.

"Look over here," said Reubair and pointed to his own face so the knight would leave her alone.

The knight looked away from the tub, then said, "News from Scottish Eilean Aonarach. Cruachan has set out to find you."

Lindsay went utterly still. Relief was so profound her eyes stung and she struggled to not put her hands over her face. Alex was coming to get her. Knowing that, all else dimmed in importance. Her husband was still her husband, and Reubair could do nothing about it. She stared at her feet under the water and continued to ignore her captor. Alex was coming and soon she would be returned to him.

"When can we expect him?"

The messenger wagged his head. "There is no way to know, for he was well gone by the time I learned it. Indeed, I expected to find he'd been here before me by the time I arrived. He left no word of the direction he would take; he could be near, or far. I cannot say."

"Can he find his way through the mists?"

"Rumor says he has recourse to Danu herself."

Reubair bit a corner of his mouth and thought that over for a moment. Then he dismissed the messenger and said to Lindsay, "Unlucky."

Lindsay declined to reply, but continued to groom herself, slowly, certain she would be sent back to the dungeon in a moment.

But instead he said, "Climb out of that tub, dry off, and restore your shift. You'll sleep in the servant's bed. Go there now."

She looked at him, then at the closet bed in the corner. Sleep here? But not in his own bed? It sounded like a pretty good deal, and she looked to him for explanation, but it appeared he had nothing further to say. Instead he turned his attention to the food on the table and took a stuffed pear to chew on. Elbows leaning heavily on the board before him, he stared into the middle distance, thinking.

Lindsay wondered what was next in his plan.

CHAPTER 5

By the time Alex reached the mainland with his small contingent, it was apparent he wasn't going to die of his wound. Not directly, in any case, and not right away. Infection was still a possibility, for the opening hadn't closed entirely yet. Mary had sewn him up like a rent T-shirt, in a neat row of black stitches. He could feel each and every one of them pulling at his skin. They itched already, and he wished he dared take them out.

As they neared the English border, headed for Carlisle where rumor had it rogue knights were harrying nearby villages, Alex realized he wasn't healing as quickly as he should. Still no visible infection, but his strength wasn't returning the way it always had before when he was wounded. The possibility of internal damage turned over and over in his mind as he rode. Sometimes, in a stabbing, a weapon would go straight in and hit nothing. Other times it would slice up everything in its path. Without enough immediate blood loss, it could take weeks to die even if the bowel was cut. Longer, if the source of infection was small and slow growing. There was no knowing what damage might have been done to his guts, and only time would tell if he could survive it.

He'd been stabbed before. Shoot, he'd been stabbed in the belly before, but this was different. This time his peritoneum had been breached and there was a deep sense of alarm underlying every thought and movement. His body knew it was in danger. His gut felt as if his entrails were ready to spill out, and he rode with one arm pressed hard against his side. Cold sweat popped up every so often. Every step of his horse was a jolt of pain, and he had to remember to breathe. Even that small action was painful, and he did it in short, panting gasps. Hour after hour, his horse plodded along the track south to the Borderlands. It didn't take long for him to sag in his saddle. More than ever in his life he longed for the days when he could have made this trip at Mach 3. The days when he might not have been so terrified of infection.

He looked around him at the knights he'd brought. Each bore scars from fights, and two of them had skin lesions from infection. Kept hidden, for sores were always thought to be leprosy, Alex had glimpsed them once or twice. More knights might have them, that he hadn't seen. Having come from a culture where even acne was considered unforgivable blemish, he'd never seen anything like this until coming to this century. Here, acne was taken as nothing. Harmless, and therefore something to be ignored. Smallpox scars were even considered a good thing, since it meant one had contracted the disease and survived it. Lesions were more common among the poor, for rich men tended to marry healthy, unblemished women, but were common enough among the knights of Alex's household. Sight of nobility bearing open sores brought home the understanding that in this century there was no recourse once an infection got hold. No antibiotics. Nothing to take down inflammation. Nothing to help his body fight off a general infection if something nasty were to take up housekeeping in his gut. Each time his thoughts wandered in that direction, the panic renewed and breaths came hard.

Father Patrick sidled close and rode next to him. "Should we find a farmhouse and obtain a wagon for you, my lord?"

Alex gathered himself and sat straight. One big, deep breath, and he held it for a moment before letting it out in a long sigh. "No. I'm fine."

"One should have a care for lying to a priest."

A corner of Alex's mouth lifted in the best grin he could manage. "I suppose you'll tattle on me to God."

"If ever I have His ear, which I admit is less often than one might hope."

Alex wanted to laugh but didn't. Instead he pressed his arm more firmly to his side.

"Is your wound still red?"

The earl nodded. In fact, it had grown redder. He'd been watching carefully for red streaks or yellow patches on his belly, but beyond lancing and cleaning any pustules he had no idea what he might do if he found them. Distilled alcohol hadn't even been invented yet, and he had no idea how to make it himself. All he had going for himself was determination to not die before finding Lindsay.

Patrick rode on beside him in silence. Alex got a sense he was praying.

He and his five men were hot on the trail of Reubair's troupe, acting on information they'd had in Lochaber, and Alex wondered how he was going to get Lindsay away from them. Pitched battle wasn't an option—not with only five men behind him. He would have to take her by stealth. He sent a scout in search of sign, and hoped if the faerie knights were found she wouldn't be heavily guarded.

Faeries. That meant magic. He hated magic, because he didn't know how to fight it. God knew what fey protections those guys might have on their campsite.

Lindsay was undoubtedly restrained by Reubair somehow, or she would have escaped from him. It occurred to him she may have escaped and be on her way back home. Alex could search all summer and never find her. He could be killing himself for nothing, but there was no way to know. All he could do was keep after the band of raiders and hope for answers when he caught up with them.

At night he lay beside the small cook fire dying to ashes as the other knights slept. One of them snored loudly enough to make Alex wonder why they hadn't been detected by those they pursued. He should go over and give the guy a shove with his boot—shut him up—but that would involve getting up, and he wasn't sure he could. He lay on the ground and listened for approaching enemy.

In the dim, barely flickering light, Father Patrick prayed on his knees atop his bedroll, his rosary woven between his fingers as his lips formed rapid, nearly breathless words. Alex watched him and wondered, as always puzzled by the man. Patrick was several years younger than Trefor, wielded a weapon as skillfully as Alex's best swordsman, and yet despite his physical energy, he embodied the sort of emotional aplomb usually found in very old men. There was none of the raw edge of youth, not even zeal for his sincere faith. Only a core of hope. Not stoicism, but real hope, which Alex had never understood in anyone, no matter how young or old.

When Patrick was finished with his prayers and hung the string of beads around his neck for safekeeping, Alex said softly, "How about a prayer for me?"

Patrick turned to him and smiled. "Several for you, my lord. Each day."

"Afraid I'll go to hell?"

"I know you won't. I've heard your confession and I believe your repentance for transgressions is sincere."

"But you pray for me anyway."

Patrick shrugged. "It's all to the good. Your spiritual life is my responsibility, and to pray for you is to know you better."

Alex wasn't so sure about that. He looked toward the fire and wished the pain in his gut would ease up. These days his spirit was pretty much wrapped up in ignoring pain in this life, never mind the next. Patrick was waiting for him to speak, so Alex said, "What makes you so sure there even is a God?"

Bald surprise made Patrick's face go slack. "Never say such things."

"You're offended?"

The priest glanced around at the sleeping knights, his expression boggled, and when he spoke his tone suggested astonishment that he needed to explain this. "I fear for your life. An enemy—or even a devout friend—would see you burned, were he to hear that." It went without saying he thought enemies could be anywhere, for his eye was on Alex's four other retainers who, with luck, were truly asleep and not listening.

Alex gave a wry chuckle. "Aye. If I die, then where would you be?"

Patrick raised his chin. "Serving God as always, but someplace other than Eilean Aonarach. However, I've grown fond of the place, for its laird is a rare good man and I would hate to see him brought down by a careless word. Never let anyone hear you express such doubt."

"You're my confessor. You won't tell anyone."

"And that is your salvation, my lord."

"Seriously, Patrick, surely even you've had moments of doubt."

"Moments. Very brief and under severe circumstance. I'm as flawed as any other man."

"How do you cling to hope then? With all the flawed men everywhere, how do you keep thinking all is right with the world when you see horrible things happening all the time?" Alex wanted to ask how Patrick could be so infuriatingly calm every minute when the world was going to hell in a handbasket, and Alex knew it would continue to do so for at least seven more centuries, if not forever after. No end in sight. It was a terrible thing to know so surely.

Patrick shrugged. "Faith."

"And why is that such a good thing?"

Now the priest smiled. "Because the alternative is constant doubt and worry. Worry corrodes the soul. It gives nothing but pain. Have faith, and the pain goes away. Fear is defeated."

"So you think it's a good thing to be purposely stupid?"

"Purposely stupid? No. Ignoring the circumstance isn't the same as being certain of something for which there is no evidence. What one can see, touch, and hear is undeniable and requires no strength of spirit to understand, but not everything is knowable. What one cannot sense, except within one's heart, is the purview of faith."

Alex thought about that for a moment, then Patrick said carefully, "Tell me, my lord, are we talking about faith in God, or might we be talking about someone a little more down to earth?"

Trefor? Lindsay, even? Alex gazed at the priest, then replied, "Easy enough to talk yourself into thinking a well-meaning God will make things turn out well in the end, but people are nearly always a disappointment."

"True, it's more difficult to depend on a flawed relative than on an omniscient being who is always right because rightness is defined by His actions. But often your very faith and influence—your strength of spirit—will help that flawed man want to make the right choices."

That made Alex chuckle, and a shot of pain pierced him. His eyes shut and he said, "If I believe in Trefor, he'll like me better and want to please me?"

"If you believe in him, he will believe in himself and be stronger for it. He will be a better man and therefore better in your eyes."

Alex gazed into Patrick's utterly sincere face and considered his words. Then Patrick said something that nearly made Alex's jaw drop.

"You are his family, after all. He seems closer to you than a cousin."

Alex's attention on Patrick sharpened. What did he know? What could he have heard about Trefor?

But Patrick continued, "It's plain he wishes he were more closely related to you, and holds you as more of a brother than a cousin."

Brother. Alex could accept that. Patrick hadn't said "son." Alex said, "He doesn't show it much."

"On the contrary, he fairly shouts it. All you need is to listen."

"He does nothing but argue with me."

"Indeed he does. If he cared nothing, he would ignore you entirely."

Alex blinked in surprise, for he realized the priest was right. He rolled onto his back and stared at the dim pattern of tree branches overhead as Patrick prepared his bedroll for sleep.

Just short of Carlisle, the weather turned suddenly cold, a light drizzle of snow hearkening back to winter. Alex's scout rode into camp in the evening, in a hurry and his horse nearly blown. Out of breath himself and filled with excitement, he reported to Alex, "I saw them. Faerie knights encamped not far from here."

Alex struggled to his feet, his arm as ever pressed against his side. "Did you see their ears?"

"Aye. And I smelled them." He nodded hard, and his lanky brown hair fell into his eyes. When he tossed it from his face his goofy grin reminded Alex of one of the Beatles, though he couldn't remember exactly which one.

Alex frowned. "Smell?"

"Indeed. Did you not know that faeries have a smell? Particularly when they are massed as these are. 'Tis similar to a freshly turned furrow. No matter how long they've been aboveground, they smell strongly of their burrows. Like plowed earth or dug moss."

That tidbit of information had eluded Alex and interested him now, but he didn't pursue it and merely grunted in reply. "Did you see the countess?"

The knight blinked in distress. "No, but she must be there, my lord. They've tents; I couldn't lay eyes on all of them."

Alex figured Lindsay must be in one of the tents. "Tell me the layout of their camp. Have they pickets posted?" He called for Patrick and the others, and the six of them gathered around their fire to map out a plan to creepy-crawl the camp. Moving with utmost stealth, they would locate and extract Lindsay without disturbing the sleeping enemy. With luck, the faeries would never know they'd been breached until Lindsay went missing the next morning. Snowflakes danced around them and hissed on their small fire. Then they slept until the moon was nearly set.

At full dark, when the moon was gone and the sun not nearly risen, snow was still falling. Alex and his contingent approached the camp of Reubair's knights on foot. Stealthy and silent, they went downwind, for faerie hearing and smell were nearly as acute as an animal's. The cold air was lucky, for dampening their scent. This was like sneaking up on a wolf pack, and at least as treacherous. Alex stopped at a rise where he could see nearly the entire arrangement of tents, and a scattering of men in bedrolls who had no tents. Lindsay wouldn't be one of those, not if Reubair had an interest in her. She would be in one of the tents with him, under guard, and the question was which one was most likely to be his. Alex and his men would have only one chance at this, and they needed to nail the right tent the first time.

The big one in the middle. That would be the leader, and that would be Reubair. If Lindsay was in this camp, it would be in there, Alex was certain, for Reubair would want her where he could see her and control her himself. Sloppiness in dealing with Lindsay was unwise, and Reubair would know that. An image of her in chains flashed before him, and red anger colored it. Alex would kill the faerie, he was certain. Never mind whether she was hurt or not, he was going to kill Reubair on principle.

He pointed to the large green tent pitched near the crumbling embers of a good-sized cook fire and gestured for his men to follow with their swords drawn.

Hair stood up on the back of Alex's neck as he led his contingent between sleeping bodies dusted with snow, toward the heart of the camp. There was no picket, and the band of raiders was overconfident in its numbers. One thing Alex had learned about knights in this time was that they tended to arrogance to the point of carelessness, and in fact took pride in it. Safety measures and conservative action deemed mandatory by his modern training were sometimes seen by knights as a form of cowardice, which made them vulnerable to stealth attack and avoidance tactics in battle. Military men would one day learn better, but in the meanwhile Alex, as a commander, was seven centuries ahead of his time and had the edge on these guys. He went straight to the heart of their camp, quickly, quietly, in a maneuver they would have found appalling, cowardly, and unfair—bordering on insane—had they been conscious to see it.

Nevertheless, he failed to reach the tent he'd targeted.

Not far from the cook fire, a booted foot shot out from one of the bedrolls and kicked him in the shin. He stumbled and recovered, and pain pierced his gut like a fresh sword stroke. Father Patrick, just behind him, ran up and dispatched the faerie knight with his sword, but as the wounded defender lay dying he shouted a warning through a throat gurgling with blood. Reubair's men lying about the fire came awake and to their feet, swords drawing with the sounds of metal on metal and leather. A cry went up. With sinking heart, Alex knew he and his men were doomed.

They fought anyway. Better to go down in a struggle than to be captured. Faeries weren't men; there was no telling what they might do to a human prisoner. Alex turned to defend Patrick, but the priest had already moved on to another opponent, and Alex found himself assaulted by two other faeries. He wailed against swords in the darkness and reeled when one knocked him sideways. His left shoulder went numb. Probably broken. He turned and swung, but it was useless. A mace knocked him to his knees, then all went black.

The pain was monstrous. As Alex rose toward consciousness, he struggled back into oblivion, but it was useless. He found himself astride a horse, draped over its neck and secured to the saddle with a rope. It was too tight and bound his kidneys like an iron barrel band, and when he tried to sit up he discovered a rope tied to his wrists and run beneath the horse's neck. Just as well to remain lying over the saddle, for he couldn't feel his left shoulder except when he tried to move it. When he did, it screamed such pain that nausea hitched in his gut. The old wound flamed agony. Something had happened to it, but he couldn't tell what. All he could tell was that red pain radiated from deep within him. Though the air was freezing and snow floated past his face, beads of sweat on his forehead rose and dribbled down. Drops shook from the end of his nose in rhythm with the horse's tread. He felt a vague disappointment he hadn't died, and his mind turned with thoughts of how it would feel when he finally did.

A horse sidled up to him, and its rider spoke. "You've awakened."

Alex tried to see who the speaker was but couldn't turn his head far enough to see high enough. He replied, and blood spattered from his lips onto his sleeve. "Reubair."

"No. Who are you, and what do you want with my master?"

A glimmer of hope sparked in Alex. They didn't know who he was, and that suggested the possibility of escape. They might not think he was important. "Money, of course. We're itinerant knights in need of funds. We seek gold and silver like anyone else." He tried to make his voice suggest this should have been assumed in the first place.

"But you found a fight. Not terribly wise of you to come around us, I think."

"Apparently not." It was an admission calculated to appease, but Alex couldn't deny the truth of it.

"How did you know Reubair is our liege?"

"You're fey, yes?"

The knight snorted, and Alex wished he could see the face. "That means nothing. Many knights fight under the banner of the Dagda, rather than An Reubair's."

The Dagda. Alex had heard the name before. King of the *Tuatha Dé Danann*. He said, "But not you. You're Reubair's men."

"True." This faerie drifted into a conversational tone, as if glad to relieve some boredom. "But we fly no banner even when he is here, which he is not."

Reubair wasn't among these men? Alex lifted his head in an attempt to see his surroundings again, but the effort brought on more nausea and his gut felt as if it would squeeze from his wound onto the ground. If Reubair wasn't there, then Lindsay wouldn't be, either. He shut his eyes and hope waned. If Lindsay wasn't with this group, then he had no idea where she would be.

But his chatty companion said, "In any case, you'll regret your action last night. No ransom for you; we're taking you to Ireland."

Alex frowned in an effort at concentration. His mind was a mess, and all he could think of that related to Ireland was Robert's efforts at eliminating the threat to Scotland from the Irish nobles loyal to England. "What's there?"

"Reubair's lands. Castle Finias."

"He's fighting on Robert's side?"

The faerie knight laughed. "Reubair fights on his own side, always. And Robert, human that he is, has no idea these lands even exist except in legend. Reubair, for his part, is far more concerned with his relationships with Nemed and Dagda than with any human." The faerie uttered the last word as if it were a pejorative.

Nemed. Suddenly Alex was interested in faerie politics. But his brain hurt with the effort of sorting out who was who and what was what. "What's Dagda got to do with Nemed and Reubair?" Alex longed for a piece of that elfin sonofabitch, Nemed.

"Well, he surely wants his tribute from the lands of Finias."

"And Reubair is worried about Dagda? Do they not get along?"

"Nemed is an elf, and was once king in his own right, before his people were destroyed. Reubair is a Christian. What would you say are the chances of accord between the three?"

Not knowing how Danann felt about elves, Alex couldn't say. But since he knew they didn't generally care for Christians, he guessed. "Not good."

"Not good at all. It stands to reason the Dagda is not happy for an elf to place himself between a faerie king and his vassal. By all accounts he is less than amused by Nemed."

Nemed controlled lands that rightly belonged to Dagda? It figured. Alex knew Nemed to be an angry, bitter, uncooperative guy, and it wouldn't surprise him if the nasty old bastard had pissed off every Danann on the planet. Possibly even Reubair, but as this knight had said, Reubair was on his own side. Always.

A wave of nausea rolled over Alex, and his stomach heaved. A dribble of bile eased from his throat, and he spat it onto the ground under his nose. It landed and fell behind on the trail as the horse walked on. The pain made him wish he'd died in last night's fight, but he clung to a single shred of hope. They were taking him to Reubair, and where Reubair was Alex was certain he would find Lindsay. That glimmer would keep him alive for a while, at least.

CHAPTER 6

Trefor made the voyage away from Eilean Aonarach with his own and Alasdair an Dubhar's men under his command, landing the first night for a stopover on the island of Tiree. He accepted the hospitality of a landholder loyal to Robert he knew only by reputation, who lived at a place called Clachan Mór, a fair-sized keep and village at the north end of the island. He and his men were welcomed heartily for the night and were put up in quarters Trefor thought a mite plush for his bunch. He appreciated that his host was enthusiastic about his support of Robert, for the laird of this place talked much of the struggle against the English king.

His name was Maclean, and though his rank was only the Scottish title of "laird," his clan was large and consolidated, and his wealth obvious. The castle was solid, well-appointed, and well furnished, a far more comfortable establishment than Eilean Aonarach. He also seemed to have been taking notes from the Normans in his neighborhood, for the manners evident in his household were as gracious as what

Trefor had seen in gentlemen's homes on the mainland. Of course, that didn't say much by modern standards—even the bare-bones manners taught to him within the state foster care system—but these folks were less crude than the rough Highlanders of Trefor's experience.

Trefor sat at table, near the head of the room in a place of honor but not so high as to encourage him to think he was above himself, and found himself impressed by the arms displayed about the walls. Maclean was related to some powerful men. Ross. Buchanan. Very powerful. Trefor also recognized the arms of James Douglas's father, and wondered just how closely Maclean was related to the first Earl of Douglas. Sometimes it seemed to Trefor that everyone in Scotland was related, for the clans kept close track of all alliances, but it was apparent Maclean's pedigree was exceptional.

Trefor envied it horribly.

While he was lost in his reverie, a cluster of giggly girls blew into the Great Hall like a gust of wind, aflutter with something one of them had just said that had struck them all as terribly funny, and they fell silent at sight of the visitors. All four were striking, even from across the room, decked out in fine, fashionable dresses and graced with a bit more than the average amount of jewelry. They glittered like fresh snow in sunshine.

"Deirbhile!" Maclean called out from the head of the table, and the prettiest, most glittery of the girls turned her attention to the laird. Her neck was long and pale, and her cheeks blossomed with bright pink roses. Large, bright, round eyes lit up a heart-shaped face. "Come and sit! Your meat grows cold!"

Jer-vil-uh. The unusual name caught Trefor's attention, and he mouthed it silently. Deirbhile. He liked it. One thing about the people here was their talent for naming. Eilean Aonarach—*Lonely Island.* An Reubair—*The Robber.*

Cruachan—*Mountaintop*. He liked that people here pro-
nounced the "F" in his name, where folks back home in
Tennessee had insisted on calling him "Trevor." He watched,
intrigued by this Deirbhile.

The girl smiled again, and dimples popped into her
cheeks. She curtsied like a proper Norman lady, then took
an empty seat at table, above where Trefor sat, while one of
her attendants hovered behind to serve her. Deirbhile was a
family member, no doubt, and he guessed she was the
laird's daughter. There was enough resemblance between
her and Maclean to make a case for it, and Maclean's young
heir who sat to the laird's right had the same coloring as
she. Deep chocolate brown hair peeked from under her
headdress and veils, and her bright eyes were a pale, pale
blue that Trefor found spooky. When she glanced his way,
he had to turn his attention to his trencher, from which he
picked bits of crust and laid them absently on his tongue.
Not too cool to gawk at her. If she was the daughter of his
host, it was best to not be caught staring.

The conversation at table was of the weather, for a late-
season storm was on its way and everyone present wondered how bad it would be when it hit. Trefor wondered
when it would, for he needed to be on his way in the morning. With his knowledge of the fey arts it would be a fairly
simple matter to make certain it would lay off until he was
gone, but he hated to spend the effort if it was going to do
that anyway. Magic didn't wear him out so much as it used
to, but it still wasn't much fun and carried risks he didn't
care to incur unnecessarily. In magic, as in everything else,
every action brought reaction. But with magic the response
was usually neither equal nor opposite, and impossible to
predict.

But, even as the laird expressed his hope for clear
weather to hold out, there came a crack of thunder so loud
it seemed to shake the heavy beams overhead. Everyone

looked up. Rain slammed against the narrow, glazed windows of the Hall. Any chance for good weather was ended, and the men in the room expressed a hope that the storm would be brief and the skies clear in the morning.

That hope died the next morning when Trefor awoke, dressed, and sought the nearest arrow loop to look out. Alarm galvanized him. It had snowed during the night, and the stuff was still coming down. The nearby hills were covered in an unbroken blanket of white. Piles of it along the castle battlements reached heights of a foot or more, and it was falling in large, soggy clumps under a low, leaden sky. Trefor ascended a tight spiral stair to another loop, where he could see his ships in the bay, and his heart clutched at what he found.

Two vessels had clashed in rough water, and though the distance was too great to assess the damage, it was plain the rigging was a mess and at least one mast was broken. Trefor's stomach dropped as he noticed one hull seemed to lie a bit lower in the water than it should. He turned and hurried to the castle bailey and called for a horse and one of his men to accompany him to the shore.

There he found the damage was even worse than he'd feared. The boat with the broken mast had also jarred a leak in the side of the vessel next to it. Two of Trefor's three vessels were no longer seaworthy, and one of those was shipping water at an alarming rate. Enough to sink it within a day. The boats were still banging into each other with loud, hollow, wooden thuds that made Trefor flinch. Bailing crews already hard at work to stave off losing them entirely shouted to each other as they tossed buckets of water overboard and climbed about to find the leaks.

"Crap." Trefor's mind flew to find a plan of action. He called to one of Alex's knights, who directed the bailing efforts. "You! George!" George, clinging to the broken mast to save his balance in the chop, turned to hear his orders.

"Have some of the men unload the supplies and weapons while you're also unloading water. Everything we get off that ship is to the good if she sinks."

"Aye, sir," George replied, then turned to see who among those present he would assign the task.

Maclean rode up, accompanied by several of his attendants, and dismounted. "Bad luck, Pawlowski." His tone conveyed genuine concern, as if they were his own boats sinking. A frown creased his aging face, and he glanced at Trefor before continuing on down toward the quay. Maclean's merchant boats, and the fishing boats anchored up and down the harbor shore, seemed to have escaped intact, though equally as icebound. Trefor's were the only ones with obvious and crippling damage.

Trefor followed, at a loss for what to do, for his resources consisted entirely of those ships and the men he was transporting. He'd counted on acquiring cash and barter goods on meeting up with Robert. Now, not only did he not have wherewithal for repairs, the loss of his ships would put him in a bad spot for getting any.

Maclean shouted to a few of his men that they should bring some smaller boats around to tie up Trefor's sinking ship and keep it afloat until the breach could be repaired. "Get some pitch boiling!" he shouted, an edge to his voice that suggested he was annoyed there wasn't already a fire on the shore and a big pot of sealant warming on it. "Lachlan! Hie yourself to the carpenter and have him bring lumber for a patch! Hurry, lad!" One young man separated himself from a cluster of spectators near the quay and took off running toward the castle.

A wave of relief washed over Trefor, and he was then able to order his own men to keep bailing and ready themselves to patch the hole. Hot pitch could be prepared, a patch nailed over and sealed, and the ship would be saved.

"It'll be some days before your boats will be of use again,

my friend," said Maclean. He looked around at the sky, then to the horizon out to sea, and added, "Not to mention the prospects of the weather being anything but frozen for the foreseeable future appear mighty slim. You can see where the ice has already formed along the rocks and blocked the mouth of the harbor. If this storm doesn't abate, you'll be locked in until there's a thaw." Maclean sighed, as cheerless as Trefor felt. "I'm sorry, but it appears you'll be trapped on my poor island for a time."

Trefor was inclined to agree that it was a poor island, for he was eager to present himself to the king in Ireland and had no interest in Tiree, but he kept that sentiment to himself. Instead he said, "If you can stand to have us impose on your hospitality for a while longer, I think 'trapped' might be too strong a word for it."

The laird laughed and watched the workmen scurry back and forth. "My hospitality is beyond question, lad. Stay as long as you like, and never mind the circumstance. And pay me for the repairs once you've come into your rewards in Ireland, whatever they may be. I'm always glad for the company of a man dedicated to Robert, particularly one related, however distantly, to the MacNeils of Barra and Cruachan. Tarry as you will, and enjoy the stay."

The freezing wind blustered and tossed the men's hair around, along with the descending snow, as they watched the work. Huge flakes became a barrage of cold and wet thrown at a sharp, stinging slant. Trefor checked the security of his hat and the green silk bandanna he wore under it, ostensibly for warmth but really to cover his ears. Then he hugged himself within his coat against the icy air and stifled a sigh. Robert wasn't going to like this delay any more than he did. Trefor could feel his opportunity with the king slip through his fingers with every moment.

There was no rush to repair the boats, for the weather did not improve that day. In fact it worsened, and that evening

Trefor found himself in the Great Hall beside his host's
fire, listening with half a mind to the castle bard tell stories
of past glories of Clan Maclean. No matter where Trefor
went in this century, the stories all seemed the same,
though the older ones usually involved a little more magic
than did tales of recent struggles and victories. A good
bard could always put a new twist or slant on an old tale
and make it seem fresh, and this guy had a talent. With a
nimble tongue and expressive voice, he expounded on the
demise of a sea monster that had lived centuries or millennia ago. But Trefor had heard it before, told as a MacNeil
adventure, and his knee bounced up and down in an antsy
tic. His eye wandered around the room in spite of the sto-
ryteller's excellent efforts to keep it on himself.

   The women sat apart from the men, a custom that struck
Trefor as strange since it meant they were farther from the
warmth of the hearth and he didn't think that a way to treat
women. Even in his postmodern, twenty-first-century
world of equal opportunity there would have been some
sense of chivalry about keeping girls warm. But these guys
were heavily invested in the idea of the high-ranking men
taking the choicest spots, and who was Trefor to argue with
his host? Certainly not him, certainly not today, as in-
debted to Maclean as he was.

   Most of the women had sewing in their laps and chatted
amongst themselves in low voices, but some listened to the
bard. Trefor noted the laird's daughter was rapt at the story.
Her mouth had dropped open, a little "O" between her lips,
and he couldn't help noticing how red they were. Around
here, red lips meant health as well as beauty. No makeup.
Rosy cheeks were rosy cheeks, and there was no hiding a
sallow complexion. This girl was truly beautiful. Trefor indulged himself and stared.

   At a pause in the story as the bard plinked a bit on his
lyre, the girl glanced at the men and caught Trefor ogling

her. He looked away and his face warmed. The bard once again became the center of his attention, and Trefor frowned with the effort of concentration on the epic. The story thread was lost to him, but he struggled to find it no matter how dull it might be. All thoughts of Deirbhile were stamped out like sparks from a pine fire, with the same sense of emergency. He raised his chin, crossed his arms, and ignored the girl.

For a while. The bard's voice held no interest for him; it had become a low background noise to Trefor's thoughts as he resisted the urge to look toward the women again. But the more he tried to ignore her, the more he wanted to look. As if his eyes were being drawn by a magnetic force. Finally he looked.

He found her staring at him and he blinked, then looked away again. Had she been watching him this whole time? Could she have seen him struggle to keep his attention away from her? Once again his cheeks flamed, and he was astonished they still could. Not since high school had he blushed like this, and it mortified him. Now, having been busted twice and with little to lose, he looked back over at her. Her eyes were still on him, and now the dimples dug into her cheeks. Her teeth were large, and the whitest he'd seen in this century. Which wasn't saying all that much, but at least she had no gray ones up front like most folks here. And she kept them clean, another habit not common for humans except among the very rich.

Her pale eyes sparkled with silent laughter, and Trefor didn't know whether to smile or look away again. This wasn't fun; she made him feel like a boy again, a period of his life he'd fought long and hard to forget. The feeling was creepy, and he looked down again at his hands. He wished he could leave the room but couldn't risk being rude. He was stuck.

Another glance at Deirbhile, and still she stared. But the

dimples were gone. He sighed and returned his attention to the bard. Whatever had just happened, he was certain he'd ruined something. Not that he could have any clue what that might have been.

The storm worsened, a blizzard now that dumped sheets and mounds of ice all over the north end of Tiree. Work on the ships was at a halt, and everyone in the castle and village hunkered down and hoped the firewood would hold out till a thaw. Ice in the harbor threatened the ships of both Trefor and Maclean, and crews were kept by the quay to knock loose thin ice and throw fire embers on thick. The risk of setting fire to one of the vessels was high, and Trefor kept a watch out castle arrow loops in his worry. All he needed now was for Alex's ships to go up in flames. He sure didn't care to have to send for help from Eilean Aonarach and explain how he couldn't even make the trip to Ireland without mishap.

Two days into the blizzard, at the end of the evening when darkness and quiet descended on the castle, Trefor went to his bed annoyed with himself for exhaustion over an unproductive day. No progress on getting out of there, just a lot of sitting around, listening to the boasting of his host and his host's underlings of past wartime exploits. Never in his life had Trefor known how much energy it took to live in tedium. Tension across his shoulders made his neck sore, and he stretched and bent to work it out. He undressed by the fire, draped his clothing over the drying rack, though he hadn't been outside and they were not wet, and hurried across the cold room to slip into the bed.

Something moved beside him in the blankets, a shifting of what he'd thought was a lump in the mattress. He leapt up again. Heart pounding, he scrambled for his belt and the dagger hung from it, but a familiar voice from the bed made him pause.

"Trefor, 'tis myself only."

Relief washed over him, and he straightened. "Morag?" The shadows in the bed on the other side of the room moved, and he could now see a person-sized shape under the wool cover.

"Aye." The girl sat up and rubbed her eyes. She'd been asleep, and now peered at him through a haze of slumber.

"Where did you come from? Where have you been?" Then the real question occurred to him. "How in God's name did you get here?" Nothing and nobody had come in or out for two days. Had she been here all along, or had she flown in on a broomstick?

"I have ways of being places, as ye ken well enough." She stopped rubbing her eyes and tried to organize the mass of curly red hair that spilled over her shoulders.

It was true. He knew she could do things he only wished he could do. And he wished for one of them now. "You can leave the island if you want, right?"

"Aye."

"Then help me get out of here. I need to meet Bruce's army in Ireland."

Her eyes narrowed at him, and he realized how stupid his request was before she even spoke. "You yourself, or you and your knights? Do you wish to be in Ireland without your men?"

Trefor's hope failed again. She could go places, and might even be able to send him somewhere, but not necessarily. Beyond that, it was another thing entirely to transport an army, and he knew she didn't have that kind of power. Nobody did, as far as he knew. And even if the power did exist and she were to accomplish the task, there would be explanations to be made, and he was certain he didn't want to deal with that. The prospect of being burned at the stake was at the least unappealing.

He sighed, set aside the dirk, and slipped into bed beside her where it was warm and she was soft against his

skin. One great thing about Morag was that her body fit
him well. Every bump on him had a corresponding soft
place on her that welcomed him without question. She was
a pain in the ass in every other way, but in this she was his
perfect match. Settling in next to her, he kissed her and she
melded to him as if she were his other half.

He'd missed her, and only now did he realize how
much. A fire lit in his belly and warmed his groin so his
mind went up in a puff of stupidity. All intelligence wafted
away, and the only care he had in the world just then was to
taste of delicious Morag and live inside her as long as he
could stay. It was a pleasant stay, and long, for one of the
things he'd been taught by the Bhrochan was control over
his body. He moved fast, then slow, then quickly once
again for a while, until she pled exhaustion and soreness,
and he finally relented with a final rush and his own growl
of nearly pained satisfaction. Propped on his elbows above
her, pressed to her, panting and grinning, he wished he
could go again right away. It had been far too long, and he
had far too much he longed to give her.

"Where have you been, Morag?"

"About."

"Why did you leave me down that hole?" Why, indeed,
had she led him to the hole to begin with?

"Can ye deny you needed what they gave you?"

"You wanted me to learn the craft?" A chuckle burbled
from him. "You wanted me to learn this?" Again he
pressed himself between her legs, where it was now damp
as well as warm.

She giggled. "Aye, but not only this. I could have taught
you how to make love to me without the help of my wee
relatives."

"Then what?"

"The knowing will come in handy someday. 'Tis inevitable."

Ah. "Fate. My destiny."

"Indeed. Brochan told you."

"He mentioned some things. I don't believe him."

She didn't reply, except to gaze into his face and utter a reflective hum.

Trefor shifted to the side and lay beside her with his head propped on an elbow. "He didn't tell me much."

"So, what's to believe or not believe?"

"That there's such a thing as undeniable destiny. I believe in free will. Nobody can tell me what I'm fated for, or that I have no control over my actions."

"But who's to say that what you do is not what your fate was to begin with?"

"I am. I'm the one who chooses."

For a moment she gazed at him in the flickering light of the fading hearth, and he wanted to kiss her again. So he did. She responded with familiar passion, then said, "If only you understood the true power, my love."

That puzzled him, but he had no desire to pursue the question. He was the captain of his fate, and that was all he cared to know. He kissed her again and deep within himself found the power to enjoy her again. It didn't matter where she'd been, or why. She was here now and he would make the most of it.

In the morning she was gone. It was unsettling to awaken, knowing the castle was snowbound, and find her not only not in his bed but not anywhere on the premises. Nor in the village. Without appearing too much as if he were in search of someone who couldn't possibly be there, he cruised the likely spots and didn't find her.

Huh.

On a fretful climb to a vantage point in the castle, where he could observe the state of his ships, he encountered Deirbhile gazing out a glazed window in a chamber high in the keep. Trefor was surprised to see her, especially alone.

Girls like her were never alone; they surrounded themselves with waiting ladies or friends who kept them entertained. Trefor looked around for a companion or chaperone of some kind, but there was none. He suddenly wasn't sure whether to apologize and withdraw in haste, or to stick around and see what he could learn about her. Keeping the boredom at bay sounded like a pleasant idea, and Morag having disappeared, it seemed the laird's daughter was his best bet for interesting conversation. He smiled and gave a slight bow. "Good afternoon, my lady."

"Good day to you . . . Sir Trefor Pawlowski, I believe?"

She knew his name and had it correctly. He liked that. "Aye. Pawlowski." Okay, it was his mother's maiden name, but it was the one he used among people who couldn't know who his parents were.

"Such an exotic name. Nearly musical. I'm Deirbhile Maclean; my father is your host." Trefor knew that, but only nodded in acknowledgment. She continued, "You and your men seem to be in an unfortunate situation."

Though he agreed heartily, he said instead, "On the contrary, we are quite fortunate for this to have happened while visiting your father, whose hospitality is incomparable and whose support has saved not only my property but the king's fighting men as well. I'm grateful for his intervention."

A sly light came into her eyes. "Nevertheless, you wish to embark at the earliest opportunity."

The tension in him showed. Damn. "I have a job to do and must go to Ireland to accomplish it."

"Surely you could relax and enjoy your time here when you know there is nothing to be done about the weather."

Trefor slipped his hands behind his back and straightened to look out the open window. It was bitch cold in this room, though a fire burned merrily in the hearth, and the wind from outside bit his cheeks and numbed his nose. All was white as far as he could see, off down the hills and rocks of the island. The village lay in a scattering of dark bits below, the houses nearly buried in snow, and the stuff descended in a relentless dump that made hissing noises as it landed on drifts. "My duty to Robert is pressing. I would hate more than anything else to disappoint the king."

"Terribly admirable of you, but surely there is no sense in making yourself miserable over what you cannot change."

That made him smile, but it wasn't all that amusing. He'd been able to change very little in his life, and it seemed the more he tried the less success he had at it. If he was tense about this voyage, it was because so much rested on it. And he'd wasted so much time with the Bhrochan. He needed to get on with his life. "Is it so obvious?"

"One might think you weren't so grateful for my father's help, or that you're not enjoying the company."

Trefor hastened to reply, "Oh, you shouldn't think that. I enjoy the company very much." He did at that moment, in any case. Very much.

The dimples popped into her cheeks, and they were a pleasure to see. It also struck him she was more pleased by his reply than one might have expected from a girl who didn't know him or like him. He concluded she must like him, and that sent a warmth through his belly that stood against the chill from the window. She said, "I watch you fret over your ships, and wonder if you might be trying to melt the ice in the harbor by mere will."

He could have explained to her that his will had been known to prevent or encourage events, but never to undo them, but left it unsaid for fear of giving himself away as fey, the same reason he kept his ears well covered by his hair. He never cared to discuss his heritage, even with those who knew. Then there was that his mother was a descendant of

Danu herself, which, were he to confess that, might be seen
as bragging. He never knew how someone might react to
those things and always thought it best to never let them be
an issue. With a sigh, he replied, "Perhaps you're right. I'm
giving too much attention to something that will work itself out with or without my help. I should enjoy the company even more than I do."

"I would certainly like that."

Now he had to smile. That was a bold thing to hear from
a girl her age. Was she hitting on him? Had she purposely
sought him today to be caught out without a chaperone?
"So, tell me a bit about the company I'm keeping now.
What do you do for fun around here?"

"Oh, nothing so enjoyable as fighting the Irish nobles."
Trefor chuckled, and she giggled at her own joke. "For the
most part I have my embroidery, my friends, and next year I
shall have my husband and his household to keep me busy."

Amusement fled, but Trefor kept his smile in place. She
was engaged. He turned to the window again and wondered
why she was rattling his cage if she was spoken for. "You
have a fiancé?"

"Of course I do. We've been promised to each other
since we were children. I can't remember a time in my life
when I wasn't engaged to Geoffrey."

Now he peered at her. "It was arranged?"

"Aren't all marriages? All worth having, in any case."

Trefor was aware arranged marriages were common
here, but he'd never thought they could be so blithely accepted by the bride. "No. Not my parents', at least." Never
mind that Alex and Lindsay were not of this culture. As
much as he'd learned about this place since last year, it was
still nearly impossible to wrap his mind around the medieval
attitudes of love and marriage. "They were in love with each
other. Still are, I think. Neither was promised to anyone."

Her smile was, he thought, a bit condescending. "You

are from Hungary. I think the Continent is more permissive in these matters." Her voice conveyed that she didn't think much of such permissiveness.

"Perhaps. Nevertheless, I don't think I would care to be engaged to a stranger my whole life." Nor would he have wanted Alex or Lindsay to choose his wife. Especially he wouldn't want that.

She laughed. "Certainly not. I will be married for most of it."

"A happy wife?"

"A wife, and therefore happy. He is rich, and he's Scottish. There is nothing more to ask."

"One might ask for respect."

"He will respect me for being my father's daughter. The Maclean is a great man, and I'm proud of him." It seemed she thought these things were self-evident, and a puzzlement lit her eyes as she explained carefully to poor, clueless Trefor how things were and always had been.

Trefor next took a conversational risk, in hopes of finding out what she was doing talking to him alone in a remote corner of the castle where they both knew they would not be disturbed. "And what about the bedchamber? Do you think you'll find happiness there?"

"Does anyone?"

"I would expect it."

The puzzlement deepened. "With your wife?"

"Of course."

For a moment it looked as if she would say something, then she changed her mind and turned toward the window to look out. Thinking. He let her spin out the thought in her head and waited for her to speak, and when she looked over at him again she said, "You have a great deal of faith in your future."

That was news to him. "How so?"

"To be so certain the woman you marry will be suited to

you so perfectly and will never change. Such a trap to be in if you discover she isn't all she appears. No man or woman is so transparent that another can see what he or she will become."

"The more reason to be careful whom one marries."

"The more reason to not depend on marriage to fulfill one's hope for love."

"You're advocating infidelity?"

Shoulders lifted in a gentle shrug. "It will be a fact of my life whether I advocate it or not. If I expect my husband to never stray I will surely be disappointed, and the more wealthy and powerful he becomes, the more likely and obvious the dalliances will be."

Trefor hesitated before asking the bold question that leapt to mind but said it anyway. "And what about yourself?"

There was hesitation in her as well, then she said, "I haven't the same faith in my future as you do. I cannot say."

Trefor uttered a neutral grunt and examined her expression. She was more wise than the girls her age where he'd come from.

She continued, "The idea of giving my heart so permanently, to someone with so much power in my life . . . I don't think I could do it."

He said, "I suppose the trick is to try to grow in the same direction."

"And which of the pair changes direction for the other?"

Now Trefor had to grin. All of a sudden she was sounding like the girls back home. "It can be mutual."

"Can be and would be are two different things. What man would change himself for a wife?"

"I would. If I loved her enough."

Her lips struggled with a smile, but she stifled it. He couldn't tell whether she was intrigued by his personal confession or thought it was a lie. She said, matter-of-factly, without a hint of bitterness or even an edge to her tone, "Men never love. They covet. They lust. They respect. But love isn't in them, though they would protest it is. Tell me, Sir Trefor, have you ever been truly in love?"

He thought of Morag, and for an instant thought he could tell her he was, but suddenly he wasn't sure. The Bhrochan faerie woman had consumed his thoughts from time to time, like fire that burned all else from his mind. But there were other times when he never thought of her at all. Like now. He could easily push Morag from his mind and think only of this girl.

Or perhaps he loved his mother. Lindsay, only a year older than himself, was an issue he gnawed on frequently. His feelings for Morag paled beside the heart-stopping need he often had to know Lindsay as his mother, a need he figured would never be satisfied. So, in that sense, he'd not only never been in love, he'd never loved at all. The realization choked him and he had to clear his throat.

His answer was, "No. I've not met the right woman."

"Good luck to you in your search. I hope your match is not living in Hungary, lest you never meet her at all."

"And who's to say she's not right here in this castle even now?" His mouth shut hard. He had no idea why he'd blurted that.

A giggle burbled from her, and he was relieved to see she thought his comment a flirty joke. "Fate will say."

I say. "Perhaps it will."

Voices drifted up the stairwell from several stories below, and Deirbhile picked up her skirts to flee. With a quick curtsy, she said, "It has been a pleasure to pass the time with you, Sir Trefor, but I fear I have duties elsewhere just now."

Trefor bowed and said quickly, "Indeed, I must watch out this window for a while, to make certain all is well with my boats below. God be with you, my lady."

"And also with you, sir." With that, she hurried down the spiral stair toward the voices.

Trefor watched her go, then turned his attention to the busy harbor where his men were repairing the broken mast on his boat. He glanced at the stairwell as the voices below faded, then away, and considered what an odd girl Deirbhile was. So young and beautiful, seemingly innocent, but at heart terribly cynical. He wondered if all girls in this century were that way. He'd seen plenty of whores here, and many faerie women, but this was the first he'd ever spoken so candidly to a human girl of Deirbhile's rank. She wasn't at all like what he'd expected of the sheltered daughter of a wealthy laird.

He glanced over at the stairwell again and wondered. As he wondered, a warmth settled in his heart.

CHAPTER 7

Lindsay was let alone at night, though she slept in Reubair's chamber. The first night she was kept awake by the certainty of hearing the creak of the cabinet bed door, waiting for her captor to take advantage of his prize. Alert for the sound of footsteps in the room outside, she waited. But the door stayed closed and the night was quiet.

Oddly, when she realized he wasn't coming there was a vague sense of disappointment, but she shook it off. So vain of her, she thought, to be offended that he didn't force himself on her. And so . . . nuts, as Alex would have put it, to be disappointed in such a thing. The man had kidnapped her and imprisoned her. Then he'd chained her naked to a rock, to be gawked at by passersby. She hated him. She'd always disliked him, but now he deserved her hatred and it filled her. Every bit of her soul despised him and wanted him dead. She longed to kill him herself.

Although, there was that he hadn't touched her. He'd never touched her, nor even attempted it.

When she finally slept, and slept through the morning,

she went undisturbed until she herself opened the door of
her bed and found the morning well on its way to midday.
Reubair was not in the chamber, but she figured he was
somewhere close by. She glanced around the room before
venturing from the bed, then shut the door behind her
softly. She checked to be sure the tie at the neck of her shift
was secure.

The table was set for two, but no food had arrived.
Clothing lay draped over a rack near the fire, and she went
to examine the dress. It was different from the one she'd
had on the night before—more fancy—and the silk under-
garments were clean. On inspection, she discovered they
were newly sewn. They'd never been worn, and the stitch-
ing had not settled in or the hems flattened. Before donning
them, she washed up in the bowl and dried with a soft linen
towel. She'd thought her own household had been plush,
relative to most who lived in these times, but Reubair's castle showed her that one didn't have to be royalty to enjoy
extreme wealth.

It made her wonder why Reubair bothered raiding
worthless little villages in the Borderlands. Fun? Certainly
not much profit, relative to this. Perhaps the comfort of this
place was another aspect of the same principle of magic
that accounted for the lack of even the smallest speck of
dirt on the knights who had brought her here. Iain, for instance. As a raider, working for Reubair last summer in the
north of England, Iain had been barely distinguishable
from his filthy and ragged human compatriots, including
herself. But here in Reubair's hidden Irish lands he was
nearly regal and utterly spotless, his mail so shiny it might
have been crafted from silver. Reubair himself had changed;
he nearly glowed with the magic he'd denied in England.
She wondered whether it was a willful change, or if merely
being here made the difference.

Just as she was struggling one-handed with the buttons

on the sleeves of her dress, Reubair entered the room. She turned to address him, but changed her mind and only gazed blandly, waiting for him to speak. His head tilted in a look of appraisal, then without a word he stepped forward and took her arm to help her with the buttons.

Her first urge was to pull away, but she decided against it. If asked, she wouldn't have been able to say why, but it just didn't seem the thing to do at the moment. She watched his fingers slip the buttons into their holes and noted his hands were strong and slim. Funny how she'd never seen that before. A callus marred the large knuckle of his right index finger. It was where his sword hilt rested; she'd blistered there enough times to know all about that. Her own sword callus was smaller, more prone to further irritation, but his appeared sturdy. As if it went clear to the bone and had been there since childhood.

Then she caught herself staring and looked away, embarrassed. She thanked him in a mumble for his help.

"The midday meal will arrive shortly. You've slept through breakfast," he informed her.

"I'm not very hungry."

"You will be once you've smelled the dishes I've had readied. My cooks are the best to be found in these lands, and even the worst here will outshine the best among humans." He gestured for her to have a seat by the fire.

It seemed that by a change of clothing she'd transformed from a captive held in a servant's bed to the lord's guest. It didn't matter much to Lindsay they were alone; she could take care of herself and wasn't afraid for her reputation or her person. Not after what Jenkins had done to her and what she'd done to him in response. She now faced Reubair as the Countess of Cruachan, wife of Alasdair an Dubhar MacNeil and knight of the Scottish realm in her own right.

Perched in a chair by the hearth, she now found herself

noticing the way his blond hair shone in the flickering of the fire. Had she ever seen that before? Had it ever been anything but a dull mess before? Today it was so blond as to be nearly white, shiny, and sleek, and the long ends of it drifted in the draft created by the fire nearby. The delicate tips of his ears poked through the fine strands ever so slightly, curving forward as if pricked to hear her every word. She found it pleasing.

His attempts at conversation faltered, and finally stopped, for it was only small talk and she wasn't listening, in any case. She snapped out of her reverie and looked into his face.

"Something on your mind?" he asked.

Her mouth twisted to a wry smile. "Home, perhaps? Where I should be but am not." Of which she should have been thinking, but had not, and the realization made her ashamed. What was wrong with her? Her cheeks warmed.

"This is your home now."

"My husband lives. My home is wherever he is." A pang of longing pierced her heart, and tears rose to her eyes. She fought them back and succeeded. Reubair had never seen her cry, and she was determined he never would.

His face clouded over with anger, and his voice went low. Venomous. "You'll be widowed soon. I swear it."

"You sound as if I should want it."

"You should, for it is inevitable. And preferable, all things considered." He gestured to the room. "See what you will have. That mean little island keep can't possibly compare to the wondrous life I offer."

It was true. No matter how cozy Alex might one day be with the king, the lifestyle on Eilean Aonarach and Cruachan would never be as lush and comfortable as this. There was also that with some hints here and there Reubair's magic might produce wonders to measure up to life in the twenty-first century. Properly preserved food, hot showers, central heat . . . it could happen here.

Lindsay shut her eyes against the thought, and a flush of shame came over her. Her loyalty was to Alex, not to her own comfort.

Food arrived, carried on a large platter by the human servant she'd seen yesterday. He placed it on the table, then exited without a word or a glance. The meat smelled wonderful, and there was a fruit pie of some sort. It smelled tangy, but she didn't recognize it. She and Reubair moved to the table to eat, giving pause to the conversation while he filled her plate. She tasted the pie and still couldn't recognize the fruit. It was a berry of some sort, but larger than any she'd ever seen. Smooth like blueberries, but not nearly as purely sweet. As if they'd been crossed with something tropical. Pineapple, perhaps. Or mango. But that was impossible.

"This is delicious." Her resistance to her captor and her determination to hate him were no match for just how delicious this pie was. "What is it?"

"You wouldn't know it, I'm certain. It only grows here."

She noticed his plate held only the meat dish. "You're not having any?"

"I've no sweet tooth, but I understand you like a bit of fruit or honey with your meals."

Lindsay fought back the surge of flattery that he'd taken note of her preference. So she liked a sweet with dinner. Big deal. She ate the pie and pretended she didn't care what he thought. Easy, since she didn't care what he thought.

Reubair said, "I've given you free movement within the castle."

That caught her attention. "Free movement?"

"You can go anywhere you like."

"Except home."

"You are home."

She emitted a snort of disgust and continued with her meal. They ate in silence after that.

As soon as she was finished, she rose from the table and announced she was going for a ride. The protest never came, not even a warning that she shouldn't try to escape, and Reubair only gave her a bland stare as she looked to him for resistance. There was no resistance at all, even as she moved toward the door. She donned his offered cloak and exited without hearing so much as a murmur. This couldn't be good.

It was easy enough to find the stable, for it wasn't far from the keep entrance. A saddled horse waited for her there, held by a squire waiting patiently for her arrival. Definitely not good. She didn't know whether Reubair had a communication system in place, or if he'd just guessed well and ordered the horse in advance. The squire was impervious to her enquiries on the subject, so she figured she'd never know. She mounted and rode toward the portcullis.

It was no surprise she never found it. Though she was certain she remembered the rather direct route from the stable to the gate, and several times glimpsed the guard towers from a distance, she was never able to come upon them. Each time she turned a corner and expected to find herself in the outer bailey, instead she found herself somewhere else. Up an alley, or headed back the other way in the main street. Soon her bearings were in such a confusion she wondered if she could properly find her way back to the stables.

But just as that thought occurred to her, she looked up and found those stables. As if a request had been fulfilled. If technology and magic could sometimes be confused, they could be compared, and she wondered whether the communications technology of her own century paled in comparison to what she was witnessing among the faeries of this century. Reubair must think of her as a terribly cloddish human, and just then she was inclined to agree.

Not that she cared what Reubair thought. Or ever could care. She turned to leave, in search of the portcullis again, but reined in once more as she realized it was hopeless. She was never going to find the exit.

"You had to know there would be no escape."

Lindsay jerked with a start and turned to find Reubair sitting his horse to her right. She hadn't heard him approach and didn't know how he'd managed to sneak up on her like that. "You're right. I should have known."

"You will learn."

A shiver skittered along her spine. No, she wouldn't learn. Either she would escape or she would keep trying until she was dead.

A shout went up from a distance, and Lindsay turned to listen to the commotion coming from the direction she'd guessed was the portcullis. Someone—a large group, it sounded like—had arrived at the castle. Reubair raised his head to listen as the gate ran up, clanking and rattling with chain against wood, and urged his horse in that direction. Lindsay followed.

"If I go with you, will you also find yourself circling back away from the gate?"

"Come with me and find out."

Lindsay followed, just to screw with him and see if he would lead her to the exit. He glanced back at her and rode more slowly, and she understood she wasn't going to see the gate, with or without his help. She also understood the answer to her question was "No." Had he gone to the gate, she could have followed him through it. Now the trick was to get him to lead her through.

Voices in the distance rose in joyous reunion, and some also in abject grief, and Lindsay gathered that the arrivals were returning knights who had been gone a long time.

Those related to the dead and missing wailed their anguish,
an eerie keening that wasn't quite human. The word "ban-
shee" came to mind, though Lindsay heard male faerie
voices in the mix. The sound made her want to fall behind
Reubair and not follow any farther, but she kept with him.

When they came to a row of shops, Reubair paused before them and waited while voices approached. The towns-
people gathered, watching up the track to see who would
come. It was a parade of knights. They filled the narrow
street, riding slowly among throngs of welcoming people.
Lindsay recognized many of the men she'd known as a
mercenary the year before. This was a much larger company than before, and there were more of the *sidhe* among
them than there had been. Like the group Lindsay had ridden with, they disguised themselves as human, keeping
dirty and covering their ears with helmets and hair. When
they spotted Reubair standing his horse along the side of
the street, they removed their headgear and saluted him. He
acknowledged with nods.

Then, among the raiders, Lindsay spotted several horses
with men tied to them. Two of them were slumped over in
their saddles and had ropes around their waists and wrists.
One was bent so far over his pommel he was almost lying
on it. He appeared nearly dead. No helmet, no weapons,
his mail hauberk was black with dried blood, and his red
and black surcoat was in shreds.

With a charge of horror, Lindsay realized it was Alex.
The bottom seemed to drop out of her stomach. Breath
wouldn't come. Tears sprung to her eyes, and she widened
them so none would spill.

She looked over at Reubair, who continued to review
his troops without a flicker on his face. Had he recognized
Alex? Lindsay prayed not. There was no way to know if he
was pretending to not know who he had in his custody.

Lindsay took heart in the belief that if Alex had been recognized Reubair would have ordered his death immediately. A weird thing to be glad of, but just then it was her
best hope. Surely Reubair would make haste to murder the
only man who stood in the way of the forced marriage he
desired.

Wouldn't he?

Lindsay made herself not look at Alex again. Not even
to see who had been captured with him. She gazed off
down the street as the prisoners passed, pretending to be
more interested in glimpsing the portcullis than in watching the parade. When she finally had to blink, she touched
a finger to the corner of her eye to brush away the tear that
escaped, as if she were removing a speck. Then she looked
to Reubair, whose attention was on the last of the returning
company. He didn't seem to have any reaction to the prisoners. Not even a spark of a gloat.

Good.

Without a word she reined her mount around and returned to the stables.

A lex shivered miserably, but not with cold. It was the
deep ache of fever, and he wished he could fall back
unconscious for some blessed peace. Sleep. He would sleep,
and at the moment he didn't care if he ever woke up again.

A voice came from nowhere, at a whisper. "She's here,
my lor—*sir*."

Who? But it was too much to say the word aloud.

"Are you with me, sir? Can you hear me?" Not a voice
from nowhere. Father Patrick. Dying. They'd summoned
the priest because he was dying. Good.

"Sir, she's here. I saw her."

Why was Patrick calling him that? *Sir?* What happened

to his title? Alex managed to get his eyes open. *Her.* Her
who? He spoke, but his lips didn't seem to want to form
words. "Whaaa . . ."

"The countess. Your wife. She's here."

Lindsay? Here? Where was "here"? It took an effort to
open his eyes, but he did it, and spoke her name. "Lindsay . . ."

"She's here in the castle."

"Lindsay home." Oh, good. Lindsay was safe. Home.
All was well. "Thank God." Alex closed his eyes again and
drifted into blessed unconsciousness.

A fter turning the horse over to the groom at the stable,
Lindsay went back to the keep and to Reubair's bedchamber, there to gaze out the window and watch the castle
settle into routine once again. One by one or in little clusters, faerie townsfolk and their human servants wandered
back to their lives, chattering about the men who had returned, and the ones who had not returned. The lord of the
castle lingered at the stables, and Lindsay followed his
blond head among the figures below, loitering in the bailey
before the stone building.

Patience. Lindsay would need a great deal of patience to
not rush to the dungeon. If she gave away Alex, Reubair
would kill him. If Reubair so much as suspected Alex was
his captive, nothing she could do would save his life. Her
heart sped, aching to see him but knowing the danger. She
stared out the window as the sun moved to the west, and
willed Reubair to stay away so he wouldn't see her sweat
and tremble.

But before enough time had passed for her to be able to
slip away to the darkened corners of the keep, Reubair returned to the bedchamber and came up short as he passed
through the doorway and found her at the other side of the

room. For a moment he looked as if deciding what to say, as if he'd not expected her to be there, then apparently decided to say nothing and shut the door behind him. She watched him cross the room to warm himself at the fire, then she returned her attention to the window, where the sun threw red streaks into the sky and she wondered idly whether it was the same sun she'd known in the human world. The silence between them spun out and spun out, until she thought it might break for being unwieldy.

Finally he said, "You aren't taking advantage of your freedom?"

"What freedom?"

"You're not locked in this room. You choose to spend your time in my bedchamber?"

She cut her eyes toward him. "I'd rather be in the dungeon." It occurred to her there was more truth to that than she wanted Reubair to believe.

"It can be arranged."

With a grunt of disgust she turned back to the window and crossed her arms over her chest. "Very well," she said. "I'll make use of this freedom you've so generously allowed. See me take a walk now." With that, she turned and strode from the room.

Heart pounding, she kept a steady, leisurely pace down the spiral steps to the bailey. It wasn't nearly dark yet, so she couldn't go directly to the dungeon. There was no way to be certain her movements weren't somehow monitored, but that was a risk she would have to take. Once it was dark, she would slip back into the keep and make her way to where it was even darker.

It seemed to take forever. Too much light; always too much light. She wandered about, half looking for the portcullis though she knew she would never find it. Wasting time, even hoping that perhaps she would accidentally find herself in the dungeon.

Good cover story. If Reubair wanted to know why she
was there, she could tell him his confusion spell had
worked too well and sent her back to her cell.

Finally, when the streets were dark and only scant can-
dlelight shone from windows here and there, she let her
wanderings take her back to the keep and downward into
stone-lined chambers. Where the walls were slightly damp
all the time, and the cells cold enough to be a danger to
anyone weak. Lindsay thought of the blood on Alex's
hauberk, and the extreme paleness of his face, and knew he
was at risk. Her heart pounded and skipped around in her
chest, and her mind tumbled with what to say to the guard
when she might find one.

"Halt!" *Right.* There he was, a big, lumpy fellow covered in acne cysts and old scars, and sporting a nose
roughly the size and shape of a small potato. Human, more
or less. At least, his ears were round, but Lindsay herself
was part Danann and knew round ears sometimes meant
little. She wasn't sure whether she'd seen this fellow before; the guards in this place seemed to be all the same size
and there had been very little light in her cell.

"The prisoners brought in today . . . An Reubair sent
me to learn who they are."

A dark gleam of suspicion lit in the guard's eye. "I've
sent Andre with that information." Lindsay opened her
mouth for a protest that Andre hadn't arrived and she'd been
charged to deliver the information, but the guard continued,
possibly out of simple gabbiness, or a desire to cover his ass.
"The raiders have brought back four prisoners: a priest, two
squires, and a knight. The squires are from Carlisle, and the
priest and knight were taken when they tried to rob the company of its gold." The guard laughed heartily, as if it were
the funniest thing he'd heard all year. "The two thought they
could sneak into camp and make away with the treasure
gathered at such cost by the men of An Reubair."

Lindsay laughed, relieved to hear Alex identified as not even an earl, let alone the Earl of Cruachan. She hoped this lumpen human couldn't hear the false note in her voice. There was no chance that Alex had been after plunder; he must have been in search of her. The priest captured with the knight would be Father Patrick, and she was glad to know he was alive. She said, as much chuckle in her voice as she could manage, "Silly of them."

"Oh, aye, my lady."

"Where are they? Reubair will want to have a look at such confused men, for the amusement of it."

The guard pointed with his chin to a door to her right. "In there. They're not much to look at, nor to speak to, for the one is weak from a wound and the priest maintains his silence for now. He's surely taken a vow, but I'll cure him of it."

Lindsay knew Patrick, and knew better on both counts, but said nothing and only smiled. "Do let me see them. I'm dreadfully curious. Where did they come from?" The guard didn't move, so she gestured to the key ring at his belt. "Open the cell. I want to ask them who they are. Perhaps they'll tell me what they wouldn't tell you."

The guard puffed up with offense and flushed dark, blotchy red, like some irritated undersea creature. "Och, I'll get the word from them soon enough. In the morning that priest will be in here, a-bleeding, and a-wailing his confession to me." He nodded toward a wall where hung the tools of his trade: tongs, chains, whips, and some devices so arcane and torture-specific that she couldn't even imagine how they were used. Her stomach flopped. The guard continued, "The other will have to wait until he's healthy enough to not simply die before he's said his piece."

Panic rose, and Lindsay acted on an instinct she never knew she had. She went to the cell door to look inside through the peep window, though she knew the actual cell was beyond a series of doors, and her voice took on a childish, petulant quality. "Oh, please let me see them! I would so love to see what they look like. I heard they have horns!"

"Horns?"

She turned to him, wide-eyed. "Yes. Lovely horns growing out of their foreheads. Like this." She gestured with her fingers to indicate goat horns.

"Like demons?" He seemed intrigued, and blinked his surprise at the idea of horns on his prisoners.

Now she gasped. "Do you think they could be demons?"

"They've no horns."

"You're certain?"

"I didn't see any when they went in."

"Could we look?"

A puzzled frown of curiosity grew on the guard's face. Lindsay bit her lip to keep an exultant grin from it as she watched the cogs clank laboriously in this fellow's head. He was actually trying to remember whether he'd seen horns on Patrick's forehead. Finally he reached for his keys and unlocked the door. "Bring that torch," he said and gestured to the light in a nearby wall sconce. Lindsay followed him in, and into the next chamber, where he unlocked the door to the final cell. She looked around at the walls and discovered a sconce for the torch. She thrust it in.

There they were, lying on the floor against the far wall, both stripped of their armor and surcoats, wearing only shirts and trews. Patrick stirred and rose to sitting, a hand raised to shield his unaccustomed eyes from the torchlight. Alex lay still, crumpled, curled into a wad and looking like a pile of rags on the dark floor. Lindsay's heart skipped that he might not be breathing. Her hands went to fists she held against her thighs as hard as she could, to keep herself from going to him and taking him into her arms.

The guard sighed, relieved. "See, no horns."

"Very good. Not demons, then. Let me talk to them."

A frown of refusal preceded the expected reply. "I could hardly allow a lady to remain alone where she might be in danger from attack."

She peered at him and knew he couldn't possibly recognize her from her earlier stay here, but whispered to him with glee she did not feel, "Let me tell them what to expect at sunrise, so they can anticipate it fully all the night through."

As a professional and enthusiastic torturer, this man surely knew the value of frightening his subjects before interrogation. He thought it over a moment, then nodded. "All right, then. Shout once you've convinced them."

She smiled and saluted him.

He puffed up again, with pleasure this time, and leaned over to tell Patrick, "And don't neither of you be touching the woman in ways Reubair wouldn't like, or I'll see to it personally you regret it. Understand?"

Patrick nodded for both himself and Alex. Neither was in a position, nor inclined, to give the woman any guff. The guard nodded to affirm his words, then left the cell.

"Be afraid, young priest," said Lindsay as the guard retreated, then once the outer door was shut she dropped to her knees beside Alex and drew his head onto her lap. "Alex," she whispered to him. "Oh, Alex, be alive. Please be alive."

He was alive, breathing, and his eyelids fluttered in semiconsciousness. His temperature was high. His skin was dry and hot. His shirt was rucked up over his belly, and her heart clutched to see a wound there, red flesh swollen around a line of black sutures. "Patrick, what happened?"

The priest stared at the wound, eyes wide, already grieving for his master. "He took a terrible wound when they captured you. I'm afraid the fever has got him now. I doubt he has long. I'm surprised he's lasted till now."

"Why did he come?"

Patrick blinked, surprised. "He could do naught else. I confess I see it the same way."

"He'll die for this."

"Better than to die while doing nothing."

Lindsay burst into tears, though she struggled to hold them back. Alex moaned and his eyelids flickered again.

"Lindsay?" Alex's voice was hoarse.

"Alex, I'm here."

"Lindsay? Don't leave me."

"No, Alex, never." She held him and rocked him gently, and held her cheek against his hot forehead. "Hang on, Alex. Live so we can get out of here."

"Lindsay? Is that you?"

Tears rolled over her cheeks. "I'm here, Alex."

"Don't leave me."

"Never."

Cold. Alex was cold. And hot. He shivered for a while, then stopped. Pain. Existence was aching. The world was pain. A howling descended. Bereaved, echoing. Inhuman. Not faerie. Beastly, lonely, coming nearer and nearer until it seemed inside the darkness. It became the darkness. It pressed to him. Smothered him. It was all grief. All loneliness. All eternity strung out in endless dark. Alex struggled for breath and hauled in a long gasp. The howling stopped, and all was silence. All was darkness. Darkness, but in it a thread of Patrick's voice. Near, then far, then silence. The words were a mental blur. Meaningless, but deep in meaning. It didn't matter that Alex couldn't follow them. They were a thread, then a rope to tether him to life.

Then another voice. A woman. Lindsay? Could it be her? Was he that lucky? Did he dare to be that lucky, for there was always a payment for too much good fortune.

But he would pay anything to hear Lindsay's voice. "Lindsay? Don't leave me."

He was going to die. Of all the wounds he'd taken over the years, this one was going to get him. Then the arms around him were gone. As if they'd never been there. The abyss opened and yawned before him. Heat and pain. Pain and heat. Cold. Monstrous cold. More arms around him. Tired, so tired. Longing for sleep. Desperate for retreat from pain. Patrick's voice, holding him, bringing him back from the yawning dark. Shadow of death. Keeping him from the relief of ending.

Alex tried to find his tongue, but words were mangled in his mouth. His voice was dry and difficult, like bad sex. "Lindsay."

"She was here."

"Really her?"

"Aye, my—I mean, sir."

"Why?"

"Reubair took her. We found his men, and they took us to Reubair. Sleep now. Go to sleep and gather your strength. We've found the countess and she us."

Alex let his eyes close. He wouldn't die now. Couldn't. Lindsay needed him, to get her out of there.

On leaving the dungeon, Lindsay went in search of the castle kitchen and found it on the other side of an alleyway outside the keep. She might never have found it, except for spotting Reubair's valet with a serving tray, crossing from the wide door in the next building. He staggered beneath the weight of the food he carried and did a double take when he saw Lindsay. But he didn't speak and only proceeded on his way. The smell of grease and burnt bread guided her from there, and she entered the kitchen to find a bustling and noise and heat of an enterprise charged with the feeding of hundreds, if not thousands, of people three times a day.

Slabs of beef, venison, pork, and mutton hung here and there, some of it carcasses and some cut into huge roasts or racks of ribs. Worktables bore stacks of fowl waiting to be plucked and cleaned. A cook scurried past her with an oven paddle loaded with bread loaves ready for baking. It was huge, and must have carried twenty of them.

Another apprentice came near with a sack of flour on his shoulder, and she addressed him. "Boy . . ."

The young teen stopped in his tracks to attend her, for she was plainly by her dress his superior. "Aye, my lady?"

"I wish to order some food and drink to be taken to some prisoners in the dungeon."

The lad's eyes went wide with astonishment. "Prisoners?"

"Yes. The knight being held with the priest. I'm a Christian, you see, as is An Reubair, and I wish to give all due respect to the Lord's servant."

He looked around, as if expecting this to be a joke for which he would be laughed at later. Then, seeing no obvious witnesses, he blinked and stammered and hefted the sack on his shoulder for balance. "Oh, ye cannae be serious."

"I am, quite."

"But I cannae comply with your wishes, my lady. With all respect, it would be my life—or at least my health and livelihood—were I to take so much as a morsel into the dungeon."

Lindsay nearly groaned. This wasn't going to be so easy as she'd hoped. "I promise I won't tell a soul."

Fear drew his features taut, and he bowed even under his burden. "Nae, not even for a mistress so beautiful and filled with grace as yourself. Nothing goes to the dungeon, ever, but the gruel. If something rots, they get that. Naught else, by order of Himself. A standing order for as long as I've lived in this castle, which is all my life. Please don't press me, lovely lady, for I would have no choice but to deny you." He seemed truly distressed, and she believed he would have helped her if he weren't certain of punishment for it.

"I see. Very well, then. Proceed with your duties."

Unabashedly glad to be released, the boy spun and hurried on his way, even forgetting to excuse himself.

Lindsay would have to find another way to get food to Alex and Patrick.

She went to the bedchamber and found Reubair at his meal. The food set before her when she sat was still hot, of course. Steaming. But she didn't begin eating right away. All she took was a draught of her mead. Then she said, as if deep in thought, "Those two prisoners the men brought in. Who are they?"

"What prisoners?" No tension in him; he really didn't remember.

"The priest and that knight. The one wearing red and black. I expect they'll bring a good ransom."

"Oh, those." He sat back and shook his head with an air of regret. "No, I'm afraid they're worthless for that. The two from Carlisle will bring something, but that priest and his companion will more than likely die here in interrogation. Particularly the knight, who I'm told isn't long for the world, in any case. They're naught but robbers and worthless to anyone." He grinned. "Like myself, but not nearly as successful." A chuckle burbled up at his own joke, and Lindsay looked away.

She said, "That's unfortunate. That you don't think they're worth anything to their people. I thought they appeared well-off. Or did your men dress them and give them horses to ride?"

Reubair laughed at that. "Certainly they did not."

"Then I'm surprised you think they're worthless."

"As far as I know, they have no people to pay their freedom."

Of course not. Patrick would never let on who they were. "It might behoove you to keep them alive long enough to determine the truth of that."

Reubair grunted, perhaps thinking over her words. "What is it to you if they live or die?"

Lindsay shrugged and reached for a piece of meat to shred and nibbled a bit. As she chewed, she said, "They're human. I know how low we are considered here, and I would hate to see them die for it unnecessarily."

He leaned forward and rested his elbows on the table to look into her face. "Is that why you resist me? You think I despise your people?"

Blindsided by this turn in the conversation, Lindsay was at a loss for a reply. Had he really thought there was even a chance of her *not* resisting him when she was already married? In the same moment, her mind foundered as it cast about for a response that wouldn't give away Alex's identity. Finally, she said, "I resist you because I have no desire to be kept by you. I make my appeal because I have no desire to see men die for no reason. They have nothing you want. They aren't your enemies. Why don't you just let them go? It would be a Christian charity."

"Oh, but they are my enemies. They tried to rob me. They've killed some of my knights. They are, by all that is holy, my enemies, and they will suffer for it. Perhaps they will die for it. But one thing they will not die for is their humanity. I do not hate them for that, I assure you."

She wondered why he thought that would make a difference to her attitude toward him but decided not to press the matter. Best not to make him wonder too much about her interest in the prisoners. She admitted defeat with a shrug and addressed her meal in earnest. "Very well, then. But if they die and you later find you could have ransomed them for a high price, I'll remind you I told you so."

He sat back with a chuckle. "I believe I can withstand that."

Foiled again. Lindsay would have to think of some other way to keep Alex alive. She scanned the table, looking for items of food she might smuggle out of the room in a kerchief, and hoped Reubair would have business to take him elsewhere before the valet came for the dishes.

CHAPTER 8

Late on his third night on Tiree, Trefor again found Morag in his bedchamber. Stretched out on pillows before the fire, she wore a loose shift of embroidered linen that covered her body in gentle folds. The room was warm, for the fire had been built high, and a sheen of sweat glistened beneath the sheer fabric. Her nipples showed vaguely pink. She didn't acknowledge his presence, but gazed into the fire as if reading it. Standing at the door he'd just entered, he stared at her, saying nothing as he slowly closed the heavy chamber door behind him. Then he lifted the bolt across it. Trefor watched, breathless.

"Who knows you're here?"

With sleepy eyes she turned to him. "Nobody."

"None of the servants have come in here to poke the fire?"

"Nae."

"How come?"

Her brow crumpled. "They simply have not."

He grunted, doubtful, but went to sit in the chair next to

her and warm himself by the hearth. "Why are you here at all?"

She rolled toward him, and the wide, gathered neck of her shift fell low on her chest. He found himself staring for a glimpse of the body he already knew well and knew he could see again simply by reaching out to draw the fabric aside. But he gawked anyway, as if it were a contest to see what he could see. She said, "I missed you. I missed having ye between my legs."

"You came all this way to get laid?"

She laughed. "Such a way you have with words, my love. And, aye, I wish to have you. Last night was a joy, and worth the travel."

As much as he would have liked to believe she thought him a masterful lover and had made the effort to come to Tiree just to play patty fingers with him, he could hear the tinny note of a lie in her voice. He hadn't the patience for this game. "Why are you here, really?"

An irritated sigh deflated her, and she gave him a look. "Your destiny, Trefor. Ye ken your destiny is before you."

So many women so interested in his future; he should be flattered. He could recall a time when no girl cared about his prospects, because everyone believed he had none. "There is no such thing as destiny. I told you that."

"There is, I promise it. 'Tis fact that your destiny is to inherit the kingdom of the Bhrochan."

That made him laugh. "The Bhrochan. And where is old Brochan going that I would have his kingdom?"

"I cannae say, because I do not know."

"But you know I'm going to be their king."

"Prince."

"Ah. That's what Brochan said. I didn't believe him, either." His patience with this was thinning. Now he wished she really had come here just to get laid.

She rose to her knees before him and leaned between

his to kiss his unmoving mouth. "Believe it, my love. When the time comes to act, you will do exactly what Brochan says you will."

"Which is what?"

"I said I do not know beyond that the result will mean more power and wealth to you than you've ever dreamed."

"Convenient enough to say."

She shrugged. " 'Tis the truth. Receive it or not; it makes no difference."

Trefor liked the idea of great power and wealth. If his destiny brought him that, he might not mind it. He kissed her, then took her in his arms and slipped with her to the floor to undress her in front of the fire.

Once the shift was off her, and his own clothing was tossed aside, she said, "More to your liking than that silly mortal woman whose father is the laird here?"

Trefor paused in his attentions to the softness of Morag's breasts, and looked into her face to determine the reason for this question. She seemed quite serious. He planted a kiss right at the center of her chest and relished the soft flesh against his cheeks, then said, "I wouldn't know what hers are like."

"Not as full as mine."

"Not as available."

"Is that all you care for?"

He leaned up over her on one palm and looked down at her face. Firelight flickered on it, brightening her hair to appear as if it were in flames, and for a moment he flashed on hell. He shook that off and said, "What's Deirbhile got to do with anything?"

"She's beautiful."

"Yeah. You think you've got the corner on that?"

A frown creased Morag's brow, and he clarified, "I mean, you think you're the only beautiful woman in Scotland? Or even Tiree?"

"Nae. But I think most days I would be the only beautiful woman with whom you pass the time."

"I can't imagine you never talk to other handsome men." Or have sex with them. But that much he didn't want to know. She had a right to bang anyone she wished, but he didn't want to hear about it. "I'm not your husband."

"No, you are not. Nor do I truly care whether the wee princess's breasts are more attractive than mine. I would only know whether my presence is desired, or if I should leave and not come back. Are you planning on having her?"

He smiled, and wasn't sure whether he was amused by her silly question or enchanted by the idea that he might one day find himself in bed with Deirbhile. "No. She's the daughter of my host, she's engaged, and as soon as I can get off this rock I'm going to Ireland and won't be back this way until she's quite forgotten about me."

"She'll want you when you become a prince."

He snorted and buried his nose between her breasts again to blow noisily against her skin. Prince. Right. And it sounded more like it was Morag who wanted him for that. The thought was unappealing, for nobody liked being used, but for the time being he was happy to let her think he was stupid. He urged her legs apart and settled between them to enjoy her, then afterward fell asleep with her next to the fire and stayed there till morning.

Trefor never knew what Morag did with herself when he wasn't around, and today he didn't care. If she were discovered in his chamber by the servants there would be explanations needed, but he suspected she had put up a warding of some sort to keep them away. It surely wouldn't take much effort to make servants forget to maintain the fire or make the bed in a guest chamber.

Trefor spent the day in the Great Hall, whiling away the hours in conversation with his host while his men spent their attentions on the ships in the harbor. The snow had stopped falling, but the harbor was still ice locked. It could be days or weeks before the temperature would rise enough for the ships to make their way through it. Frustration ate at Trefor, nibbling at the edges of his soul and making him not very talkative. He sat and listened to others go on in speculation about Robert's progress in Ireland. With no communication in or out, and no new information, it was hash and rehash. Trefor chafed with the desire to fight in Ireland rather than talk about it.

Deirbhile sat next to him at table that day. Trefor flushed with pleasure, though he suppressed the feeling, as he always had with girls who were out of his league. The ones who made him feel like a rat in a maze, who paid him attention just to see how he would react, who expected him to blush and stammer and who always seemed disappointed or surprised when he didn't. At the midday meal he kept a cool front.

"You're awfully quiet," she said.

Trefor was not inclined to explain the quiet, which made him all the more silent. But he did say, "I've little to say."

"Have you been thinking hard about our conversation yesterday?"

It took him a moment to remember which bit of conversation she meant, then he said, "About marriage?"

"About love." She shrugged. "And about marriage, I suppose. About having a balanced life."

That concept made Trefor smile. Wife and mistress equals balance. What a guffaw that would have brought in his own time! "Having cake and eating it, too."

Deirbhile grinned. "Indeed. I would say that loving one's wife or husband, and expecting that love to be returned, would be like having and eating. With two pieces of cake, one can have one and eat the other."

Trefor sucked on the inside of his lower lip as he puzzled over this girl. What was she up to? Once more it felt as if she were hitting on him. Yesterday he'd thought it was a bit of naive teenage flirting. But now he thought maybe it wasn't. He said nothing, but looked into her face for answers. She looked straight back at him, and it was unnerving. This girl didn't seem a teenager. She was as worldly as any woman he'd ever known, and this felt like a genuine pass. Big trouble.

"Why marry at all, then?"

"Why, for children, of course. Legitimate heirs. And for property. A good match, to someone of means, is worth far more than love."

Trefor frowned, and had to think a moment to grasp what she meant. To him, a "good match" was always for love. But she was talking about money. Influence. To her, marriage was for social advancement. Upward mobility. "You would marry a man you found repulsive if he were rich?"

"If he were rich enough and not so repulsive as to cause nightmares. And if he were in a position to benefit my father's standing with the crown."

"And your fiancé is all those things?"

"Geoffrey is terribly rich; his father is influential. But whether he is repulsive or not is to be seen. I've never met him, and have no idea what he looks like."

"You've never asked?"

"They say he's handsome, but they would say the same if he were a humpback troll with a bleary eye and no teeth, lest I protest the marriage. What I'm told is of little consequence, since I will learn the truth soon enough."

"And you will give him legitimate heirs."

"Of course." She glanced around to be sure she was not overheard but lowered her voice anyway. "I don't expect I'll take a lover until my children are grown. If luck is with

me, I may even outlive my husband, though he's not so
much older than myself that it would be a certainty."

Trefor thought he'd seen jaded women in his life, but
this one had him speechless. Furthermore, he found himself disappointed to realize she wasn't making a pass at
him. Not unless she was making plans for twenty years
down the road when her legitimate children would be
grown. His mouth opened to crack a joke about that, but he
changed his mind and shut it.

It was probably a good thing the girl's father interrupted. "Sir Trefor! When you get to Ireland, say hello for
me to the wee folk there!"

A surge of apprehension made Trefor give Maclean a
sharp glance. What did he know about the wee folk, and
why did he think Trefor knew any of them? Had someone
seen his ears? He touched a finger to the bandanna-covered
hair at the side of his head, but, no, his ears were well covered. The laughter of the others around the table gave him
to know his host had been joking. He laughed with them,
but his heart wasn't in it. "The wee folk, you say?"

"Aye, lad. Were you to find yourself in the mists and
come across some of the fey, give them my regards and tell
them I could use a bit of luck. Or gold, if they've any to
spare."

Trefor knew all about faerie luck, and it amused him to
think how surprised Maclean would be to learn how close
he was to one who could provide it. But he kept silent
about his skills and replied, "In the mists? Fog? What's
there?"

"Why, the lands, of course. Hidden faerie lands that go
on and on but cannot be found on any map, for no human
has ever seen them."

Another of Maclean's guests said, "Or them as have,
have never returned. Stolen babies and such."

Trefor blanched. Stolen babies.

Maclean allowed as that was true and nodded vigorously. "Like death, no man has ever returned to tell the tale."

"Then how does anyone know they exist?"

Maclean snorted. "Why, 'tis common sense. Those who never return must have gone somewhere, aye?"

Trefor had been around enough to know that "common sense" was one or the other, but never both. However, this idea intrigued him. "You've heard stories?"

"Of course. They say to never go into the mists in Ireland, for ye may not come back. The wee folk hold sway there, and they protect their domain with magic."

"Naturally."

"No man can know what goes on there."

Trefor's thought was that he could know. He knew things most men didn't. Curiosity kicked to life in him. He'd seen where faeries lived. The Bhrochan lived underground; he wondered why. Did they also have lands aboveground? He burned to ask Maclean but knew he would get no satisfactory answer. Even if the laird knew, he would find Trefor's questions suspect. Too much familiarity with the fey might get him kicked off the island, if not arrested and put in the gatehouse. He said, "Then I wouldn't care to seek them out to give them your regards, would I?"

Maclean laughed. "And that would be the joke, lad."

Trefor laughed for the sake of form but wasn't terribly amused. This guy didn't know half of what he was talking about, and this talk skirted uncomfortably close to things Trefor didn't wish to address in the company of humans.

Deirbhile said, "You didn't know of the faerie lands?"

"Until now, no."

"That surprises me. You seem the sort of fellow who would know all that was knowable of them."

Again, a skittering of alarm chilled his spine. What did she see in him? "In what way?"

Her eyes narrowed at him as she considered. "Just . . .

there is a look about you. I cannot say for certain what it is, but I sense something about you that speaks to me of magic. Something special."

"Something not unappealing, I hope." His heart pounded that he might be revealed as Danann.

Dimples appeared, and crinkles of amusement showed at the corners of her eyes. "Very appealing. So terribly attractive I must restrain myself around you."

Now he had no clue what to reply and so said nothing. This girl was touching him in places he'd never known he had. He shifted in his seat as if he were avoiding an actual finger poking at him. Excruciating discomfort. Leaving the table on a pretext might have been the thing to do, but like picking at a sore spot, he couldn't just let it alone. He wanted to know what her game was and so looked straight into her eyes, in search of anything that might indicate what she was up to if she wasn't hitting on him.

All he saw there was blithe interest. Curiosity, perhaps. A desire to know him. He liked that, and it made him smile at her. She smiled back. Aware of the danger of being seen making eyes at her, he turned his attention to his trencher and ate as if starving.

The shivering went on and on. So cold. For Alex the effort required to do anything more than breathe was too much. There were arms around him, but he barely felt them. They weren't any warmer than his own cold skin. Not Lindsay's. Lindsay wasn't there, but she was near. Somewhere close by, and that was the most important thing. That was what kept him struggling to draw breath. Lindsay was there, and she wanted him to live. So he did.

A voice came to him. A man's voice, and for a moment he thought he'd died. What man? Where was he? Then he remembered. An Reubair. They were in Reubair's domain, in his dungeon, and Patrick was there. It was the priest who held him. The priest spoke to him, and he swam up through the depths of unconsciousness to hear. Pain and cold assaulted him, and it would have been relief to sink back into unconsciousness, and then possibly into death, but he fought it. Fought the pain. Fought his way toward life.

"Patrick." His mouth was dry. His lips stuck together, and he curled the upper one to separate them.

"I'm here." There was light now, and a small warmth of a torch lying on the floor before him. It was nearly expended but gave off enough light to see the walls of the small cell.

"Am I going to die?"

The moment of hesitation told Alex what Patrick thought, but the priest said, "No."

"Liar."

Patrick chuckled and adjusted his hold on Alex to put him closer, to keep him just a little warmer.

Alex said, "Lindsay is here."

"She was."

"Not here now."

"Not in the cell now. She had to leave."

"They took her out." He panted from the effort of speaking. "How did she get in?"

"The guard let her in."

Alex fell silent, and through the thick haze of fever the implications of that slowly seeped in. "Why?"

"I don't know why."

"Not a prisoner."

"Certainly she is. You know her better than that."

The old doubt tried to return, and Alex fought the despair. He did know her better than that. He had to; she was his wife. But he asked, "You sure?"

"They don't know who we are. She's the only one here who has recognized us. She's not betrayed us to them, or we would be dead."

"Ransom."

"Not for you, my lord. Certainly none for me. But as for you, were Reubair to learn your identity, he would execute you immediately. The countess has told me what he has planned for her on your death."

Alex waited for Patrick to continue, and when there was only silence he urged, "Tell me."

The silence continued, and Alex waited. Finally Patrick said, "Reubair would assassinate you to clear the way for a forced marriage."

Alex turned to look into Patrick's face. It was an outrage. Nausea rose and waves of shivering took him. Marriage? Reubair wanted to marry Lindsay? "Over my dead . . ."

Right. That was the plan. Alex sagged as all the air left him. His eyes closed, and the pain once again began to gain the upper hand. He sank toward the blackness and peace.

"No, my lord. Don't give up. Stay with me."

Alex breathed again, but kept his eyes closed. He didn't want to see Patrick. Or the walls of the cell.

Patrick said, "Don't let him succeed. The only way he can take her is if you die. You must live, and return to Eilean Aonarach, to save her from him. She's protecting you by keeping her silence. If he learns you're here, he'll execute you."

The priest was right. But something in the dimness of Alex's fevered mind didn't ring quite right. "Why forced marriage?"

"Certainly she wouldn't marry him voluntarily."

Alex shook his head, and the world swam. "No money." Lindsay had no property, would inherit nothing from Alex because with no descendant heir his lands and title would revert to the king on his death, and she had no influence independent of Alex. There was nothing for Reubair to gain by forcing a marriage that would be legal in only the most technical sense.

Again Patrick hesitated to answer, but then said, "An heir, my lord. He wants a legitimate heir."

Anger brought Alex's mind into focus. "He's a bloody faerie. Why legitimate? What does he care for human law?"

"He's a Christian. He wants a child legitimate in the eyes of God."

Fool. "Why Lindsay?"

"I cannot say. She's not enlightened me on that question."

The thought of Reubair with his hands on Lindsay brought fury that made Alex's head swim beyond the fever. "I'll kill him." He drew a deep, strained breath and coughed it out. Then he drew another.

"I expect you'll have to. The sooner the better, if you don't want to risk an illegitimate heir in your own household. Get well soon, my lord." There was an annoying note of smugness in Patrick's voice as he settled in with his arms around Alex.

The torch guttered out, leaving them both in darkness.

CHAPTER 9

Morag came to Trefor again that night. He'd given up waiting for her and had rolled over to sleep when a warmth snuggled up to him beneath his blanket. There had been no sound at the chamber door. Her hand snaked around his waist and she pressed herself against his back. He took the hand and kissed it, then turned over again to face her. She pressed her face to his chest and her belly to his, and lay there in the crook of his arm. It was moments like these that made him a sucker for her. Warmth glowed in him, and usually he wanted to stay like that forever. But tonight he needed something besides warm fuzzies.

"Tell me of the faerie lands in Ireland," he said. "The territory beyond the mists."

She lay back to look him in the face in the dimming light. "Finias, you mean? The Bhrochan land that is held by the Danann?"

"Is it really? Bhrochan land, I mean. Those folks have a casual relationship with the truth, and I never know what to believe about them."

"Take care with your words, my love, for ye ken I'm of that clan."

He wished she'd quit calling him that. She didn't love him, and he knew it. "You're only a little more Bhrochan than I am Danann. You look human and should call yourself that."

She only grunted in reply.

He continued, "Tell me about the lands. What's the story there?"

"They once belonged to my people, and now they don't."

"Who controls them now?"

"The Danann raider, An Reubair."

Stunned, Trefor kissed Morag's forehead so she wouldn't sense the sudden tension in him. He murmured, "I can't resist you."

"No need for resistance." She kissed him in return. But he wanted to know what he could learn about these lands, for he realized Alex had gone the wrong direction in search of Lindsay. An Reubair wasn't in the Borderlands; he'd surely taken the countess to Ireland to hide her where the human Alex would never find her.

A soft moan, and he said, "An Reubair? So the hidden lands are really Danann territory?"

" 'Tis King Nemed who is Reubair's liege."

That was a surprise. "Nemed isn't Danann, nor Bhrochan. He's an elf. The only one left of his kind, I think." Alex and Lindsay had crossed Nemed before; Trefor had heard stories, and they weren't pretty.

"Indeed, he's an elf among faeries and humans, and therefore he depends on his alliance with the Danann king, Dagda, for protection of the land he controls."

Trefor's ears perked at mention of the Dagda, and his pulse picked up. This was probably not good news. "So, how come Nemed controls it and not Dagda or Brochan?"

" 'Tis Nemed as took it from the Bhrochan."

"How?"

"He tricked us."

Trefor laughed. "Right. That wily old faerie let himself be tricked. How did Nemed do it, really?"

"No, 'tis true what I'm telling you. He promised the lands as dowry for his daughter, and Brochan was to be her husband."

"I'm guessing the marriage never took place."

"In proxy. When the lass was a child. But never consummated."

"Why?"

"She was killed in the Fomorian war, when most of Nemed's people met their demise and just as the Danann came to Ireland."

Trefor knew little about this history, beyond that the Fomorians were beastlike people who predated just about everyone on the planet. He wondered briefly whether "Fomorian" might be Irish oral tradition code for "Neanderthal" but decided it didn't matter much. The point to this story was that Brochan and Nemed both claimed the land within the mists and somehow Nemed prevailed. "So old Brochan didn't get the girl?"

Morag lowered her voice to a whisper. "There's talk that Nemed may have arranged the demise of his own daughter to keep him from the land."

"No way."

"Aye. For 'tis how the Danann gained their foothold on the land. Nemed gave over large parts of the island, those that are now outside the mists and are controlled by humans, to the Danann. His alliance with them is much more valuable to him than the one he'd promised to the Bhrochan."

"But it's crazy. Nobody would have their daughter killed just to get out of an engagement."

"Well, indeed it would have been easier on the girl to have married her off quickly to a Danann prince, or perhaps to Dagda himself, but Nemed has never been one for niceties, and I think he relishes shocking others in the world."

Niceties. The way she said that so casually made him wonder about her as well. "I don't believe even he could have done something like that." Trefor assumed the horrible stories he'd heard about Nemed were true, but this was beyond anything he'd heard.

"Believe what you like. It's nevertheless true that he reneged on his arrangement with Brochan and has denied us the land. He's given over the tenancy to An Reubair, who husbands it to the advantage of King Dagda and the Danann. And, of course, himself."

"But if there was no marriage . . ."

"Consummation or no, the land belongs to us, for the marriage was by proxy. 'Tis no matter that the girl died; the covenant was made."

"Why would Nemed want to trick the Bhrochan?"

"Why not?"

"What has he gained? He had the land to begin with."

"It matters not what he may or may not have gained. He's tricked us, and we want our land."

Trefor said nothing more. One of the irritating things about Morag was that she often thought like a Bhrochan, in circular logic and specious vaguenesses. If she wanted to think her king had a right to Nemed's land, there would be no convincing her otherwise.

But then she said, "The elf has reason to forsake us for the Danann. His alliance with Dagda is far more useful to him than the one he would have had with Brochan. The Danann, who often pass for human, are far wealthier and more influential among them. And 'tis humans as rule most of the world anymore."

"Sounds to me like Nemed made a bad deal with the Bhrochan. How did he know back then that humans would one day rule the earth?"

"Why is Brochan so certain you will go to the castle of An Reubair to meet Dagda?"

Destiny. "Okay, if he knew, then why did Nemed make the deal to begin with?"

"Lapse in judgment?"

"Bhrochan spell?"

Morag laughed. "Nae, Brochan only wishes to have that sort of influence over the elfin king. Nobody, man nor faerie, has so much power as to push Nemed with magic. I cannae say why the elf wanted the marriage to Brochan. All I know is that he changed his mind."

"Or the daughter was killed in a fight he couldn't stop, and he didn't feel obligated to hand over his last chunk of Ireland to the truly wee folk."

She made a soft sound of impatience and changed tack. "You must go to An Reubair's castle."

"Why?"

"To fulfill your destiny."

"We've been over this. There's no such thing."

"Dagda will be there."

"So?"

"You must go there, because that is where he'll be."

"I absolutely will not go there, because there's no such thing as destiny and I'm going to prove it."

"Ye'll go."

"What makes you think I will?"

"Because," she said with the thinnest possible patience, "it is your *destiny.*"

"Well, if the weather doesn't improve, I'm not going to make it to Ireland at all."

She glanced toward the door as if looking outside. "Och, this storm will end. And you'll arrive in Ireland in search of the mists, which you will find, and you will go to the castle of An Reubair. There you will meet the Danann king, Dagda."

"How do you know all this stuff?"

She said nothing, but only gave him a look.

"Right. Destiny." He said, "Hm," then kissed her and shifted on top of her. This conversation was annoying him, and he figured it would be better to wear her out so she would sleep.

Afterward, he settled into the sheets to sleep himself but then jerked awake with a realization and his heart sank. Alex was in the Borderlands, chasing after An Reubair, who wasn't there. Dad wasn't going to save Mom this time. If Lindsay was in Ireland, hidden in the mists, it was left to himself to go get her.

Morag was right. Trefor had no choice but to go to the castle of An Reubair.

The following morning Trefor went to the window in the keep tower to have another look at his ships. He would go to the harbor later in the day, but for now he needed to make certain they were still afloat. What he found was promising. The snow had stopped falling, and a sudden rise in the temperature had already done some damage to the ice in the harbor. Decaying piles of snow everywhere were beginning to resemble lace, and the sun glanced off it in blinding streaks. Morag had been right; he was going to make it to Ireland before too long. On the one hand his heart lifted with relief, and on the other he dreaded reaching Eire and having to decide which direction to take his men: to Robert or to find Lindsay.

There were footfalls on the steps below, and he recognized the tapping tiptoe as a woman's. His pulse surged with hope, and he immediately chastised himself for it. Too much interest in the laird's daughter was an incredibly bad idea, and it might not be Deirbhile, in any case. He looked out the window and waited to find out.

It was she. She came into the room from the spiral stairwell and paused when she saw him standing by the window.

Aflutter with feigned embarrassment, she nevertheless approached rather than retreated, and looked outside with him as if she were there specifically for the view. He could tell, though, that her purpose was to visit with him. She knew he came here every morning to observe his ships; any surprise on her part must be a lie. He let her think he didn't know she'd sought him out.

"It would appear your ships will be free to leave the harbor within a day or two."

"It would. The snow is slush already and will soon be water."

"Spring can be like that. Deep ice one day and cold runoff the next. We've enjoyed your company; you should come again next winter and be snowed in for more than a few days only."

Trefor chuckled at her wit, then gazed out at his ships again. "It would be a pleasure." No, it wouldn't. Were he to return to Tiree and be snowed in for any length of time, it would be an unmitigated drag. By next winter she would be married to that Geoffrey guy and living somewhere else. On the mainland, more than likely. Then Trefor would be stuck here, wishing to see her pretty face. Nope, next winter he wouldn't be coming back.

Then he blurted, "Tell me, if you had to make a choice between duty to the king and duty to your mother, which would you choose?"

She considered for a moment, then said, "That would depend. Would doing my duty to the king help my father's prospects with him? Would doing my duty to my mother hinder them?"

"That's what's most important to you? Your father's prospects?"

"You've asked a vague question, and I'm giving a vague reply. Be more specific if you want a better answer."

Trefor sorted through his situation and cobbled together

a question that wouldn't give too much away. "Very well. Which would you choose: tribute to the king or preventing physical harm to your mother?"

"Would the king be able to help my mother out of her predicament?"

Trefor smiled. This girl certainly wanted to have it all. "No. The king cannot even know about the other situation."

Deirbhile frowned over the puzzle, an academic one as far as she knew. "So there would be no excuse for not paying the tribute. The king would not be very understanding."

"No, he wouldn't." It wasn't his own tribute that would go missing—it would be Alex's—but Trefor would miss the benefit of the service he intended. The notice of the king was to be valued, and Trefor wanted badly to join Robert's army.

But Deirbhile said, "I would certainly choose whichever course would benefit my family's prospects. The tribute would be the more important."

"You'd sacrifice your mother?"

"She would understand."

"That you value your own skin more than hers?"

She shook her head, impatient at his lack of understanding. "Not only mine. That of the entire clan. My father, my brothers, my uncles and cousins. Indeed, everyone who lives on this island. She would understand that the greater good is more important than her life."

"That would take a great deal of understanding."

She peered at him and smiled. "I should think it a matter of course. The family always comes first. My father leads the clan with every thought to its betterment. Family is everything."

"The king is not a member of my family. How does obeisance to him become a duty to family?"

"Over the long course, the favor of the king sustains us. Lack of favor would hurt us. One life cannot make up for that. Even my own life would be forfeit in such a predicament as you describe. I certainly would understand. My duty is to the advancement—and therefore the protection—of my clan."

"That's why you don't care whom you marry?"

"Of course it is." Her tone suggested she thought he might be putting her on that he was ignorant of this. "Why are you asking me these things? Did nobody teach you of family loyalty when you were a boy?"

That struck him as an awfully strange thing to say. Having had no family growing up, he also was stung by it. Nobody had taught him much of anything when he was a boy, particularly not family loyalty. "Loyalty? How is throwing my mother to the wolves family loyalty?"

"Helping her in lieu of obeying the king would be unutterably selfish. You would be 'throwing to the wolves,' as you say, the entire clan to save someone for the sake of your own love for her. Terribly selfish."

Trefor gazed at her as he puzzled over this. Selfish? The look in her eyes was of deep caring that he didn't already understand this. He might have expected a dull, cynical glaze, but it was plain she was alarmed for him.

She said in a voice soft with concern for him, "What has happened to your mother?"

"I'm speaking only in speculation. Hypothetically."

Her lips pressed together, and he knew she didn't believe him. She waited for him to speak again.

"All right," he said, "I have word she's been abducted by someone."

To his chagrin she sighed in relief. "Well, then simply pay the ransom and have her back."

"He doesn't want a ransom."

Now Deirbhile frowned. "What else could her abductor want? That is . . ." Then something struck her. "Oh, dear. Could they have eloped?"

"No. My father is alive." Barely, but last time Trefor saw Alex he was still breathing.

"Then he should go after her."

A lie leapt to Trefor's lips, a little more easily than it should have, perhaps for wishful thinking. "He's a very old man."

"Then, what?"

"I don't know."

"Perhaps she wishes only to be a mistress."

The thought curdled Trefor's blood. Lindsay willingly with An Reubair. But that didn't make any sense, either, as quickly as she'd bailed from the faerie's company of raiders last year. Since then she and Alex had been joined at the hip, rarely out of each other's sight, twining fingers and whispering into each other's ears with secret smiles at every turn. It was enough to make Trefor want to barf sometimes. Lindsay wasn't so fickle as to go running back to Reubair's raiders; that much, at least, he was sure of about her. "I can't believe that."

"I don't expect you would, if you're a good son."

"I know her well enough to know she's not like that."

"It's a puzzle, to be sure." He thought she would leave it at that, but then she asked, "Would you return to Hungary, then, to attend to the situation? By the time you get there it may have resolved itself." Meaning, Deirbhile thought his mother might already be dead.

But Trefor knew Lindsay was neither in Hungary nor was she likely to have been killed by An Reubair. Not yet, anyway. "No. He wouldn't have murdered her. If that were the plan she would have died in the attack. They nearly killed my father."

"Does the abductor know they failed to kill him?"

Trefor opened his mouth to answer, then peered at Deirbhile, surprised and impressed by her perceptive question.

He'd not thought to ask it himself, and he should have. "I don't know."

"If they intended for your father to die in the attack in which your mother was abducted, then perhaps marriage is the goal after all."

"But she wouldn't want—"

"Of course not." Her tone suggested she was only placating, that she believed his mother may have been complicit, but then she went on. "But there is the possibility of forced marriage."

Now Trefor was truly confused. "Huh?"

"Perhaps your mother's abductor has forced her to marry him."

"He could do that?"

"Of course. 'Tis little better than rape, and when it's not a sham and the woman is not willing such marriages tend to be very short, but it sometimes happens. And if that is your mother's fate, then you must seek retribution immediately. And your father. The both of you must retrieve her and make the abductor pay for what he's done."

That was a quick turnaround from the idea that saving his mother would be selfishness. "I thought you said I shouldn't rescue her."

"Och, but this is an offense you cannot simply let go. 'Tis a slight to not just yourself and your father, but to your entire family and clan. It would be most shameful to endure such a thing and not have vengeance. You could not hold up your head among other men if you let live the man who forced himself on your mother."

Something deep in Trefor's gut not only agreed with her, but urged him to find a way to Ireland immediately— that very day—even without his men and boats if necessary. Again the image of Lindsay with a stranger rose before him, and the rage it brought colored his vision. "I think you're right," he said. "I've got to leave."

"For Hungary?"

"No. She's here, in the north. She was taken from Eilean Aonarach and is probably in Ireland."

"And your father is here, as well?"

"He's searching for her on the mainland, if he hasn't died from his wound. There's something I've recently learned, which he doesn't know."

Deirbhile uttered a soft, "Och."

"I'll have to find her myself."

"Then go quickly. The longer you dally, the more likely it will be you'll not like what you find when you reach Ireland."

Trefor sighed and sat on the windowsill to cool his heated face on the winter wind. Like Morag, Deirbhile also was right.

CHAPTER 10

A lex swam up from the depths of darkness once more. How long he'd been gone from the world was hard to tell. Darkness and cold had become only cold, and he could sense the torch from where he lay, its heat a beacon of life. He wanted to embrace it, to let the fire consume him. Burning sounded lovely to him just then, far better than this incessant cold.

Lindsay was there. Her scent filled his head and his heart. An earthy smell he'd loved from the first moment he'd ever been close enough to her to detect it. She knelt next to him, and he struggled to raise his head. She gathered him into her arms, hugged him close, and he continued to shiver there. Her gentle hands touched his face and smoothed the cold sweat from it. Everywhere she touched, the pain eased. A wave of comfort washed through him. *Heaven*. He was in heaven now, and Lindsay was there with him. It didn't even bother him that she must have died to be there. The only important thing was that they were together.

Something touched his lips. Wet. It ran to the corners of

his mouth, and he opened up to lick it. Broth. Food. He sucked it eagerly. Yes, he was in heaven. Somehow, against all logic, he'd made it. There was a spoon, and it dribbled soup into his mouth. Heavenly spoon. Wonderful broth. Lindsay's voice came to him in a whisper.

"Alex, hang on."

Hang on to what? All was well. What could he possibly need anymore? She was there, and that was all that mattered. He swallowed, and could feel the lovely warmth make its way to his belly. All the way down. There it spread to his nooks and crannies, and his shivering calmed. There was some talk in the room, but it was too much effort to follow the words. They didn't matter, anyway. Lindsay was there with him, and that was all that mattered. His hot body shivered and he swallowed.

"He asks after you when you're not here," said Patrick. Lindsay fought back tears and reached to the small copper pot for another spoonful of lukewarm broth. The torch burned merrily on the stone floor, as near Alex as she dared put it, so it would warm him. She cradled his head in her lap and took care that all the food went into his mouth.

"He knows you're here." The priest spoke around a mouthful of the bread she'd brought for him. His eagerness bespoke his hunger, and she wished she could come every day. But smuggling in the pot and loaf had been a nightmare of subterfuge with the potato-nosed guard. Were Reubair to hear of this, he might look into the identities of his prisoners. She might not be killed for it, but Alex and Patrick certainly would. There was no telling when she could safely return with more food.

"He's got to live," she told him. "Don't let him die. Don't let God take him. If he doesn't live, I can't either."

Patrick sat up straight, alarmed. "You wouldn't do away with yourself."

A sigh took her, and the tears tried to come again. "There's suicide, Patrick, and there's failure to live. Without Alex, I would no longer care whether Reubair became angry enough with me to kill me." Suicide by cop. Common enough in her time, and picking a fight with a superior opponent was appallingly easy in these times. "If he dies, and Reubair takes me to a priest, there will be a fight and one of us will end up dead. Perhaps both."

"The earl will live. Each time you come, he's stronger for it. The fever is gone." Patrick exaggerated. Lindsay could see the only improvement in Alex's condition was that his temperature was down a little. He was still barely coherent, semiconscious, skin clammy and pale, and his breathing came in shallow, ragged fits. He would probably die without enough food, and she wasn't certain how many more trips she was going to be able to make to the dungeon without attracting attention to him.

"I can't come too many times. Possibly not even one more time."

"He'll live. He lives for you."

Lindsay had heard people say that before, but they had no clue what that really meant. Patrick knew, and she knew what he said was true in a literal sense. Her throat closed, and for a moment she couldn't even breathe for her desperate concern for this man who had made her his life. "Pray for him." She nodded toward the floor in front of him, in a "start now" gesture.

Patrick nodded, rose to his knees, clasped his hands and bowed his head, and began speaking to God in Latin. In a conversational tone he prayed for Alex's life to be spared until he could finish his job on earth as Lindsay's husband, the father of her future children, and the laird of his people.

Lindsay found the plea soothing, and continued feeding Alex as tears ran down her cheeks.

Later, leaving the cell with the tiny pot and wooden spoon hidden in her headdress, having left the torch behind again, she had to pause in the dungeon antechamber, in a dark corner, to gather herself before going back upstairs. But instead of calming down, she burst into uncontrollable tears like a hysterical idiot. She hated herself for it. At a loss, she leaned against the wall, each sob a rip in her heart. She was no crybaby. This wasn't her, and she was appalled that she couldn't stop bawling. This was not the behavior of a knight, dubbed by the king on the eve of battle. For years she had passed as a hardened male warrior among men who prided themselves on their lack of fear in the face of death. She should be able to brave this through without falling to pieces. But she couldn't and continued crying.

Then realization struck, like a wave of cold surf that washed over her and left her choking. *What if she were pregnant?* What if this were hormones run amok? Frantic, she thought back to count days, but realized she couldn't. She had no clue how long she'd been in the cell, where she'd not seen the sun at all. It could have been days, or weeks. There was no telling. She continued to gasp and glance around the dim chamber, looking for the answer as if it might be found lurking in the shadows like something evil, at once terrified and thrilled. What would Reubair do if she were? Would he kill it? Would he kill her? Should she surrender to him and try to make him believe it's his?

That last thought appalled her for even thinking it, but somehow the more she turned it over in her mind the less horrible it seemed. Survival. It would mean life. Tears came again, and she sank to her heels against the wall behind her. She couldn't be pregnant. She couldn't have

Alex's child here. That would be too much to bear. She
hugged herself and continued crying.

It took an awful long time for her to pull herself together enough to leave the dungeon. Even fear of discov-
ery couldn't stop the tears, though she didn't want to be
caught weeping too near Alex, lest the connection be made.

Once she was able to stop, she stood and dried her eyes
on her sleeves. Then she hurried via back alleys and narrow
passages to the kitchen, where she splashed cold water from
the cisterns onto her face in hopes of reducing the redness
and swelling of her eyes and nose. Cooks and their helpers
watched, some staring openly, some glancing from the corners of their eyes. She ignored them. A few were human, and
though she didn't trust them, she did know that humans
weren't taken seriously here and few were ever in communication with Reubair or anyone high enough to have his ear.
They would mind their own business, and nobody would
speculate within hearing of a faerie as to why the Countess
of Cruachan had been crying. She thanked the nearest cook
for the water and went for a walk to let her eyes rest.

By the time she returned to the keep and the bedchamber, Reubair was seated at the table for dinner. He'd started
without her, had finished in fact, and was lounging against
the arm of his chair when she arrived. Though she thought
he might be irritated for her lateness, she was relieved to
note he was taking it in stride.

"Why don't we ever eat in the Great Hall with the
household?"

He smiled and settled further into his rather large chair.
"I wouldn't care to share you with anyone, let alone such an
enormous audience." It was probably meant as a compliment, but for her it only brought a feeling of being trapped.
She sat at the place set for her, and he offered her a platter
of beef he shoved toward her without speaking. It was still
warm, and as tasty as if it had just been delivered, though

Reubair's own plate was empty of all but a bone he'd picked clean. The food had been waiting for some time. The cooks may have been human, but they certainly knew their way around the spells that kept things clean and fresh. She took a large draught from her cup, already poured, and the spiced mead set up a pleasant glow in her belly.

When she looked over at Reubair again, the feeling of claustrophobia had passed. He leaned back in his chair, one elbow on the arm of it, and watched her eat. The gentle smile he wore was pleasant to look at, and suddenly the thought of surrendering to him wasn't so horrible.

Her heart clutched, and she looked down at her plate. *No*. Thinking that way was wrong. Not just a bad idea, but simply wrong. Reubair was not her friend; he did not have anyone's best interests at heart but his own; and she was not attracted to him. She was married to Alex, and would be married to him until one of them died. Further, she hoped she would be the one to die first.

A small voice at the back of her mind told her that wasn't likely, that Alex would probably be gone within a few days. Or even within hours. With horror, she realized the thought brought no tears.

Now she was afraid to look at Reubair. Something was wrong. There must be something terribly wrong with her to think this way. She picked at her meat, then took another drink. The horror went away. It was a welcome relief, and she drank more deeply of the honey wine. Her tolerance to alcohol was usually much higher than this, but for now she welcomed the dullness it brought. She looked over at Reubair again, and the bright look in his eyes made her smile. Not a fake smile this time, but a genuine feeling of pleasure. Embarrassed, she returned her attention to her dinner and ate more quickly than she might have. There was bread, and she tore a piece to soak up the beef juice on her plate. Then she said the thing she said at every meal.

"I want my wedding ring back."

He didn't reply. He never did. But today he reached into his tunic and pulled out a dangling bit of gold. Her ruby necklace. He tossed it onto the table before her. "Here."

"The ring, please."

"You know I can't let you wear it."

"I must wear it, as the wife of Alasdair an Dubhar Mac-Neil, Earl of Cruachan."

"You're being absurdly stubborn."

"The ring, please."

"Take the necklace. I can afford to let that go." Meaning, he was so rich he didn't need this heinously expensive piece of jewelry for his own use. Meaning, also, that he understood her emotional attachment to the symbol of her marriage. What he didn't know was what that necklace meant to her in terms of Alex's willingness to sacrifice for her. She reached out to touch it. The gold was still warm from having been inside Reubair's tunic. If she took this back, she would never see the ring again. But then, she was unlikely to ever see the ring again, in any case. She picked up the necklace and clasped it around her neck. The gold band could be replaced. The far more costly necklace would serve as the symbol of her marriage just as well.

She considered the possibility of being pregnant and decided it would be best for her to slip into Reubair's bed as soon as she was sure of a baby, the better to convince him it was his. Another glance at him, and she noticed how pleasant his smile was. The clean lines of his face and the brightness of his hair were a pleasure to look at. His shoulders were broad and his bones long and straight, his body a study in grace. Before, she'd thought him lanky and lazy, but now he seemed slender and relaxed. Aristocratic, in the modern sense of "Never too thin and never too rich." Even his ears seemed interesting and provocative, the tips curling forward as if he found her interesting.

For a fleeting instant she hoped it would be necessary to sleep with him.

Then she flushed red. "Excuse me," she said, then touched the edge of the tablecloth to her greasy lower lip, wiped her fingers, and rose from the table. "I'm quite tired, and believe I'll retire early tonight." As she made her way toward her closet bed, she reached behind for the ties of her dress, but her fingers couldn't find them. Clumsily she grappled, unwilling to ask for help. She wished Reubair weren't even in the room and would have simply climbed into the bed fully dressed if he hadn't risen to help her.

"Come, let me," he said in the softest voice imaginable.

She started to dodge, but the voice calmed her and she allowed his nimble fingers to loosen her dress. His hands at her clothing were maddening, as they tugged, pressed, held her at the waist to release ties. She was at once pleased and horrified. Part of her wanted him far away from her body, but part of her wished the hands to slip inside her dress. One rested on her hip, and she very nearly pressed her own palm over it to keep it there. When she didn't, he moved it and tended to removing the dress. He lifted it over her head and set it aside on the drying rack. Quickly, then, she threw off her slippers and ducked into her bed.

The door thumped closed behind her, and she moved to the foot of the bed, farthest from the door, and leaned against the wooden wall in the darkness. In a welter of confusion, she pressed her face to it and once more began to sob. It was all too hopeless. She was at a loss to understand what was happening to her, and she hated herself for it being so unclear.

What had just happened? What had she been thinking? How could she think of Reubair in this way? Were her hormones betraying her so badly she could no longer tell right from wrong? Did she have some sort of weird chemical imbalance that caused her to lose all sense of who she was and what her place was in the world? She'd been pregnant before, and it had never been like this. This wasn't pregnancy. This was . . . something different.

A sick feeling stole into her gut, like poison. In that moment of wanting to surrender, she'd been perfectly willing to betray Alex. In that instant she'd wanted Reubair to rip her dress from her, and the intensity of it terrified her. And, even more frightening, the more she thought about the idea, the less resistance she could muster. Until now there had never been any question but that Alex was the center of her life. But now it was different. She was different, and she didn't know why. She wished she were home. It would all be so much simpler if she were home. If only Reubair would let her go home.

But, then, how would she get Alex out of the dungeon?

CHAPTER 11

Trefor sat at breakfast and studiously avoided Deirbhile's eyes across the table, speaking only to his second in command, George, who sat to his left. Together they
worked out some details of the trip, and Trefor found himself feeling out the knight, testing him to know whether he
was steady enough and knowledgeable enough to take the
men on to Robert once they'd landed in Ireland. Only then
did Trefor realize he'd decided to go in search of his
mother, and it was enough of a shock that he told himself
he might still go to the wars with the Bruces. Dagda and
the Bhrochan idea of his destiny awaited him in the faerie
lands, and Trefor was loath to take a chance on proving
them right. Even taking Deirbhile's advice into consideration, it was a difficult decision.

A trumpet sounded from the quay side of the castle, and
everyone at the table looked up. Trefor especially, for earlier
he'd taken a good look at the harbor and seen the ice was not
yet cleared enough for a boat to pass. If someone was coming from seaside, he was curious who it might be and how.

When he found out those things, he would become even more curious to learn the why.

Once the boat had landed, with great commotion and uproarious greeting, there entered the person and entourage of a man about Trefor's age. A Lowlander, it seemed, with much Norman blood, and Trefor had a creepy feeling who this must be. He was right.

"Geoffrey!" Maclean greeted the visitor with enormous pleasure, open arms, and a hard, open-handed thump on the back. "Macfie, what a pleasure and a surprise!"

Geoffrey. *The* Geoffrey? Trefor looked to Deirbhile. She sat as still as a rock, staring hard at the visitor, pale and unblinking. Trefor guessed this must be her future husband, whom she'd never before met. Huh.

The newcomer blinked in puzzlement. "I sent word. Did my messenger not arrive?"

"Och, there's been naught in or out of Tiree for days. The surprise is not so much that I had no word of your approach, but that you arrived at all. What business has brought you to us so early in the season?"

Still appearing a bit puzzled, Macfie replied, "No business, my friend. I simply had an urge to travel and found myself here. Quite by accident, I'll say, but a happy one, I think."

Maclean laughed with a joy that was sincere enough to reverberate from the walls. "Indeed! That your boat should toss up onto my shore is the best of luck!"

Luck. Trefor was certain he knew better than that and wondered where Morag was just then. Watching? Laughing, more than likely, wherever she was. He glanced around but didn't see her. If she was observing his reaction to Geoffrey, it was from a position invisible to himself. His eyes narrowed and his attention returned to the visitor.

"Come!" said Maclean to his new guest. " 'Tis late in the morning, but surely you must be hungry. Come eat with us." He herded Macfie and his companions to the table, made space for them near the head, and they all sat to await food. Those who had finished eating, including Trefor, settled back in their chairs as well, to hear whatever news of the outside world Macfie might have brought. Big entertainment, after so many days of isolation from the world.

Deirbhile, sitting not far from her father, was barely breathing and appeared coldcocked. It struck Trefor as rather cruel of Maclean to not let his daughter formally meet her fiancé right away. The shock of his presence, after so many years of anticipation, must be terrible. She must be even more curious than the rest of the castle.

Including Trefor. Like everyone else he assessed Geoffrey at the head table, and unlike everyone else, hated him with an unreasoning gut reaction so violent even he was shocked by it. He tried to shake it off like an unwelcome spell, but it stuck. It was real, and there was no getting rid of it easily. He coughed and his eyes narrowed, and he wondered why he gave a damn about this guy.

Though Trefor wasn't a connoisseur of handsome men, Macfie's good looks were obvious. Undeniable, though Trefor found himself wishing he could. Deirbhile's intended had the smooth grace of the privileged class, the wide shoulders and deep chest of a successful outdoorsman, and a deep, strong voice. Had Geoffrey been an American, he would have been one of those guys who in school had excelled at everything. He would have been the class president, the three-letter jock, the guy who made girls giggle when he walked past. He would have been the sort Trefor and his friends had sneered at, secure in the knowledge whatever they might say would never be heard by him, because they moved in entirely different circles and were quite invisible to such as him. Trefor felt that was true now, as well.

Geoffrey's masterful, confident voice echoed from the windows of the Great Hall as he spoke to his host. The

entire room was treated to their conversation, as if they
were putting on a show for the gathered household. Which,
it struck Trefor, might be so. A show for Deirbhile, in any
case, and she was hanging on to each word. Then Maclean
addressed the room at large, and Trefor found himself riv-
eted to hear Maclean tell of his future son-in-law.

Deirbhile's father said, "Oh, but Geoffrey has proven
himself many a time on the hunt. Not nearly the prowess of
myself, you understand, but he's been known to take a boar
single-handedly and with not so much as a scratch to himself."

"A boar? By himself?" Trefor had hunted deer and
never boar but had heard how wily and deadly the creatures
were. Macfie, to his credit, said nothing himself but sat
back in his chair with a polite smile on his face and let
Maclean speak for him. Not that Trefor thought it was out
of modesty. He knew these Scots well enough to understand that had Maclean not volunteered the story Macfie
would have provided it himself. But so long as someone
else was willing to sing his praises, Macfie benefited from
the credibility boost of having the tale told for him.

"Aye," said Maclean with more enthusiasm than Trefor
had ever seen in a man speaking of a future in-law. " 'Twas
on a hunt a number of years ago, on his father's property
on the mainland. Thick forest, it was, and far from any
dwelling. He was after a hart, ye see, and ill equipped for
an encounter with a vicious boar." His voice lowered and
became filled with the drama of his tale. The rapt attention
of his audience seemed to encourage him to lay it on thick.
"He came upon it quite accidentally, and it charged him.
There he was, naught but a single sword between himself
and the raging monster. To run would have been the end of
him. Quick as a flash, he drew his weapon and attacked the
beast. Charged him in return, and ran him through."
Maclean gestured with an imaginary sword to illustrate.

"Caught him straight between shoulder and throat, and the blade found the heart as sure as if God had put it there. Dropped the beast in its tracks, he did. And good thing, for had it lived a second longer it would have gutted young Geoffrey with its enormous tusks."

Trefor found himself wondering if he could have succeeded in taking a boar like that. He'd never even attempted such a hunt properly equipped, let alone faced the deadly animal with just a sword and his own wits. But he decided it couldn't be any more difficult than the men he'd killed in battle. Surely people were even more wily than a stupid pig. But rather than compete with this obviously well-loved guest, he said, "That's awfully impressive."

Maclean continued, "He wears the tusks around his neck on a thong. I'm told he never takes them off." He turned to Macfie with a questioning eye, and Geoffrey obliged. He reached into the neck of his tunic and pulled out a thong bearing the famed tusks. Yellowed, and streaked with brown, they were mounted with gold caps and tied a few inches apart on the leather. A silver medallion embossed with a cross hung between them, and they framed it like parentheses. Trefor watched to see if Geoffrey would return it to his tunic, and noted that he didn't. The trophy was left in full view of everyone, and Trefor guessed it would remain there for the duration of Geoffrey's stay.

Deirbhile said, "We'll see whether he ever takes them off, next year."

Maclean let go a hearty laugh. "Aye, and you're already thinking like a wife!" The room chuckled, even Trefor.

He eyed Deirbhile, whose eyes were bright with amusement. She didn't seem like a girl being forced to marry. She seemed to look forward to wedding and bedding the Mighty Hunter who so impressed her father. It was in her entire posture, the sparkle in her eyes, the lilt of her voice. If she wasn't in love, she certainly expected to be soon.

Trefor thought of his own prospects. He was a warrior, a knight, and would make his reputation in battle. In Ireland. No boar for him. His adversary was human. By the time the meal was concluded, he'd again convinced himself that staying with his men was the best way to go.

But then later in the day Deirbhile cornered him on his way to his chamber to oversee the packing of his personal things. Waylaid in the anteroom outside his door, he had no choice but to talk to her.

"You will return to visit on your way back to Eilean Aonarach?"

He shook his head and started to decline, but she continued, "My father likes you well. It would behoove you to show yourself often." Disappointing as it was that she wasn't the one who liked him well, he realized she was doing him the favor of alerting him to opportunity. It had nothing to do with her own feelings about him, or even lack of feelings. It was a little like being told, "Let's just be friends." A nice thought, but not what he would prefer. He would have liked for her to want him, and an ache came that she didn't. At least, not enough to do anything about it. She smiled up at him with her sweet dimples, and eyes that seemed to touch him in places more private than he'd once thought, and suddenly he wanted to put a love spell on her. Gently, but enough of a push to make her wait for him. One to keep her from marrying that Geoffrey guy too soon, so Trefor could make his name, return for her, and talk her out of it. If only he'd met her on the return trip instead of headed toward the war, and then he would have been loaded with cash and imbued with the goodwill of the king. Probably then she'd have been all over him like ugly on an ape for all that money and influence. And he would have been glad for it.

"You were right; your father is a great man, and terribly perceptive. Tell him I'll return as soon as I can." He was telling her he would hurry back, and didn't really give a damn what she told her father. If there was any chance of her having ideas about him, then maybe she would hesitate in her wedding. One could dream.

"I wish you excellent luck in finding your mother."

He started to tell her he was going to join the Bruces but instead said, "I expect to find her very soon." If she thought he was only going on a quick foray against a single land-holder, she might dawdle for him. The war would take much longer, and she certainly would be inclined to forget him then. The urge to place that love spell was maddening. A gift of food or drink to be sent back from Ireland would do it. He could cast it in a small jug of mead or dried fruit. A personal gift from himself tied up with a bright bow to flatter her, and small enough she would eat or drink it all herself.

"Family is everything," she told him. "You have a duty to your father and your clan to redress this wrong."

Trefor still didn't get what the importance was, but something in his gut agreed with her that his mother was more important than anything else. His conscience tugged at him to not follow his men to the war, though he was convinced blowing off his promise to fight for the king would be the worst form of cowardice. He figured his men would think so, too. Not a very good leadership choice.

A love spell, and she would wait for him. He liked the idea. Then he could join the Bruces.

But what of Lindsay? The thought of her even touched by that faerie knight choked him with rage. That the woman was so besotted with Alex was bad enough; the earl, at least, was his father, and Trefor had to acknowledge the necessity there, or he wouldn't exist. But Reubair had taken her from Eilean Aonarach against her will. Surely it was against her will. The faerie should die for that, and if he forced himself on her, then there should be torture first. Trefor would be pleased to do those honors. Suddenly he wanted to send

Robert his regrets and go in search of the Danann lands. He nearly whimpered in his frustration to decide, and simply nodded in reply.

Then Deirbhile stood on her toes and kissed his cheek. "God be with you, Sir Trefor. I see a goodness in you uncommon in men. You strive to find the right path among difficult choices. I wish you all the best in what lies before you." Then she turned, picked up her skirts, and left the room.

He watched her go, and knew he would never cast that spell. It would be wrong, and he couldn't betray the thing this girl with such a big heart saw in him.

The voyage to Ireland took a couple of days, during which Trefor thought and rethought the issues before him. Slowly he came to the conclusion that, regardless of how others felt, regardless of what the current conventional wisdom demanded of him, his own convictions were what mattered, for he was the one who would need to live with them afterward. Deirbhile was right; family was everything. But not for the reasons she thought. Economic issues were less important than personal duty. Honor, of a sort. Trefor was only a year younger than Lindsay, and she had not raised him, but she was still his mother. He owed her his life, and owed it to her to defend hers with it.

In the final analysis, he had no choice but to send his men onward with George and venture into the mists after his mother. Alex's wife—Alex's responsibility—but for all Trefor knew old Alasdair an Dubhar might be dead by now. It was up to himself. He landed in Ireland with his mind made up. As the men unloaded horses and weapons from the ships, Trefor took George aside to give him orders.

"I want you to go ahead with the men. You're to follow the track south and west, and ask in the towns to find Edward Bruce's army. I'm told this territory here is held by

Scotland, and take care you don't wander into lands held by those loyal to the English king."

A skeptical light, somewhat puzzled, came into George's eyes. "Where will you be, sir?"

"I am charged with a duty elsewhere I can't avoid."

"More important than that duty you owe the king?"

Trefor raised his chin, for this bordered on impertinence. "I owe nothing to the king. The tribute is due from my cousin the earl."

George dipped his head to acknowledge the truth of that but said, "Nevertheless, there was a promise. To the earl, at least."

"Not that you need an explanation, George, but the new duty is also an errand left to me by my cousin, who is indisposed to accomplish much of anything this summer, as you well know. I would much prefer to please the king, and would have you stress that point to Robert when you speak to him, but my greater obligation is to the countess. I will rejoin you and the Scottish forces as soon as I am able. Tell Robert that, as well."

"Aye, sir."

"Take good care of my cousin's men, and you'll be well rewarded."

George nodded, for what Trefor said was a given. "God be with you, sir."

"And also with you." Trefor watched George return to the unloading, then went to gather his horse and pack mule. Robert would understand his absence. Especially since he would still have nearly all his fifty men.

There was no doubt Trefor would be able to find the faerie lands in spite of the various spells and whammies that would necessarily have been used to hide them. Powerful ones, to have been effective against human incursion for so long, but with vulnerabilities because the wee folk themselves needed to penetrate them. And he was one of those folk, not so wee but trained in the art. Piece of cake.

Trefor left the quay and the small town surrounding it and rode to a nearby wood to seek a good thickness of trees. Not a geographical center, nor even a hiding place, but a spiritual gathering where the energy would be strong. He found it on a bit of high ground, away from running water and surrounded by thickets of gorse. Here among the closely growing oak and birch the underbrush was thin, and he found a space at the top of the low rise where there was only thin grass and a bed of decaying leaves. He dismounted, hobbled his horses, and found an elder tree. Good. Some deadfall sticks from beneath it would be just right for what he was about to do. He climbed the rise, then paused to listen.

The birds had gone silent at his intrusion, and there was no wind to rustle the leaves. Peace filled his head, calming the noise there, and he closed his eyes to take deep breaths of it. One thing he appreciated about the training that had been forced on him was that it had given him the means to master the anger that had filled him all his life. Rage had always caused him to do stupid things, and though he knew it would never go away, now he was able to control it. Usually. He took more breaths of the sweet, calming air in this place and knew his spell would work today.

He knelt and cleared a hole in the damp, mushy leaf bed. The sticks of old deadfall made a tidy pile for a fire. Elder for the sake of seeing that which would hide itself. Especially faeries. He could have lit it with a gesture, but that was a heinous amount of power for an incidental thing he could accomplish with the flint and steel in the bag at his belt. He lit some dry leaves and spent some time rather than power encouraging the flame.

Then came the part he sometimes liked and sometimes hated. Today he hated it, for the air was cold and the fire was small. He stripped, piling his clothes and weapons to the side. Dang, it was cold! The icy air played over his skin, and goose bumps rose to cover him. His balls tried to crawl up into him. He hurried to do what he came for, in hopes of getting back into his clothes before too much shivering would set in. He'd been raised in Tennessee, and as far as he was concerned, weather this cold was just evil.

He took his water skin and the small scrying mirror he kept for this sort of thing from his saddlebag. No larger than a small brooch, it was a piece of glass painted black on the back and sides. A small, woolen, drawstring pouch protected it from scratches, for the paint was fragile and would scratch off. He knelt by the fire. This would have gone faster if Morag were here; the more *maucht* with more people, but he looked around at the trees surrounding him and didn't find her. It didn't appear she was going to make a timely surprise appearance, though he was sure she would if it suited her purpose. He wondered what her purpose with him was. No telling. All he knew was that she had one. Everything she did was for a reason; sometimes it seemed her whole life must be ulterior.

The spell was neither lengthy nor complex. He simply summoned the energy from within himself and visualized the thing he wished to find, a drill he'd been made to do hundreds of times before. He'd hated the training as much as he'd hated learning multiplication tables in the third grade, and this was ultimately as simple. Today he shivered as he gazed into the mirror, glad when the dark reflections of trees around him resolved into an image of Irish countryside. Then more images. Landmarks. And as he gazed, he felt a pull. A direction, but not a direction. He realized he was going to need to maintain this state of focus throughout the rest of his journey to find what he sought; otherwise he would be kept going in circles forever.

Finding the faerie lands beyond the mists wouldn't be as

simple as reading a map or following a series of turns.
More like having a GPS unit in his head that would tell him
which fog would take him there and when to work his
maucht to slip through the barrier in the midst of magical
confusion. Not simple at all. No piece of cake. It would require huge, appalling amounts of power, and he wondered
if he had it in him.

There was only one way to find out, and that was to proceed.

In a hurry now, for he could already feel the effort of focus draining him, he pulled on his clothing, the silk, linen,
and leather somewhat the worse for dampness from the
ground. The damp and cold seeped into him, for he had little enough body heat left to warm them. A huge shiver took
him and made him growl with annoyance, and he rubbed
his arms and hopped up and down a little to warm himself.
A while back, he'd seen some Scottish men walking around
in snow, wearing nothing more than tunic and shoes, with a
wool plaid wrapped around themselves to keep off the
wind, and had no clue how they could stand it.

Once he stopped shivering, he extinguished his fire,
stowed his mirror among his things on the pack horse,
mounted, and headed off in the direction indicated by his
faerie GPS.

Ireland didn't seem as green as he'd always heard.
Spring was still new, and the bracken was winter dead and
brown. The snow here had gone, and the countryside looked
soggy. Dank. There was plenty of fog nestled among hills
and drifting within the forests, but Trefor could sense these
were not what he sought. It wasn't until he came upon the
same thicket twice that he knew he had to be near his goal.
Instead of retreating the way he'd come, as would have a
human trying to find his way, he pressed forward a second
time and paid sharp attention to his gut urges. Part instinct,
and part awareness taught to him by the Bhrochan, it was as

true as a compass. He walked his horse slowly now, his head tilted as if listening, though it wasn't sound he sought. He guided his mount in the opposite direction of where they both wanted to go, and found himself entering thicker and thicker mist. The way became treacherous, and the animals began to snort and balk. Their unease was a good sign, and Trefor kicked his mount forward. Slowly, they made their way through the forest and the mist, dead of sound and damp enough to plaster Trefor's hair to his face. He no longer had any sense of direction; his only guide was the pressure to turn around and go back.

Then suddenly he was in the clear. His horse stepped out onto a meadow, from a wall of mist so perfect and flat it appeared as a stone wall that rose to the sky. The bank was the height of a skyscraper, and Trefor looked up at it like a New York tourist. He'd made it. This was the faerie land, which Brochan claimed but Nemed held. It was morning, the sun low in the sky and the grass still glittering with dew, though when he'd entered the mist it had been late afternoon. Had he ridden all night? It didn't seem so. It seemed no more than a couple of hours since he'd entered the thick mist. It should be dark now. The mist had been dark but had never gone the complete black of night.

But that was no real matter, and could more than likely be chalked up to the same magic that kept humans from finding this place. He relaxed his focus, and his body went wobbly from exhaustion. A small but persistent headache thudded just above the back of his neck. He rubbed the spot with his fingers and rolled his head. He took his bearings, free of the warding influence. The trail he'd been following was now clear, and the horse and mule no longer balked. Trefor kicked his mount to a trot to follow the trail and looked around at the empty countryside.

It didn't look much different from the human territory of Ireland, though perhaps more sparsely populated. Trefor saw no farms, no smoke from cook fires, not even sign of domestic animals. The only indication of habitation was the track he followed, so wide it almost was a road. Many horses had come this way, the most recent ones headed the direction he was going.

Soon he came upon a signpost, little more than a thin pole stuck in the ground. It didn't look much like a sign. The only reason he knew it as such was that he'd been taught the occam alphabet and he recognized the slash marks cut along the pole. His fluency in the old tongue taught by the Bhrochan was recently acquired and poor, but the pole bore only one word: *Finias*.

The track led straight through a glen, where hills on either side rose to become mountains. Then he turned a bend, and there, on the floor of the valley and sprawled across the pass through the hills beyond, lay a castle so perfect he knew it must have been built by magic. He'd arrived.

CHAPTER 12

Lindsay and Reubair were at breakfast when a faerie retainer knight entered the chamber to announce a lone rider at the gate.

"His name?"

"Sir Trefor Pawlowski."

Reubair gave a sharp glance to Lindsay, who struggled to maintain her composure though she allowed herself to express a reasonable amount of mild surprise for Reubair's benefit. *Trefor*. She might have guessed why he was there, but that he'd presented himself so openly was a puzzle. And disturbing. That man always seemed to have something up his sleeve and had never had any respect for Alex or herself; Lindsay wondered what was on his agenda this time, and figured it couldn't be good. Particularly not with Alex so vulnerable. "A relative of yours?" asked Reubair.

"A distant cousin, actually." Obviously she must know him. It would have been madness to deny it, for the Polish name was otherwise unheard of in this country.

"What could he want with me, I wonder? And how did he find me?" There seemed a slight edge to his casual tone.

Lindsay shrugged, as if she didn't know, and could never have known, the answers to those questions.

The messenger spoke up. "He bears the mark of the fey."

That raised Reubair's eyebrows. "Indeed?" His fingertips went to his own ears, and he looked askance at Lindsay. His meaning was clear; how did she know this cousin and not have known all her life she was of faerie heritage?

Her response was equal puzzlement, though she knew full well where Trefor had gotten his ears. "He does? The ears, you mean? Surely they aren't so very pointed. Though I can't say I've known him well, and have only met him once or twice, surely I would have noticed a genuine faerie mark, were it that plain."

"It is, my lady," said the knight. "However hidden his ears may have been before, he now has them displayed to be seen." He pulled back his own locks to indicate how Trefor wore his hair behind his ears.

"Ah," said Reubair, "he kept them hidden." It seemed he was glad to accept the theory and let Lindsay off the hook. "What does he want, then?"

"To see you, he says. A request."

"Of what nature?"

"I confess, my liege, I was unable to determine his wishes."

Reubair grunted. "Bring him here."

Lindsay's heart began to pound and dance, and her mind rushed to sort through the many aspects and implications of this visit. How had Trefor found this place? Did he know Alex was here? Did he even know she was here? What would he tell Reubair when he saw her? But the most important question was, what did he really want?

It was nearly half an hour later that Reubair was informed

the visitor awaited him in an antechamber. The faerie lord stood and said to Lindsay, "Come with me." Not a question, nor even a request, but an order, and Lindsay obeyed.

In the anteroom Trefor stood near the hearth and turned when Reubair and Lindsay entered the room. His smile of greeting was bland, and didn't change when he saw her. It didn't even flicker. She gathered he'd known she was there. Good. Perhaps the situation was controllable.

Or else it was already lost.

Trefor bowed to Reubair, and the faerie lord responded with a nod. Then Trefor acknowledged Lindsay's presence with a nod and said, "What a pleasant surprise to find my cousin here! It's good to see you, Lady Cruachan."

Relief made Lindsay's legs go wobbly, but she locked her knees to keep them from shaking as she offered her hand to her son. He grasped it, the first time she'd touched him since . . . since he was a baby. His hand was rough with calluses from riding and fighting, and there was a scar across one knuckle that looked like it should have had stitches but hadn't. Her heart tore in a way that made her wish he would go away and not make her feel so inadequate. "And you, sir. How have you been in your travels?"

"Well enough. And yourself?" A darkness filled his eye, and his lids drooped as if to shield them. It was an angry expression and made Lindsay wonder what he was thinking. She wished mightily for a chance to speak to him alone. To explain. But that wasn't likely to happen soon enough for damage control, and she wasn't sure what would be safe to tell him, in any case. She was at the mercy of whatever Trefor knew or didn't know about her situation, which could be anything, or nothing. Oh, how she wished he had never come! And beneath that was a dark, awful, secret wish he'd never been born.

* * *

Trefor was stunned to find Lindsay at Reubair's side, dressed in finery even Alex couldn't afford for her, and appearing as calm and comfortable as if she were the lady of the manor. She even wore a ruby necklace of astonishing cost, and he wondered what she'd done to earn that. Betrayal had always been a fact of his life, and his parents were no paragons of loyalty to him, but one exception had always been their feelings for each other. The earl was a fool for his wife, easily manipulated for it, and Trefor would never have dreamed the countess could cross her husband this way. It was appalling. He very nearly dumped the idea of rescuing her, and began to cobble together in his head a story that would have him on his way back to his men and King Robert in the morning.

But he was exhausted from his travels and the scrying spell, and knew he wasn't thinking straight. A niggle at the back of his mind made him think twice. Something didn't ring properly here. Though Lindsay's behavior told him nothing other than that she had thrown over Alex for Reubair, something in Reubair's demeanor wasn't quite right. In addition, there was an energy somewhere in the castle that was even more wrong. Not just wrong in the way that every castle had bad spots touched with evil or grief, but wrong in a way that was particular to him. It spoke to him in ways he understood on a gut level. As if to say to him that if he ignored it he would cease to be the man he thought he was. Whatever that might mean, he didn't know; all he knew was that he needed to find out what was really going on here. So he went with his original plan.

"I seek the Dagda, to pledge myself," he said. "I'm told he's expected here."

It seemed to surprise Reubair that Trefor would be so well informed. "Indeed he is, but how did you know? And why do you wish to pledge yourself?"

"I learned his itinerary from the goddess Danu, when I began my search for the king. I wish to pledge myself as Danann, which you can clearly see is my right. I tire of human folly and wish to join the faerie realm."

Reubair's eyes narrowed. "There's very little about you that is Danann."

"There is enough. Not just my ears, but also my heart, which is not so very little."

The faerie lord grunted provisional acceptance of that. "Well, your information is correct; Dagda is expected here shortly. In fact, we wouldn't have been surprised to have seen him as early as two days ago. But I'm told he travels from the Continent and may be delayed by circumstance. Weather, or unanticipated concerns." Trefor glanced at Lindsay and noted mild surprise on her face. Apparently she hadn't known of the impending visit. If she was the lady of the manor, she was an ill-informed one.

But then a look filled with meaning passed between her and Reubair. It was only then that the lord of Castle Finias let drop his reluctance and continued, "Do stay with us until he comes, and you may pay your respects then." Trefor looked from one to the other, astonished anew. Danged if they weren't acting like a married couple!

"Thank you, sir," he said.

Reubair turned to one of the human servants. "Show our guest to a chamber in the tower. See that he wants for nothing."

"Aye, sir." The retainer wearing Reubair's livery nodded to his charge and led the way from the room. Trefor gave Lindsay a searching glance as he left and wished the others would simply disappear for a time so he could question her freely. But he was stuck following the program, weird as it was, and wouldn't have a chance to talk anytime soon. And now that she knew he was here, she would surely avoid him. She must be ashamed to be found in Reubair's bedchamber. He would need to seek her later on, to make her explain herself. Oh, yeah, his mother had some explaining to do.

He went with the servant and mentally focused on the bad thing he sensed within the walls of the fortress. Like a knot in his consciousness, he picked at it and hoped it would unravel and reveal itself. He tried to visualize, but nothing came. Something wasn't right here. It just wasn't right, and he needed to figure out how it was wrong.

L indsay clasped her fingers together, her knuckles aligned with each other and pressed hard in a way that kept Reubair from seeing the tension in them. She arranged her face in the most relaxed smile she could manage and watched Trefor retreat with the servant. "Lovely to see Sir Trefor again."

"Quite a coincidence."

Now she smiled at Reubair, and held her expression when she saw his knitted brow. Her voice conveyed only mild wonder at that coincidence. "Not so much, I think. He apparently knows himself to be of Danann blood, and you chose me for that same blood; perhaps it was only a matter of time before each of us would end up here. The only co-incidence is that we are here at the same time." She sighed, but hurried to continue, "Though I knew he was in the north, I had no idea he wished to join the Danann. To be sure, last time I saw him I hadn't the foggiest notion of them at all, let alone that he was one."

Reubair had no reply to that beyond a bland gaze that settled on her like . . . like a warm blanket. She blinked, shocked at the pleasure it brought. This was so wrong. Terribly wrong. The fuzzy heat that rose in her belly shocked her, a disturbing evil she must resist. She took a deep breath and looked away to the window, toward the portcullis and freedom. Escape was imperative. She had to take Alex and get away from there before Trefor could give them away. God help her if Trefor found his father before she could find a way out of the castle. With no love lost between father and son, Trefor would be only too happy to reveal Alex to the man who would murder him. And gain favor for it as well, with Reubair and therefore Reubair's king. No downside for Trefor. Another deep breath, and she said, "I would like to take a ride."

"Then by all means you should."

"It would be a greater pleasure if I could ride through the forest rather than up and down alleys and baileys."

Reubair's eyes narrowed. "I imagine it would."

She waited for him to offer a solution, but he said nothing and his gaze didn't falter. Finally he said, "I would accompany you, to relieve your boredom, but I have business in the dungeon."

Cold sweat popped out all over her. She struggled not to show the panic as her mind flew to think of a way to keep him away from there. Begging him to ride with her wouldn't work; he'd already declined. So she said, "Perhaps you would care to take some exercise with your weapons? I like to keep in practice but haven't had the opportunity lately." She turned to watch his face.

He chuckled. "You expect me to hand you a sword?"

"You're threatened by that?"

"I've seen you fight. I know what you can do to a man. I've sparred with you, and I've even taught you a thing or two. I have every right to find you threatening." He said it with enough respect that she found herself flattered and smiled. Her reply was almost teasing.

"If I were a man, would you decline my invitation?"

"That would depend on how pressing my other business was. And I do have things to attend to in the rooms below."

"Surely they can't be so very dire that you won't spare

some time for me." Playing his own attraction to her against him. A cheap maneuver, but anything was fair in protecting her husband. *Anything*.

She bit her lip and her smile widened. *Come on. Forget the dungeon.*

Nothing on his face, but she sensed the tension in him rise. Her gaze was steady. She wasn't going to let him shrug her off, and he knew her well enough to understand that fully. And it was plain he wanted to spend time with her. He said, "Very well." A shout to his valet, and an order for swords to be waiting for them in the bailey, and then he stood. "Come." He held out his hand for her to take it.

"I'll need proper attire."

His lips pressed together, and though he didn't say "Rats," he might as well have. She wasn't going to let him hobble her in skirts for this, either. "Very well," he said, and nodded to a trunk in the corner. "Borrow some of mine."

She smiled and went to change.

The chamber given to Trefor was small but well-appointed. He had no entourage with him, so there was no need for a larger room, and he might not have gotten one, in any case. It contained a bed large enough for comfort and a deep feather mattress, sheeted in silk and covered with an enormous comforter of velvet embroidered in silver and gold. A servant's cot was tucked in a corner, its mattress rolled up at one end, and it would remain unused by him. A small but highly polished table and two chairs stood near the hearth, and two walls bore colorful tapestries. No window here, nor even an arrow loop, but Trefor didn't mind. No window meant nobody could look in. He set his rucksack and his belt purse on the bed and proceeded to relieve himself of his weapons. He needed sleep, but his sword also needed cleaning, though he hadn't used it since the summer before. His dagger always needed cleaning because he ate with it, and a quick wipe at the supper table wasn't quite enough to suit him. He pulled a rag and his whetting stone from his sack and went with his blades to sit by the fire.

The sword lay across his knees as he drew the stone along the edge with care. It was a calming, centering job. The zing of stone on metal was nearly musical, and his mind drifted to his father. It was Alex who had told him to buy this sword. The one he'd obtained on his arrival in this century had been too large. He knew that now, but at the time he'd thought Alex was just bullying him when he said to buy another. Controlling him. Trefor had liked the larger sword. He'd thought it was impressive, but since then he'd come to understand Alex was right. In moments of total honesty, Trefor had to admit it was possible the advice had kept him alive. Certainly it had saved him from lugging around more steel than he needed to carry. And this sword was as impressive in its own way as the bigger weapon. Smaller and lighter, but the hilt was of gold and the blade etched with a prayer in Latin: *Domine, dirige nos.* "Lord, direct us." Not what he would have chosen, but those who saw it seemed to approve.

The rhythm of strokes against the blade was steady, his hand practiced after those months of living by the weapon. He'd not touched a sword while with the Bhrochan but last summer had done his share of fighting in the Borderlands. Alex had taught him a lot about fighting with a sword, though Trefor had thought he knew it all. He'd known nothing. At least, not nearly enough to survive a battle. Again, he wondered if Alex might have saved his life by that teaching.

Alex. Thoughts of his father seemed to twang against his skull. *Alex.* He sat up straight and looked around. The

walls around him seemed to resonate with those thoughts.
He said the name aloud and nearly heard the vibration
within the stone. It seemed to come alive for a second, then
settled back to stillness like a plucked guitar string. He'd
never experienced anything like this before. This place had
something to do with Alex, but Trefor couldn't grasp what
it might be. Unless it was simply Lindsay's presence doing
it. As tight as those two were, Trefor could easily believe
Alex's core energy had accompanied her here. Perhaps,
even, his entire spirit was here and his body decaying underground along the road to the Borderlands.

But, no, Alex was still alive. The alternative was unthinkable, and Trefor was certain he would know if Alex
were dead. This wasn't death he sensed; it was suffering.
Longing. Pain. Things of life. So Alex was certainly still
alive, and a hefty chunk of his essence was hanging around
Lindsay. Trefor wondered whether Alex, wherever he was,
knew what his wife was up to.

A quick knock came on the door and a servant entered
unbidden, with a tray bearing a wooden platter of meat, a
small loaf of bread, and a pewter goblet filled almost to
overflowing with mead. He set the food on the table before
Trefor, then retreated without a word. Trefor, more hungry
than he'd realized until now, took a mouthful of a particularly fatty, drippy piece of meat and chewed as he bent
again to his work.

Deep in thought now, he concentrated again on this castle's spiritual bad spot, the ugliness he'd sensed earlier.
There was a center to it, reaching out and exploring the
chambers and alcoves of the keep. He could taste it, like a
sourness at the back of his throat, of indigestion or nausea.
Distress. Illness. During his time with the Bhrochan he'd
been taught that most people, even humans, had this sort of
sensitivity to what some called "vibes." It was a sharper fa-
cility among the fey, but some humans could be taught to

be alert to it and use it. In modern times it might be called a sixth sense, or even just a gut feeling or hunch, and those who paid attention to it would be denigrated for superstition, but Trefor had always known it to be a true sense. Even as a child his hunches had kept him out of trouble more than once. He'd recently honed that, and now he knew how to put it to use in a skilled manner. Now he focused on the feeling at the back of his head and explored its corners for whatever information it would provide.

He paused in his work, laid the stone aside, and rested his palms on his thighs. His eyes closed gently, and he imagined himself outside this room, in the anteroom that led to the stairwell. He grounded himself there, picturing clearly every detail of the stone walls and wooden floors, the fabric of the wall hangings, the rushes scattered across the floor that collected in the corners like backwaters. Then he took himself down the stairwell. Spiraling down past doors, to the exit to the bailey. Pausing for bearings, he felt the sense was farther downward, where—

Wait. There was Lindsay and Reubair. In his mind he glimpsed his mother in the Great Hall, wearing men's clothes and being handed a sword by one of Reubair's servants. *Prisoner. Right*. The two passed him on their way out to the bailey, chatting amiably, and Trefor followed them.

"Be gentle with me, my dear," said Reubair. He was joking, of course. Lindsay was a good fighter, for a woman, but was still only a woman. Surely she would be no match for him, even in harmless sparring where she knew he wouldn't hurt her.

She said nothing in reply but walked to the middle of the bailey, turned, and faced off against Reubair in a high guard. A sucker stance. She was inviting attack by leaving herself open. Reubair smiled and went for it with full strength and without hesitation.

Of course, she was put on the defensive, and in a wild

clanging of swords he backed her up several yards. But
then she dodged and ducked around to wallop him from
the side with the flat of her blade. He stood down with a
laugh. Some passersby in the bailey stopped to watch,
gawking openly at the woman in men's clothing.

"A touch! Excellent move, lovely lady!"

"Stop calling me that."

"You are a countess, yes?" He strolled, and Trefor could
see he was looking for an opening, though it seemed he'd
stopped the sparring for a moment. Lindsay wasn't buying
it and held her sword forward in expectation of an attack.
Defensive. Good. Trefor wasn't entirely certain Reubair
wouldn't hurt her accidentally-on-purpose. *Oops, so sorry.
I thought you were ready.*

"I'm a countess, but no lady when I've got a sword in
my hands. You should know that. Don't expect me to fight
like a girl."

"Never."

"Then quit your wanking about and get on with it."

A puzzled light flashed in his eyes at her strange vocab-
ulary, then disappeared as he said, "As you wish." He spun
the sword in a mulinette and attacked with blinding speed.
But she stood up to him this time and swung her weapon
with full strength. He couldn't back her up, and when they
disengaged he was panting. Trefor smiled. She was his
mother. Of course she was tough.

Now she came at Reubair and caught him off guard. He
parried madly, backing in a circle, but she laid off before
he could put the sun in her eyes. A quick run to the left, and
she again had the light advantage. Reubair's mouth pressed
in a hard line, and he panted hard. He came at her in a
flurry of flashing metal and backed her up against a rocky
rise near a high garden wall. But she negotiated the uneven
ground without having to look down.

She laughed, with a flash of anger. "You're fighting me

on home turf, you know. I lived here in this bailey, chained to that rock. Sorry now?"

He had no reply to that, and Trefor was disappointed, for he was deeply curious what she'd meant by it. Lived there? Chained? The sparring continued, and Lindsay now had an advantage of a higher ground she skipped around on as if she were the full-blooded faerie, dancing from knob to bulge. Reubair attacked and tried to cut her at the knees, but she was too quick for him, and laughed at him for it. The more she laughed, the angrier he became. It wasn't long before he was making mistakes for that anger. Telegraphing his intention. Swinging wide, attacking before he was ready. And tiring himself.

Then she tried to stab him. For real. In the midst of an exchange, she hauled back and aimed her sword right at his solar plexus. Only by a hair did he fend the attack and save himself from being run straight through.

"Ho!" Surprise and shock colored his voice and his face. "What was the meaning of that?"

Anger flashed in her eyes as well, and she said tightly, "Oh. Sorry. I'm getting a bit tired, I suppose, and my sword slipped."

No, it hadn't. She'd been in complete control, and it showed on Reubair's face that he knew it. Mouth pressed into a thin, white line, he said nothing but went to take the sword from Lindsay's hand and turned it over to his servant. He gave the servant his own sword as well, threw Lindsay a look, then went back into the keep. Trefor wondered what Reubair had expected from Lindsay if she was his captive. Chained to a rock? And she was okay with that? Nothing here made any sense.

Lindsay watched him go. Trefor was dying to know what she was thinking, but her expression was blank.

* * *

L indsay let Reubair go ahead of her, not trusting him after what she'd just done. He'd need a few minutes to
get over being angry.

Trefor preyed on her mind as she waited. His presence
was not a good thing. God knew what he would do to Alex
if he found him. She needed to talk to Trefor alone. And
quickly, regardless of whatever spies Reubair may have set
on her to report her movements. She realized there would
never be a time when that wouldn't be a danger. She
needed to approach him immediately. Once she was certain Reubair had disappeared into the bedchamber upstairs, she also went into the keep.

I n an instant Trefor was behind her, to see where she was
going. Maybe to look in on a conversation with Reubair,
if that was where she was headed.

But she only went one flight, entered the anteroom on
that floor, and knocked on the door of his own guest chamber. The knock, heard also from inside the room, wrenched
Trefor back to his body. A pain shot through his head and
made him groan. Man, he hated when that happened! He
ran his fingers through his hair, picked up the whetting
stone, and said, "Come."

Lindsay entered the room, and to Trefor's dismay his
heart surged to pounding at her presence in his space.
Since the day he'd come to her as an adult rather than a
baby, she'd hardly spoken to him, let alone sought him out.
The shock of this attention shook him to his toes. Even
red-cheeked, drenched in sweat, and wearing a man's tunic
and trews—perhaps even especially then—her beauty
throttled him, a situation he found untenable. He'd just
watched her win a sparring match with a larger, more experienced, and masculine opponent, and she'd done it by
being meaner than he was. This was the only woman who

had ever rendered Trefor speechless, and his cheeks warmed for it now. She stood there near the door, her hands clasped together, as relaxed as a queen and somehow still feminine in her borrowed clothes, and she smiled at him in a way he'd wished for all his life. She was young. She was the beautiful, perfect mother he'd dreamed of as a little boy, but he was no longer a little boy. The crippling confusion of it made his heart race, and he had to clear his voice to speak.

"Have a seat." He nodded toward the other chair by the table.

She drew it away—a little farther away from him than he thought truly necessary—and sat. Graceful, poised, long-boned and aristocratic, but with a solid strength he found captivating and which he was proud to own himself, she held his gaze fast. The rubies around her neck peeked from beneath the tunic, like a regal nature beneath a rough exterior. He couldn't take his eyes off her, though he tried to concentrate on his work. It wouldn't do to let her know how she was affecting him. That was a vulnerability he couldn't afford. Ever. He eyed her, ran the stone over his sword blade, and thought of how cozy she was with Reubair. And how disgusting that was. "What can I do for you?"

"That is an excellent question. Why are you here?"

Her tone stung him with its implication she didn't want him there. Some of the edge disappeared from his worship of her, and he replied as sharply. "Another excellent question. I heard you'd been kidnapped and came to save you from the big, bad wolf. It would appear you don't need saving."

She leaned forward in her chair. "I assure you, I do need it, and badly." Her voice was lowered to be barely audible, and he glanced at the chamber door. She was behaving as if afraid of eavesdroppers.

He was skeptical that it might be an act. "Then let's bolt. Now. Let's go to the stables, get my horses, and be on our way."

Again disappointment came when she hesitated. Apparently he was right. She didn't really want to leave. She said, "I can't. There is a spell keeping me from exiting the portcullis. Whenever I approach it, I find myself redirected."

"Just yourself, or does everyone have that difficulty?"

"Nobody but myself, as near as I can tell."

He shrugged. "Simple enough to counter, even without magic. All I have to do is lead you to—"

"I said I can't do it. He's keeping me here by magical means and I cannot leave." Desperation tinged her voice. This was upsetting her, though she struggled to keep it from him. It all rang wrong.

"What else has he got on you? It can't be just the one lame spell."

Once more she hesitated. He wanted her to admit what she was up to. He hated being lied to, and this nonsense was beginning to piss him off. Conscious of his rising ire, he set aside the blade in his hands, which was beginning to tempt him. She was his mother, and he wouldn't hurt her even if she was banging that faerie and lying about why she couldn't leave.

"As I said, it's magic. He's a more powerful faerie than most. I'm certain you'd be no match for him."

His chin raised, offended. "I've been studying. You might be surprised at what I can pull off these days."

Insistence rose in her voice, and fear in her eyes. "I'm telling you, it's no use. I've got to bide my time and look for a better opportunity to flee."

He gazed at her and tried to read her face for her real agenda. But it was no use, and there was no point in insisting she tell him. So he pretended to accept her story and said, "All right. Then what do we do now?"

"As I said, we bide our time."

"How long?"

That question seemed to stymie her. She faltered, then finally spoke. "I don't know."

Was she hoping for a chance to get rid of him? Discredit him with Reubair? Did she understand he wasn't really there to pledge himself to Dagda? What in the world was keeping her? What sort of hold did Reubair have on her? "We should leave before Dagda gets here. I hope you don't expect me to pledge myself. We need to get the hell out of here as soon as possible. No screwing around. Really, we should be gone already." He wanted to avoid the Dagda, to avoid any chance of fulfilling the Bhrochan prediction of his fate. It would be best for him all around if he never saw Dagda at all.

Now a shadow crossed her eyes. Briefly, but he saw it. She was skeptical as well, and it puzzled him. He wondered why she thought he would ever want to pledge himself as a bloody faerie. She said, "Why not pledge? You are Danann."

"I'm not. I'm more human than you are. My father isn't fey."

"But it manifests more in you. You have the mark, and the sense. You have a power I don't."

He was a throwback, in other words. She didn't say that, but this was more openness from her than he'd ever had, and he eagerly pursued the subject. "I didn't ask for it." The words came in a gush he couldn't control. "I never wanted it, and the Bhrochan held me prisoner to teach it to me." He skated right up next to the one subject he wanted to broach with her but never had the opportunity to before. "In fact, my whole life has been one big Bhrochan joke."

Her tone sharpened with irritation. "Which, of course, is why you've attached yourself to that Bhrochan witch, Morag."

"She's not the issue."

"She is if you're serious about her."

He laughed, a dry, angry chuckle. "What are you, my mother?"

Lindsay's face fell with shock. It was a cruel thing for him to have said, but he couldn't feel too sorry for it. She'd abrogated all parental responsibility by her rejection of him when they'd met, and had no business telling him how to run his life. Morag, however he felt about her, was not a subject for Lindsay, or anyone else, to discuss with him.

Lindsay fell silent, and her face flushed all the way down her neck and chest. Her lips pressed together, and her eyes glistened with tears. It crossed his mind he might have taken it a little easier, but there was nothing for it now. He returned his attention to the sharpening of his sword and ran the whetting stone along it in hard, quick strokes. When his mother rose to leave the room, he didn't look up, and simply let her go.

L indsay left Trefor's chamber and immediately outside the door burst into silent sobs. Her hand over her mouth, she hurried to the stairwell and went up one flight to find an empty room where she could tuck herself into a dark corner next to its hearth and recover herself.

Her baby was gone forever, and Trefor wasn't her son. Not in the ways that were important. She couldn't think of him as the child she'd given birth to a year ago. In no way but genetically did she have anything to do with him, and apparently he hated her for it. As hard as she struggled to not let that make a difference to her, it somehow did. And as long and hard as she puzzled over how it mattered, she couldn't understand why, or even in what way, it did.

Furthermore, she now had to let him think she'd betrayed Alex. She couldn't leave without her husband, but neither could she give him away to someone she couldn't trust. Trefor hated his parents for letting the Bhrochan take him, and Alex would die for that hate if Trefor found him. Now she'd given Trefor reason to think there was something funny going on between herself and Reubair. She dug her fingernails into her palms and cursed herself for an idiot. She never should have gone to Trefor's room.

There was a footfall on the stairwell, and she looked up to find Reubair in the doorway. Once more she pulled herself together, to face him, but there was no hiding she'd been crying.

"What is the matter? Why do you weep?" He sounded shocked to find her in tears.

She straightened and wiped her eyes on the too-long sleeve of her borrowed tunic. "I'm being held prisoner. Surely that's enough to justify a bad mood."

He thought about that a moment, and she wondered how it was he had to think about it. It occurred to her that he was as clueless about feelings as many boyfriends she'd had in the past. Men, apparently, were men whether they had pointed ears or round. He said, "I'm sorry you feel that way."

That made her blink. How else did he think she would feel? But his voice was soft. He seemed to mean it, sorry to have saddened her. He stepped toward her, and the red firelight threw stark shadows on his face. The light in his eyes suggested concern for her, and she wanted to believe in it. Her heart softened and grasped at the comfort of it. He surely meant what he said, and didn't want her to feel bad. A glimmer of hope kindled in her heart.

"Then let me go."

"I can't do that."

"Why not?"

"Because then you would leave, and I couldn't bear it."

"You don't love me; don't bother trying to make me think you do."

"Never presume to know what I might be thinking or feeling. I'm not the man you seem to believe me." His face leaned toward hers, and she was torn between retreat and standing her ground.

She kept perfectly still. "Not a man at all, I'd say."

"That is only an insult because I care what you think."

She couldn't help but smile at that.

He continued, his voice a whisper, "I would that you could accept me as your husband. Divorce Cruachan and marry me freely."

"That would be far more convenient for you than having to chase him down and kill him, yes?"

A shadow crossed his eyes, but it disappeared as quickly. "True enough. But not much to the point. I would have a happy wife if at all possible."

"Easier to keep under control."

"More gentle on my spirit. I am a Christian, after all, and have a care for my immortal soul."

"Not to mention your immortal body."

"Long-lived, not immortal. I know what it is to look down the corridor of centuries. That's a glimpse of eternity, and I fear spending my unending afterlife in hell. I have no desire to transgress against you. It's desperation only that makes me take extreme measures to have you and keep you. Desperation born of strong feeling."

The idea that An Reubair could love anyone, or fear anything that didn't have a sword to his throat, was a stretch for Lindsay to accept. It didn't seem possible. But looking at him now, he seemed sincere. He gazed straight into her eyes. She held them there for a moment, then realized what she was doing and looked away. Her pulse thudded in her ears and she wanted to flee. But she didn't. She stood there, staring into the fire without seeing it, and wishing he would either leave or . . .

God help her, she wished he might kiss her.

Breath left her, and she turned away to struggle to regain it. Her back to him, facing into the dark corner, she gathered her wits. Deep breaths. Several deep, cleansing breaths helped clear her head, and she was able to see this for what it was: a weak moment of identifying with her captor. Stockholm syndrome. She needed to rise above this urge for peace between herself and Reubair, to fight him and his seduction. A surge of strength buttressed her heart. Surely it would be simpler now that she knew what was happening to her, and that thought brought courage.

She turned toward him again, but when she looked up at his face her heart warmed once more. No matter what she told herself, the sight of him brought a pleasure she couldn't reject, and she hated it. Hated herself for her weakness. A trembling set up in her, and she couldn't even look away from him.

His voice went soft. "Don't fight it."

Alarm struck. He knew. He could see the struggle in her. But she denied and fought as hard as she could. "Fight what?"

"You know what. I can see it in your eyes."

"You know nothing about me. You think I'm weak. You think all it takes is food, clothing, and a winning smile to make me betray the man I vowed to love forever."

Reubair chuckled. "No, I don't think that at all. Above all things, that is one thing I am certain is not true. Your strength of will is all the more reason to have you for my wife and the mother of my heir."

"My strength of will is the one thing that will keep me from being your wife."

"Not if I find your husband and deal with him."

"More likely he'll deal with you."

"And such is life if that happens. I deem the prize worth the risk."

"Take care you don't underestimate the risk."

"Indeed, that would be as foolish as to overvalue the prize." She could see he was becoming irritated by this conversation, for an edge had come into his voice. But he touched his fingers to her chin, and she resisted the urge to lean into them. His skin against hers was electrifying and sent a thrill to her toes. Her eyes shut against it, and her lips pressed together. Something was terribly wrong with her. Thoughts of Alex rose to mind, but burst like huge, splattering soap bubbles made by a child's toy. Other thoughts of Reubair rose in their place. The only thing she could think of to do was flee the room, and she did so.

But there was nowhere to go. The Great Hall would be thronged with knights at their midday meal, and the streets of the town would be busy with gawking faeries. The only place to go was the bedchamber at the top of the tower, and that was where her unthinking feet took her. She found herself in the middle of the room, turning, looking for a place to be. To hide from him, though she knew there was no place in the entire castle safe from him. She pulled off the boots she wore and tucked herself into the small cabinet bed. The door thudded shut behind her, and she sat in the darkness with her legs curled beneath her, in hopes he would think she'd suddenly decided to take a nap.

The door to the bedchamber squeaked open, then shut with a boom of heavy wood. Then silence. He'd followed her. Her eyes shut, as if he would know it and think she was asleep. There was no sound of movement in the room outside the bed, but only a sigh.

"Sir Lindsay, am I to think this an invitation?"

Her eyes flew open in alarm. "Stay away from me."

There was a protracted silence as he thought that over, then he said, "You would find me a most satisfying lover, I promise."

Her imagination betrayed her and brought an image of just how satisfying he might be. It was at once appalling and exciting, like watching a train wreck, and made her gasp. But she said, "I'd rather be violated by a broomstick."

"That can be arranged."

"I expect you'd be happy to arrange it."

The silence then was very long, and was ended by the creak and thud of the chamber door. Alone finally, Lindsay breathed easily again. Tears rose to her eyes, and she sobbed quietly in the dark refuge of her bed.

CHAPTER 13

Trefor stretched out on the bed for a nap once he'd finished eating and had cleaned his weapons and armor. He mulled the idea of kidnapping Lindsay and hauling her back to Eilean Aonarach to present her to Alex like a prize, but in the end he deemed it not worth the effort of keeping her under control by himself during the trip. Even if she wanted to return to Alex, which Trefor wasn't certain she did, something was keeping her here, and until he knew what it was, there would be no handling her. He would have to heed her wishes and bide his time until she might tell him what was up.

In midafternoon a trump sounded from the castle gate that roused him from a slight doze. Sounding distant from the windowless room, it tickled his consciousness and he sat up, ears perked. Someone else had just arrived at Castle Finias. Someone important, by the sound of the trumpet and the scurrying of feet outside his door. Trefor pulled himself together, rose from the bed to restore his weapons to his belts, then went to see who it might be.

Downstairs in the bailey, a crowd was gathering. Faeries and a few humans milled about, excited by this development, and they all seemed to know what was going on. Trefor stood near a cluster of Reubair's knights, one of whom carried the laird's banner. Except for his time with the Bhrochan, he'd never seen so many faeries in one place, and these were not the little guys. Full-blooded Bhrochan were fairly disgusting creatures: psychotic, stunted of height and limb, and they dressed in rags. Alex called them leprechauns, and Trefor thought it fitting, though the Bhrochan themselves had no idea what that meant.

These faeries here were not leprechauns, nor were they delicate, twinkling Tinkerbells flitting about with wings. They were Danann, and of the same stature as humans. Nearly indistinguishable from humans if they chose to be. Trefor couldn't help staring. Though he had a Danann ancestor several generations back, he'd never seen a living, full-blooded one up close until entering this castle today, where there seemed to be thousands.

He could hear the commotion of approaching horses coming from the gate, and the people around him strained to see. A little apprentice boy, barefoot and dusted with flour from the kitchen, jumped up and down to see over the adults. But, unable to catch a glimpse over the heads of his elders, he scrambled atop a rain barrel and clung like a monkey to the pipe emptying into it. His eyes went wide at what he saw, and Trefor's curiosity sharpened. Particularly when he heard the murmur run through the crowd that it was the faerie king on his way. The Dagda. It was too late to avoid him now, and a sudden pique of interest made Trefor wonder whether he'd truly wanted to avoid him at all.

The procession came around a corner into sight. Dagda had arrived. Trefor's heart leapt to his throat, and he couldn't help straining to see. He rose onto his toes until he realized what he was doing and made himself stand flat-footed.

The mounted vanguard was quite colorful. They filled the street four across and eight deep, their mounts all black, shiny, and perfectly matched. They bore banners that flapped in the breeze. These were faerie knights, agleam with highly polished armor and weapons glinting with silver and gold. The riders surveyed the crowd as they rode, and appeared somewhat smug, though Trefor thought they may have been right to be a bit full of themselves. They were magnificent. The sumptuous dress and equipment showed them as high-ranking knights, which brought Trefor to wondering how the Danann hierarchy was structured. While the Bhrochan were pretty much a disorganized zoo, with one king and everyone else a scramble of undistinguished creatures sleeping together or fighting each other willy-nilly, he suspected the Danann were a wee bit more civilized. More civilized, perhaps, than humans.

A great cheering arose, and necks craned to see. Trefor as well, for he couldn't resist having a look at the guy who was supposed to be his destiny.

The Dagda turned the corner with a small cluster of companions, and a great cheer rose from the gathered townsfolk. Hats flew into the air. Everyone jockeyed for a good look. Astride an enormous white charger, the stallion prancing and barely held by his rider, Dagda nevertheless held the steed without visible effort. Straight and proud in the saddle, the faerie king acknowledged the support with nods and a wide, white smile. A circlet of gold on his head, in the form of leaves that were so finely crafted and naturally shaped as to look real, shone unnaturally. A halo seemed to surround him, around his flowing white and gold surcoat and belts, a hauberk of bright silver mail, and boots and gloves of leather dyed white. Pristine white, untouched by even a thought of worldly dirt. Magical white, aglow with the power the king boasted to the world. And it was, indeed, impressive.

As the king approached, Trefor spotted the faerie ears beneath the intricate, impossible crown. They curved as elaborately, and gracefully, as the golden leaves, their points delicate and refined. Aristocratic. Trefor touched his own ears, the ones he'd been so ashamed of as a boy, and something shifted in his gut. Like a knot of pain coming loose. The sight of the Dagda on that magnificent stallion, riding to the cheers of hundreds of people, made him want to cheer, too. Trefor watched the king pass and knew he'd been wrong his whole life. He wasn't what humans had always called him. Freak. Faerie. Fey. Especially, he wasn't "wee." He was Danann.

The procession came to a halt in front of the keep, and Dagda dismounted. Then he turned with his hand out to those accompanying him, and it was then Trefor saw clearly the woman riding with the king. His mouth went agape with shock, opened as if to cry out in dismay.

It was Morag.

Resplendent in dove gray trimmed with ermine, her mass of curly red hair flowed and bounced around her face. Trefor's heart dumped to his gut, and he could barely breathe. She was smiling into the face of the king, who took her hand as her escort and guided her toward the entrance to the keep. Trefor watched her go with him and felt as if he'd just been ripped in half. He'd never seen that sort of smile on her for himself. He wasn't a king.

For all his telling himself he wasn't in love with her and wasn't committed, this cut to his core. For a minute or so he leaned against the post behind him, not trusting his legs to hold himself up. Morag and Dagda. What was up her sleeve that she had pushed him to his "destiny" with the king? This other guy she was involved with. Plainly she was *with* Dagda. For how long? More than the week since he'd last seen her? Longer, perhaps, than he'd even known her? Was that where she'd been during the six months he'd been kept occupied by the Bhrochan? Trefor's mind turned and chewed on the questions that arose as he recovered his composure. Did Dagda know Morag was Bhrochan? Or was she passing as human? Did he know she was banging other men? The Bhrochan were far more casual about sex than humans, even humans of his own era, and now Trefor wondered how the Danann approached it. Did Dagda expect fidelity from Morag? Did he care what she did with other men?

Indeed, should Trefor himself care? He decided it was best he didn't, but also knew he was a long way from feeling nothing. His stomach soured, and he longed for a good old twenty-first-century antacid to settle it.

He waited amid the well-wishers and the rest of the entourage as they dispersed. Thinking hard, and rage burning his gut, he could barely see to know which way to go. The street slowly cleared until the crowd was reduced to the normal flow of traffic passing back and forth and into and out of the keep. Finally the crowd and his mind had both cleared enough for him to see, and he made his way into the keep and to his room.

It was nearly time for supper. He stripped to his linens and went to the wash stand to clean up. The water in the ewer was cold, but it didn't have anything floating in it, which was an improvement over most of the wash water he'd seen since coming to this century. One of the reasons Mary didn't like him very well was that he complained when there were bits of leaves or moss in his washbowl. He wasn't much pleased with that woman, either. She was happy enough to heat water for the earl's bath; Trefor didn't get why she couldn't make sure his own water was at least clean.

Colors in the room brightened at thought of Alex. Trefor looked around, his face dripping water onto his shirt. *What the hell?* It wasn't his imagination. He tried thinking of a purple cow, and the colors went dull again. Then Alex.

Colors brighter. Huh. He wiped a drip from his chin, then took the towel to dry his face. Weird.

After running his hands through his hair in an attempt to organize it, he tied it back with his bandanna. But unlike in the past, he tied it with his ears out and showing. For the first time in his life he wished for a mirror just for the sake of seeing them. He couldn't remember exactly what they looked like, and now he wondered if they were as well formed as Dagda's. Or even An Reubair's. He felt of the curve, and the point, trying to tell whether they stuck out or if they curled close enough to his head. It was with a lightly skipping heart that he pulled on his tunic, trews, and boots and went downstairs to attend the evening meal in the Great Hall.

As an uninvited guest of no great importance, and particularly on this day with the faerie king visiting, Trefor's seat at board was not very high. He was placed nearly at the other end of the Hall from the head table, but luckily near a small hearth where it was warm enough to keep him from shivering. Man, he hated the cold! He kicked back in his chair, lounging and watching the Dagda, Morag, and Reubair from this vantage point. He could see nearly the entire room from here by turning his head only a little and casually engaged the knight to his left in small talk. Beneath the chat, he eyed Reubair, who sat between Lindsay and the king. He tried not to see Morag, but that red hair of hers was like a warning light on a dashboard. Not only impossible to miss, but dangerous to ignore. He noted that Dagda seemed more interested in Reubair than in his female companion, and Trefor took heart in that. Perhaps this fling was even more casual than he hoped.

For Lindsay's part, Alex's countess presided over the meal with a stately air, formal and reserved. Indeed, her apparent detachment was remarkable. And typical of her, he realized. She took her seat with a calm grace Trefor had come to expect from her. Near as he could tell, very little

ever flustered that woman. She was like a fortress, as ma-
jestic and as glittering as the structure around them. At
table she was served her plate and cup and took a drink.
Trefor received his own plate and tried the meat. It was
venison. The strong meat wasn't his favorite, but at least it
seemed fresh and well seasoned.

Reubair was a vibrant—and loud—host, entertaining the
king and much of the room with what appeared to be his exploits in the Borderlands, plundering hapless humans for
faerie gain. He held a silver and gold drinking bowl in one
hand, and it sloshed as he gestured, as if to suggest he could
afford to waste the wine. Which, it was apparent, he could.
This place was incredible. Trefor had never seen a castle this
big or this rich. Even the keep was three or four times the
size of the keep at Eilean Aonarach. Trefor could see why
Lindsay might want to stay here. Reubair tried to engage
Lindsay in his conversation, with a leering grin on his face
Trefor wanted to smack off of him. Lindsay responded with
a warm smile that wasn't any more pleasing even for its gen-
tility. She shouldn't be smiling at him at all. Trefor took a sip
of his mead and stared, only half listening to the guy to his
left, who was one of Dagda's lesser knights. He spoke in the
old tongue, which required an effort for Trefor to follow, in
any case, and he was too disinterested to struggle with it.

But then the knight said something that caught his attention. " 'Tis our hope we've arrived in time."

Trefor turned his attention to his dinner companion. "In
time for what?" What, indeed, was the reason for Dagda's
visit here?

"To keep The Robber from stealing away control of the
land, of course." The knight in shining chain mail said it as
if Trefor should have known it already, then chuckled at his
own turn of a phrase. The faerie struck Trefor as not terribly bright, and so he prospected for more information.

"Of course. Spending too much time with that Nemed."

"Ye cannae trust an elf."

"Only good elf is a dead elf."

That brought a healthy guffaw and a grin of apprecia-
tion. "Aye, and that's the truth! Nemed has never had aught
for loyalty to anyone but himself."

"Nobody?"

"Well, and his people I imagine. Dead as they all are."
The knight took on a tone of someone talking to a hopeless,
clueless hick. Trefor was happy to be told what was what,
because he wasn't as stupid as he would have this fellow believe. There was always good use for things people would
tell him. "He had a fiery love for his people, but never did
them much good. I mean, have you ever seen a king fail his
people so fully as to lose every last man, woman, and child?
His entire race is gone. Wiped out."

"By Fomorians."

"And humans. He cannae stand against the humans.
They've encroached on him over the centuries until there's
naught left of his race but himself. Even his alliances have
failed him."

"The alliance with the Danann?"

The knight nodded. "'Tis the reason we're here. To
make certain Reubair's loyalty stays with his own people,
not the footloose elf."

"And you think there's a question of it? I mean, a serious chance of treason?"

The knight's gaze flickered, and Trefor thought perhaps
he'd lost him, but after a moment's consideration Dagda's
man leaned close and murmured, "There's been talk of a
rising."

Trefor frowned. "A rising? Against whom?"

"Against the Dagda. Reubair and Nemed have a plan to
depose Dagda."

Trefor leaned back in his seat to assess this. The knight's face seemed sincere. There was no "gotcha" grin lurking beneath the expression of outrage. "You're serious?"

"Aye, and I'm surprised ye haven't heard the Dagda tell of it."

Now Trefor's eyes narrowed. "Who do you think I am?"

It was the knight's turn to appear puzzled. "Are ye not one of Morag's guard?" As realization sunk in he'd probably been telling this to someone of Reubair's court, his face paled.

Trefor said quickly, "Yes. I am one of Morag's men. But I'm a recent recruit. I haven't been attached to her guard long enough to have heard much."

Relief came over the knight's entire body and he returned to breathing. Color, such as it could be for a faerie, returned to his face. He adjusted his seat uncomfortably and said, "Tread with care in those chambers. Make yourself invisible, particularly to Himself. The woman is as likely to seduce you as anything else—she's had most everyone in both guards—but the king is dangerous."

"She's seduced you?"

A wistful smile passed over the knight's face, and his voice softened. "Aye, and a lovely night it was. If she offers you the opportunity, do not hesitate, for she's a warm berth and an eager one. 'Tis much like being eaten alive."

Trefor thought that sounded painful, but knew what he meant. Just then he felt hollow inside where Morag had consumed him. He smiled to hide the ache. "In any case, you were saying the king is here to check up on Reubair. A rising, you said."

"Rumors. That Reubair's alliance with Nemed was just a mite too cozy and his loyalty to Dagda was weak. The people here, after all, have been under Nemed's rule since before the beginning of memory."

Trefor's eyebrows went up. The beginning of memory

was a very long time for people as long-lived as the Danann. "They've never known a ruler other than Nemed?"

"Nae. Their ancestors came here after the Fomorian war. 'Tis been millennia of peace within the mists, and those of this place dinnae wish to give that up. They feel Dagda will destroy their way."

"But they're Danann."

"And different from those Danann who live among humans. Especially those who live directly under the rule of Nemed are different. They hold themselves as better than ordinary Danann. And the Dagda is here to prove them wrong."

"And he's going to do this how?"

"By force of arms." Again, the knight seemed to think his reply obvious to even the most casual observer.

"Doesn't Nemed have a right to this land? Didn't he hold it first?"

"A ruler who cannae hold his land by force does not deserve to hold it at all. For how else can he protect his people from the incursion of other races?"

There was a certain weird logic to that, though Trefor's twenty-first-century mind didn't want to address that. And he was stuck for a reply that wouldn't sound as if he were a spy for Nemed, so he segued away from it. "Well, it looks like the king did arrive in time to prevent the rising."

"We shall see."

Trefor grunted and returned his attention to his supper and his mother.

Lindsay drank her mead, or whatever the folks at the head table were having. Trefor suspected it might be wine instead. She picked at her food, but drank deeply from her goblet as she listened to Reubair and the king.

Then, halfway through the meal, Lindsay gave Reubair a look that made Trefor blink stupidly at her in surprise. Long and lingering, it was. No way to mistake the light in

her eyes; it was affection. Not lust, nor even simple interest. The gaze was long and searching. She sought his eyes
and held them, like the two of them were newlyweds or
something. Trefor's stomach turned. He wanted to shout
she was a whore, that she was a betrayer and didn't deserve
to breathe the same air as honest people. She and Morag.
Peas in a pod. It disgusted him.

But then a shadow crossed Lindsay's eyes and she
looked away, and that baffled him. Her confusion confused
him. What was going on? Her face darkened in a flush, and
her gaze searched the room for something to look at other
than Reubair. Not the king, for he sat on the other side of
Reubair from her. A window. She found a window and
stared at the weak, overcast light coming through it, as if
the blank sky outside were the most interesting thing in her
life. Her chin drew in until her head was almost bowed and
she was looking from under a lowered brow. Trefor had no
clue what to make of it. He stared at her, ignoring the
faerie to his left, until Lindsay pulled herself together with
a deep breath and once again turned her attention to
Reubair. Once more she addressed him with the same
bland, careful gaze she'd had at the beginning of the meal.

Something extraordinary was going on here. Trefor was
at a loss to know what it could be, but it was plain there was
something wonky between Lindsay and Reubair, and not
necessarily romantic. Probably something magical, if he
understood his faeries. He looked to Dagda to see if he
might be involved, but the king seemed as oblivious as
everyone else in the room. Trefor chewed his meat and
continued to gaze at his mother, wondering.

Once the king had finished eating, he, Reubair, and the
two women rose from the table. Everyone in the room got
up as well, expecting the king to withdraw to his quarters.
But instead he moved to mingle with the faerie nobility as-
sembled in the Great Hall. One by one Reubair's vassals

came to bow before the king, and he chatted with each as amiably as if they were his best buddies. Trefor placed himself in the king's path and watched the progression through the room. He admired the grace and easy friendliness the Dagda exuded, filling the huge room with bright cheer. He looked each in the eye, and his voice rang with sincerity in every word he spoke.

Then Reubair leaned in to whisper in Dagda's ear and glanced in Trefor's direction. The king looked toward him, curious at first, then he smiled. There was a comment under his breath, too low for Trefor to hear, and Reubair chuckled. Neither Lindsay nor Morag reacted, but Trefor felt his face warm with embarrassment that they'd heard whatever it was. He figured it couldn't have been good. Reubair gestured that Trefor should approach the king, and he did so.

Dagda's face was aglow with power, like the pinkness of healthy cheeks but with red warmth like embers. Trefor thought if he reached out to touch the faerie's skin he might burn his fingers. It was a temptation to try. Dagda bestowed a smile filled with that warmth and white teeth, and said, "I've just mentioned to An Reubair here that you remind me of my youngest brother, but also that I wouldn't hold it against you."

Trefor smiled with relief as much as humor, that the comment hadn't been the ridicule he'd anticipated nearly out of habit. He replied, "I'm told I look like my father's brother, who is human, and I hope you won't hold that against me, either." That brought an amiable chuckle from the king. "All I can say is that I at least have the Danann ears."

He glanced at Morag, who was more fey than he but appeared more human. She gazed at him with the same bland expression Lindsay wore for Reubair. As if she didn't know him. Trefor's cheeks warmed.

Dagda and Reubair chuckled again, then the king raised his voice for the benefit of more than just their small cluster in the Great Hall. "You're plainly a son of Danu, and I'm glad to hear from An Reubair you wish to pledge your fealty to me. With whole heart, I would hear your oath if you care to give it."

Oh. Trefor hadn't really wanted to swear himself to Dagda; he didn't believe in making promises he couldn't keep, and the whole allegiance thing was a morass of rules, debt, and duties he didn't care to take on. He was only here for Lindsay and intended to be out of this castle at the earliest opportunity, on his way to join up with Robert's army. But now the king of the faeries was looking at him with the expectation that he would get on his knees and pledge fealty on the spot. A look at Morag caught her with a slight curl to her lips, which she wiped off in an instant. He glanced at Lindsay, and it crossed his mind that if she'd not balked at leaving with him earlier he wouldn't be standing here now, wondering what to do. And now she still wasn't any help. She glanced away from him, toward the king. It was left to him to figure it out.

Except there was nothing to figure out. There was no escape from this corner but straight ahead, to go through with the pledge. To hesitate just then would draw a shadow over him, a shadow he could ill afford with the iffy goodwill of Reubair and Lindsay's uncertain status in the castle. It would cause the most powerful fellows in the faerie world to look slantways at him, a risky situation given what he was there to do. And there was no telling what Morag would do or say if he gave her a reason and an opportunity to cross him.

So he knelt before the king and hoped his hesitation hadn't been too noticeable. He said, as boldly and smoothly as he could under the circumstances, "Then by all means, Your Majesty, allow me to pledge my fealty to you at once. I vow on my soul to be loyal to you as my liege. If I should ever break this vow, may I never have a son and may my fortunes all fail." He resisted the urge to look up at Morag and instead looked to find a smile on the king's face.

Dagda said to Reubair, "Succinct, at least. I like a man who wastes no time beating around the bush."

Lindsay said, "My cousin is a master of language. He speaks ten or twelve of them; some from so far away you may never have heard of those who speak them."

Reubair seemed unimpressed by that. "You've been to the Holy Land?" His tone suggested, *big deal*. "I know many men who understand the languages of Islam."

Trefor rose at a gesture from the king and replied, "She means farther east, but yes. I also speak some from the Near East." He was fluent in modern Farsi and figured he could understand Crusade-era Muslims well enough to get by.

Dagda said, "That is good to know, if ever the Danann care to involve themselves in human silliness." He cut a significant glance at Reubair, whose face remained impassive. Trefor took note of the undercurrent of friction. He guessed there was more disagreement between Dagda and Reubair than just the relative merits of elves as a race.

"I've not been to that particular fight," he said. "In fact, I've never been to the Far East, either."

Reubair asked, "Then how did you learn so many languages? Are you fluent in any of them?"

"All of them, my lord. I have a talent, and for one with determination and faerie wisdom there is always learning to be had by those who will pay attention." Reubair would think this to mean he'd employed his magical training to learn the languages. It wasn't true, but it was something the faeries would understand more readily than language CDs and tutorial software.

The king said, "I welcome you to the Danann fold, Sir Trefor. I trust you will be faithful and valuable to our people."

In spite of his initial reluctance, Trefor's heart swelled, for such a welcome was a rarity in his life. It felt nice. He bowed his head once more to the king and thanked him, thinking it may not have been a bad thing to have pledged himself. He was, after all, Danann, and there was no reason for him not to ally himself with the faerie king. His father certainly wasn't offering so much acceptance, and especially Lindsay was not.

Reubair, the king, Lindsay, and Morag moved on to the next conversation, and Trefor understood himself to be dismissed. He watched the progression a few minutes more, ignored once again by Morag, then made his way back to his chamber to mull what had just happened.

He sat by the fire, staring into it and watching the dancing, random flames, the throbbing glow of embers, and turned over in his mind the expressions he'd seen among Reubair and the others today. Each gesture, each inflection of voice. It was too dense. There was too much there to make sense of anything. Though he picked carefully at his memory, no one thread separated from the knot. He was exhausted from the journey and the long day, and his mind was mush. He gave up thinking, stretched out on the bed, and dropped off to sleep after only a few moments.

Alex was with her. In the closet bed. Lindsay's heart leapt, though she realized she must be dreaming, for her husband couldn't possibly be there. But it seemed real. She knew his scent, the feel of him in the darkness. Her heart ached with missing him, and she slipped eagerly into the deep pleasure of the dream for a time. He murmured to her of his love, in a soft whisper that sometimes drifted to low, deep voice. He kissed her and felt beneath her shift. Between her thighs. His hand was big and strong, and he made her want all of him there. He was healthy and whole. Insistent. With joy she accepted him, and the joining transported her. He moved carefully, slowly at first, savoring the moment and sighing his rapture. She arched against him, taking him in as much as she could. If only she could keep him there forever. To keep him safe, warm, and happy. Her arms around him sensed his trembling muscles. His broad shoulders. She laid a hand against his side to feel him straining against her. His undulating belly. She felt . . .

Someone else. In the darkness the man inside her changed to someone else. Not Alex. Taller. Thinner. Shoving her now in a perfunctory way, as if trying to reach his climax in a hurry.

"No!" Lindsay woke herself and the dream disappeared. The man left in an instant, as if he'd never been there. She sat up in the closet bed and cried again, "No!"

Another cry, of anguish, came from outside the bed. In the chamber. A frisson of alarm skittered up Lindsay's spine, and she cracked the door of her bed open to see. Reubair was sitting up in his bed, naked and panting. By the dim light of the embers in his hearth, she could discern a dark look of frustration as he stared into the dimness of his room. Sweat glistened on his bare shoulders. Thin shoulders, long, thin, aristocratic arms like the ones that had held her just a moment ago.

He looked over at the closet, glaring accusation, and she let the door fall shut silently. Then she lay back down and rolled away from that door, wondering what would have been the outcome if she had let the dream continue.

CHAPTER 14

In the middle of the night something woke Trefor. Something not in the room. Though the fire in the hearth was nothing more than dim, red coals, he could tell there wasn't anyone near. But he sensed a presence. Like a scent floating in air, nebulous and drifting. It was the thing he'd tried to follow earlier, and it was stronger now. Healthier, somehow, though he didn't see how that made any sense. Not much today had made sense, so this seemed just another part of the weirdness.

"Who is there?" he whispered. But he got no answer. He sat up in bed, and the chill air raised bumps on his arms. It was then he realized the presence was not an entity, but a trace that led somewhere. Like a string, or a trail of smoke, it led under the door and out to the antechamber. Trefor leaned back against his pillow and closed his eyes, left his body, and followed the trail. Under the door, where his soul squeezed through without any effort, and into the chamber outside. Down the spiral stairs and past the keep entry. Down and down, and farther down into the dank rooms below ground.

In that place torches were the only light, those few and far between. In a room scattered with metal tools and strange implements, a raggedy human man sat, asleep on a chair leaned against the wall on two legs. His head rested on his chest, and the snoring noise he made through his bulbous nose sounded like choking. A set of enormous iron keys hung from his belt, but Trefor had no need of those. He turned to follow the spirit trail beneath a doorway, then through that chamber into the next.

There, two shadows lay on the floor in darkness. They were men, either asleep or dead; it was difficult to tell which. Prisoners, without a doubt. Trefor, his body still in the chamber many floors above, shifted concentration like a man shifting an armload of packages to reach for his door key and produced a small glow of light in order to see. It was weak, but enough to see dark outlines.

There wasn't much here. Two men, alive and taking shallow breaths in their sleep, huddled on the stone floor of a prison cell empty except for themselves and a slop pot in the corner. He wondered what they had to do with him that he'd been contacted.

Then he took a closer look. One was a priest, his tonsure growing ragged and his face covered in a beard of a couple of weeks, but clearly a priest. And on even closer inspection Trefor realized with a shock it was the guy from Eilean Aonarach, Father Patrick.

His heart leapt and rattled so badly Trefor nearly lost his grip on his wandering soul. Back in his room he gasped and struggled for the tie that kept himself from floating away, out of control, forever. For a couple of minutes he clung to himself and slowly regained control. Once calmed, he approached the figures to look into the face of the other. But he knew what he would find, for he recognized the "smoke" now. It was Alex. The gang was all here, it seemed. Aglow with all the power he could muster, clinging fast to his essence, Trefor examined the face of his father, asleep on the floor.

Alex was barely recognizable. Gaunt, like an old man. A sense of irony tinged Trefor's thoughts, for Alex had once pointed out in anger that he would never be "old" relative to Trefor. That as he aged, Trefor would also. But the lines on Alex's face betrayed the effects of his injuries, and given that he was imprisoned by Reubair, Trefor wondered how Alex was still alive at all. He should have died at Eilean Aonarach, or been murdered on arrival here.

The priest stirred and looked up, too quickly for Trefor to escape without being seen. Patrick's eyes went wide. "Sir Trefor."

"Shhh."

"How . . . ?"

"Say nothing."

"How are you here? What . . . are you?"

"Nothing. I'm nothing."

"A dream?"

Oh, good. An explanation Patrick would accept. "Yes, I'm a dream. God has sent me to you in a dream."

The priest closed his eyes and murmured a prayer of thanks.

Trefor asked, "Do you know where you are?"

Patrick looked up at him again. "The castle of An Reubair."

"How did you get here?"

"We found his company in the Borderlands, but they overwhelmed us, killed the others, and brought us here."

"Did you find Lindsay?"

Now Patrick hesitated, but only for a second, for he was, after all, talking to a messenger from God. He replied, "Yes. She's here."

"She knows her husband is here?"

"Aye. She brings us food and medicine for his fever."

This made no sense. Why didn't she just get Reubair to cut Alex loose if she cared so much? Or let him die if she didn't? More to the point, why was Reubair allowing him to live at all?

But there was no time to grill the priest, for Trefor could feel the strain of his stupid faerie tricks telling on him. He was going to lose his soul in a moment if he didn't get out of there fast. Without another word, he let go of the light and plunged the room into darkness again, then retreated out and up the stairs to his own chamber at speed like a snapped rubber band.

"Ow." He should have known better than to hurry like that. There, restored to his body, he lay in the dim glow of his own hearth, panting and spent, and puzzled over what he'd just seen. Things were getting weirder by the minute.

A lex awoke and shivered in the cold. The fever was gone, but he was too weak to move. Almost too weak to breathe. Still confused about a lot of things. For a moment he had trouble remembering where he was, for it seemed he was in a bedchamber with a glowing hearth. But the cold told him that was impossible. The hard, bare stones beneath him were not the strewn reeds and heat-holding wood he'd imagined. And, for a moment, he thought he'd heard Trefor's voice.

"Patrick," he murmured.

"Here, my lord." There was a sound of shifting, and Alex sensed Patrick sitting up near him. His voice was

such a soft whisper as to be nearly inaudible even in the
quiet of the night.

"You're here. It's you." Alex reached out, and Patrick's
hand found his. Alex raised his head in an effort to see, but
there was no penetrating the utter darkness of the cell and
he sagged back onto the floor, exhausted. He hadn't seen
the sun in what seemed forever. Days? Weeks? Years? Not
years, his beard wasn't long enough. But it had been a long
time. "Patrick, was Lindsay here?" He had dim, disjointed
memories of Lindsay. She was somewhere near here, he
thought. Wherever "here" was. Reubair. Reubair . . .

"Earlier. The countess was here this morning."

Alex sighed and felt a tiny bit of warmth. He could live
if there was a promise of seeing Lindsay again. But Patrick
continued.

"Your cousin also came to me in a dream."

Cousin? What cousin? Then he remembered who Patrick
must mean. "Trefor was here?"

"Only in spirit."

Spirit. That could mean anything, given Patrick's religious vocation and Trefor's talents. Alex asked the real
question. "He knows we're here?"

"Possibly. At least, God knows we're here. Whether I
saw Trefor, or God with the face of him, I cannot say."

Alex was too sick to care whether Patrick saw God, Trefor, or Trefor playing God, or God screwing with Patrick's
head, or what. He said, "You saw something?"

"Aye. Your cousin, and with a light about him that filled
the chamber like a ghostly fire. Like a ghost himself, he was."

"Trefor is dead?" There was a charge of alarm and Alex
tried to lift his head again to look at Patrick's face, which
he wouldn't have been able to see even if he'd succeeded.

Patrick hesitated before answering, then said, "I hope
not, my lord. In any case, he asked whether the countess
knew you were here."

"And you told him?"

"Aye."

"Why didn't you wake me up?"

"He wasn't here very long. Surely, had he been, you would have awakened on your own."

Alex grunted and closed his eyes in an attempt to go back to sleep. But he was healing, and there was only so much sleep to be had now. He lay awake in the cell, staring into the darkness, wondering why God would send Trefor to ask such an unimportant question. A question to which God would surely have known the answer. It had to have been Trefor himself, and so wherever he was, he probably knew where they were.

A shiver took him and shook his bones as he realized it was anybody's guess whether or not that was a good thing.

Breakfast was once again in Reubair's bedchamber that morning, and Lindsay was surprised when King Dagda joined Reubair and herself. Without that shifty-eyed, redhaired mistress, and for that Lindsay was glad. She didn't know what Morag was up to, but she had never trusted Trefor's girlfriend. Nobody at Eilean Aonarach did, and now the wisdom of that was apparent.

In any case, Dagda sat with Reubair while Lindsay sipped her mead and picked at the bread and meat on her plate. The two were having a private conversation, away from courtiers and servants, and neither thought of her as having a brain. One of the few advantages of being a woman in this period was being privy to sensitive information; the main drawback being that there was precious little one could accomplish with even the most useful bits. This morning, however, the men held her rapt, for the name of Nemed was invoked. That elf was balking at paying tribute to the Danann.

Dagda sat, nearly lounging, with one elbow leaning on

the arm of his chair. "Nemed is an elf," he said, as if that explained all.

"He leads a Danann army."

That was news to Lindsay. Last she'd heard, Nemed was alone in the world, devastated by the loss of the last of his people. She'd never seen, nor heard of, any army. Unless it was Reubair's own army he meant. In which case, he had been deceiving Dagda regarding his own loyalty by not revealing until now the extent of his loyalty to Nemed. Lindsay found this incredibly interesting and listened closely to hear more.

But Dagda seemed to be aware of Nemed's army. Or, if he was surprised, he hid it well. He replied, "If he leads Danann knights, they are traitors. Every last one of them."

Reubair was now on notice that his loyalty was in doubt. He defended himself. "Nemed is pledged to you. All who follow him also follow you."

"As far as that goes. But," Dagda gestured his frustration that he had to keep saying this, "he is an *elf*. One cannot deny he is not one of us, and we have to assume his true loyalty is only to himself."

"He's the last of his kind."

"He's naught to lose."

"Then it would behoove us to give him something he wants to keep and protect, such as the land. Something we control."

"Or take everything, and leave him only his life."

Reubair's lips pressed together as he considered his reply to a comment he regarded distasteful. "Why stop there? Why not simply murder him?" It was a challenge, for Dagda to put up or shut up. Reubair was plainly disgusted. Lindsay wasn't sure exactly why, or what Reubair wanted from Dagda.

"I would that Nemed were done away with. But I am no murderer."

"And he is wily and powerful."

"That, too. Even so, if there is a way to have him off Danann land . . ." He let the sentence hang and eyed Reubair for his reaction.

There was none. Not a flicker of eye, nor twitch of muscle. Reubair continued gazing at the cup in his hand as if he'd not heard. A long silence spun out, then he said, "I have rights to nearly half that land."

"And you provide half his men-at-arms." There it was. Dagda knew.

"All of whom are loyal to you, as I am." Reubair seemed desperate to convince Dagda of his loyalty. He protested nearly too much.

"Are you? Truly?" Skepticism darkened Dagda's voice. "I wonder. How can you be loyal to your Danann king and an elf at once? Were he to attempt a coup, it would be with your men. He could wage war, using resources from my own lands. Men of my own race.

"Why do you think he intends it?"

"He's an elf." Dagda's tone of frustration became irritation. "As you said, he is wily and powerful." He leaned forward to emphasize his point. *"And he's an elf."*

Reubair eyed Dagda, clearly offended but unwilling to argue that particular point. He said, "Are you saying I should rise against my sworn liege because he *might* rise against you?"

"But there is no question of it. Sooner or later, the creature will chafe at subjugation by the Danann and he will attempt to conquer us."

"With other Danann?"

"Of course. To make himself king of our people. To lord over us. To say 'Elves are better than Danann.'"

To Lindsay it seemed Dagda's position was nothing more than fearmongering, and he was more interested in saving his own skin than in the interests of the faeries.

Since there was no elf population to displace the Danann living on his land, under Nemed they would live. But Dagda himself was vulnerable to assassination. By the look in Reubair's eye just then, Lindsay thought he might be the one to wield the knife. "I have sworn my soul," he said. Plainly he was disgusted with the faerie king.

"Pah!" Dagda made a disparaging gesture. "*Soul!* Speak to me not of your religion!"

Reubair flushed with anger but held his tongue.

Dagda continued, "Your fellows pledge themselves as they please. Don't tell me how bound you are by your meaningless oath."

Lindsay glanced toward the door, wondering if she should make her exit before the fight would begin. Reubair was sure to kill the king now. He was a thief and a murderer, but nobody dared challenge his belief in God.

Instead, he took a deep breath and said, "There are some who break their oaths, and will surely burn for it. I prefer not to burn, and cannot bring myself to rise against Nemed."

Dagda started to speak, but Reubair overrode him. "*However*, I also swear to you—on my soul—that if Nemed were to break his pledge to you I would consider him to have violated the trust on which my oath is based. Being no longer obligated to him, I would then command my men in defense of my king." He paused and looked Dagda directly in the eye for emphasis. "And the people of my blood." That seemed to mollify Dagda, who sat back in his chair as Reubair continued, "No man can accuse me of reneging on my obligations. None can ever say I have strayed from the path of my Lord, Jesus."

Lindsay blinked at that, and coughed to cover a bark of a guffaw. But Reubair probably was referring only to the issue of oaths, for he went on without pause.

"I swear to you, on my life and the lives of my future

children, that my loyalty is to my king, and you can rely on my support if ever Nemed violates his pledge to you."

Lindsay could see Dagda was still not impressed with any oath made on a Christian soul to the Judeo-Christian God, but she figured this was the best he could have expected from Reubair. Or anyone, really, for trust had to be based on faith in someone or something. If Dagda knew Reubair, he knew the oath would hold, whether Reubair was Christian, pagan, or Jedi Knight.

Dagda nodded, accepting the pledge, and the conversation segued to less weighty matters.

Lindsay looked from one to the other, and tucked away in memory what she'd just witnessed.

So . . . Alex was being held prisoner by Reubair. Trefor focused on the implications of that at breakfast as he watched Morag eat alone. Alex was surely the thing keeping Lindsay at Castle Finias, but whether that meant she wanted to save his life or have him murdered was hard to guess.

If she wanted him dead, then why not simply request it? Reubair would surely be happy to oblige. And also, why nurse him back to health? Was the intent to ransom him? To whom? Robert? Last Trefor had heard, Reubair was dependent on the king's goodwill for his operations in the Borderlands. More than likely Reubair wouldn't want Robert to even know the earl had been imprisoned. All the more reason to do away with him swiftly and quietly. Could Lindsay be making a pretense? Trefor set that idea aside immediately. No, he couldn't think of a reason for her to pretend to Reubair that she loved her husband. She must have been sincere in protecting Alex, and Trefor found comfort in that thought as he picked at his breakfast, not tasting any of the food.

But then, what was she doing there? Why had Reubair brought her there to begin with if not to imprison and ransom her? Why was she free to visit her husband if she wasn't there willingly? If Reubair wanted her at his side, which he plainly did since she *was* at his side, then why did he not just have Alex killed? All avenues of thought kept leading back to that question: Why was Alex alive?

But then, Trefor considered that since Lindsay seemed to be acting as the lady of the household, she may be fulfilling all the functions of wife and for every intent was one. There may have been no pressing need to kill Alex. Trefor knew from battle experience how hard it was to kill and figured it would be more difficult to murder in cold blood. Better to hold in a cell instead and hope for him to die of his wound. It could be Alex was alive out of mere inertia.

But, no, Patrick said Lindsay was nursing him back to health.

But, then, why nurse him in a cell? Why not put him in a room with a hearth and a bed? If she was giving cooperation to Reubair for the sake of her husband, surely she could have cut a better deal than this.

Trefor was missing something, but he couldn't get a handle on what it was, and he felt stupid for it. He decided to take a chance on a chat with Reubair and maybe gain some insight.

It wasn't easy to catch the laird alone. It seemed he never went anywhere without Lindsay, and his interest in keeping the king entertained made him busier than most folks in the castle. After a day or two of frustration Trefor finally made a formal request for an audience while Dagda was occupied with his own administrative tasks. He would have to deal with the presence of Lindsay and the attendants, and word his questions with extreme care.

To Trefor's surprise, the response to his request was an invitation to the privy chamber at midmorning. As he entered, Reubair's priest was leaving and the faerie laird was setting aside his rosary and Bible. Trefor had heard Reubair was Christian but until now hadn't believed it. He didn't know whether to be surprised or figure it explained some things.

When Reubair saw Trefor, he went to lounge in a chair by a table and gestured to another of the chairs. Lindsay was already seated in a cushioned chair by the hearth, looking at him with that bland gaze that now seemed habitual with her. Like she didn't give a damn about anything on earth, particularly him. Easy enough to believe. He sat in the indicated chair, one of the small wooden ones from the table.

Reubair asked, "How has your visit been these past days? Everything satisfactory, I suppose."

"Your hospitality is unmatched anywhere, my lord."

Reubair nodded, as if that were a given. Trefor could see his welcome in the castle was already wearing thin and his host expected him to move along now that Trefor's business with Dagda was concluded.

So he had to invent new business. "Now that my allegiance is established, I must look to my future within that pledge."

Reubair grunted in agreement but said nothing. This wasn't going to be easy.

Trefor continued, "I would have a faerie wife."

Lindsay's head turned slightly, and from the corner of Trefor's eye he could tell she was surprised by his words. Good. It warmed his heart to learn she did have some sort of interest in his life.

Reubair said, "You have no land. No prospects."

"On the contrary, I have prospects. I have relations in Scotland, connected to the king. My cousin is a countess." He nodded toward Lindsay. Now he waited to hear whether Reubair considered Trefor's relationship with Alex a plus or minus.

Reubair seemed reluctant to reply but finally said, "Have you heard from your cousin the earl recently?"

"No. I confess I haven't visited since last summer."

Reubair's mouth pressed tight, and he examined his fingernails. Lindsay turned away toward the fire. Trefor wondered why Reubair had asked the question if Alex was in his dungeon. And why had Lindsay reacted to the answer at all? What had she thought he might say? The truth? That he'd been sent by Alex to take her away from this place? Surely she didn't think he was that stupid.

Then it came to him. The piece of the puzzle that had been missing, and which when slid into place suddenly made every bit of this make sense. *Reubair didn't know Alex was in the dungeon.* Somehow Alex and Patrick had been taken prisoner and Reubair didn't know it. The realization took Trefor's breath away for the power it gave him. Lindsay was hiding Alex. She probably thought Reubair would kill him.

And she was absolutely right.

Trefor looked over at Lindsay. Was she scamming Reubair? Acting as a willing consort? Or was she truly being held by a warding spell? He said to Reubair, "To be sure, I wouldn't hope for an excessively advantageous marriage, so long as my wife were of full Danann blood. I understand that Cruachan is not your favorite human—"

"I've little fondness for humans in general. In my wide experience they've proven a disappointment."

Trefor glanced over at Lindsay and stammered a little over the insult. Then he said, "Well . . . yes. I understand that my ancestry is a drawback, and that my connection to the earl doesn't help my case much beyond that he is, in turn, connected to the Scottish king."

"True. Alasdair an Dubhar is in some power but is not well liked among the Danann."

Trefor arranged his face to appear surprised. "All Danann,

you say? I thought I heard that he was a personal acquaintance of the goddess Danu herself. His wife has a Psalter I heard was a gift from her."

Reubair looked over at Lindsay, who nodded affirmation. Trefor had a moment of relief that she was cooperating with him. Reubair replied, "The countess is, by all accounts, a direct descendant of the goddess. I'm certain Danu doesn't care who Lindsay is married to." A hesitation, then Reubair added, "Any more than I care."

The edge to Reubair's voice suggested something Trefor hadn't considered. That Reubair might be trying to seduce Lindsay, but hadn't succeeded. If that was the case, it begged the question of why. Trefor looked from Reubair to Lindsay and back, and his mind turned with what this meant to himself. That Alex was a prisoner, and that Reubair not only wanted him dead but had the means to that end at hand if he but knew it. That Trefor was now pledged to the faerie king and would do well to have the good favor of this powerful Danann. That Alex had never done anything for him, and was unlikely to in the future. Trefor's heart skipped with these realizations. He sat back in his chair and struggled for an insouciance that was imperative but at the moment seemed impossible.

CHAPTER 15

That night when he slipped into bed, Trefor knew he was riddled with bad energy. It exuded from him like an odor, but there was nothing he could do about it. The knowledge he'd obtained that day was too powerful. It pointed him in too many directions. There was too much he wanted to do with it. He lay beneath the woolen blankets, staring at the hearth, for a long time before he finally dropped off to a restless sleep.

Sometime later he was awakened in darkness by a warm body pressed against him. Morag. He recognized her by the familiar shape of her and her habit of slipping a hand between his thighs to rest there. But this time he didn't roll toward her. Instead he took that hand and held it so it would do no harm.

"Is there something wrong, my love?" She kissed the back of his shoulder, as if nothing had changed between them.

"You know there is."

"Och." The harsh expression was softened in her throat,

and to him sounded moist and intimate. "The king. He likes me because I appear human but am not entirely, and likes to show me off as a possession. To demonstrate his power over them."

"So, he doesn't know you've been sent by Brochan?"

"I wouldnae underestimate him. He might know it, but then he might not. Which is neither here nor there, for 'tis not as if I dictate policy to him." She freed her hand from his and stroked his forearm. Smoothed the hairs on the back of it.

"But you keep tabs on him."

"Tabs?"

"I mean, you keep track of where he is and what he's up to. And you report back to Brochan everything you see and hear."

"If I do, that's Dagda's concern, is it not?"

Trefor supposed it was, but having sworn fealty to him, there was a niggle of conscience at the back of his head for it. He shook it off and changed the subject. "Why are you here?"

"As you said, to keep . . . *tabs*—"

"I mean, why are you in my room? Here in the bed?"

"I wished to see you. I want you. I should think that would be plain enough." To illustrate, she reached around him again to run her fingernails across his belly. He nearly shivered at the charge that ran through him. But an image of Morag with Dagda quashed it right away. He captured her hand again.

"I don't believe you. I think you've got something else on your mind."

"And if I did? Would that be reason to not take advantage?"

"Yes."

She made another harsh noise of disgust, less soft this time, and raised up on hands and knees over him. "'Tis naught but a desire, and you need not think it a demand."

"What is it you want?"

She kissed him, and he let her. Then she said, "I wish you to kill Dagda."

For an instant, Trefor thought he would be ever so happy to kill the man sleeping with Morag, but then he shook off the thought as craziness. He wasn't so terribly enamored with the red-haired witch. Really, he wasn't. Obviously she had chosen this moment to tell him this because she knew he wanted her and figured he would be jealous. She was manipulating him, and that made him not want her so much.

But she kissed him again, and he let her again. Her mouth was insistent, her tongue an assault on his senses. She played with his favorite places and made him breathless. The longer it went on, the more he wondered why not kill Dagda. He rolled over on top of her and pressed himself to her.

"Why?" If he was going to do that for her, he needed to know what her interest was in it.

She spread her legs and wrapped them around his waist to draw him in. He obliged, and slipped in easily. "Tell me," he insisted as he began to move.

"He needs killing."

"Not good enough."

" 'Tis the land. The Bhrochan require their land back."

Again with the faerie lands. "Why kill Dagda?"

"He's a guest of Reubair, who is a vassal of Nemed."

"And I am . . . ?"

"Danann."

Trefor went still. There it was. The Bhrochan needed a patsy. They wanted him to kill Dagda, for if a Bhrochan—even one who was mostly human—did the deed it would cause a war. One the Bhrochan probably couldn't win. "If a Danann kills him, the upheaval is internal and not between the two factions of faerie. And I end up executed for murder. Treason, actually." His desire for Morag left him like a hemorrhage, and he slipped off of her and to the side, to prop on an elbow.

She pressed, with a tone of encouragement. Excitement rose in her voice. "Only if you're caught in the assassination. Get away with it, then the blame rests on An Reubair for failing to protect his guest."

Were that likely to accomplish the Bhrochan goal, Trefor was certain the king would have been dead days ago, at Morag's hand and under Reubair's protection, and Morag would have been safely away. "You want me to believe there would be civil war over bad hospitality?"

"Oh, aye! You know there would!"

"And why does Brochan think this would be a good thing?"

"The land, Trefor! The faerie lands that belong to the Bhrochan! We could take them back in the midst of the fight!"

Trefor didn't see how. A tiff over a visit gone bad just wasn't upheaval enough. It was clear to him that if he attempted an assassination, Morag would make certain he was caught and blamed, to make it clear Dagda had been killed by another Danann. And she would make it appear he was in league with An Reubair to boot. Lindsay's presence and her appearance of attraction to him would lend itself handily to that. For a moment he wondered if Morag knew Alex was downstairs, but didn't dwell on it lest the witch learn it by reading him. He said, "You want the Danann to take up arms against Nemed."

"Aye."

"Dagda is already at odds with Nemed. Because of his race."

"But the king willnae attack. He understands what the Bhrochan also understand: He cannae hold the land by himself. But if he were to die, particularly were he assassinated

while in the household of Nemed's loyal vassal—Reubair—
the Danann would have no choice but to respond. Without
Dagda, the Danann would take the land from Nemed, *but
they cannae hold it*."

"Why not, if Reubair is taken down? He's Nemed's military strength. Are the king's followers that disorganized?"

"Unstable. Aside from the fact that Finian Danann hold
themselves as better than those who live in burrows or
among humans, the king has no clear heirs. Many sons, but
none living who could take and hold the entire Danann
against Nemed, who has allies among the nobility in addition to Reubair. Brochan would make claim to the land as
his rightful property according to the wedding contract, and
it would go to him without so much as a second thought,
as diplomatic appeasement to keep the Bhrochan at bay during the Danann troubles. Neat as you please. No fight. No
blood."

"Except Dagda's. And Reubair's." *And mine*.

"Two who deserve their fate."

Fate. That word again, and Trefor knew how she felt
about his own. He hated what he was hearing. Then Morag
told him something that caught his breath and turned his
thinking inside out. She said, "And once the land is ours,
you will be the prince of it."

Trefor blinked. "Huh?" *Prince*. He'd been called that by
the Bhrochan many times, but never knew why.

"If your skill in the assassination is good, and you escape unscathed, you will receive this place as its lord.
You'll be a Danann prince to keep the Danann people at
peace with the new Bhrochan settlers, but trained and loved
by the Bhrochan, pledged to us, to manage the lands to our
benefit. And I will be your consort." She moved her hips
against him and grinned.

God help him, that made some sense and it clouded his
previously clear view of the situation. Could it be the

Bhrochan meant what they'd been telling him all along? Did Morag really expect him to take over in faerie Ireland? The prospect was heady, and his heart thudded in his chest. "You're serious?"

"Of course I am. Have I ever steered you wrong?"

"Yes."

"Never. I've always sent you where you needed to be, and told you what was true and good. I've always loved you, Trefor, and by all accounts will do so well into the future. You can trust me, my love. You can believe that everything I tell you is true, and the course I show you is in your best interest. Killing Dagda is what you must do, and it will mean prosperity for you. And for me, for I'll be right here beside you the whole time."

She looked up at him with the most sincere eyes he could have imagined. He sifted through the confusion of wanting to believe her, knowing he just wasn't lucky enough for this to be real. He'd learned early on in life that anything that looked too good to be true probably was a lie, but this had just enough credibility to ring right. And he figured he had just enough control over the events that he might be able to make her prediction happen. All he needed was to get away with the assassination, and he could maneuver himself into the very position she promised him. He could make it happen, and that boggled him.

He kissed her again and pressed himself against her once more as excitement filled him. He felt good. For the first time in his life he felt in control. He had a power he'd not had before his months with the Bhrochan. This just might work.

Alex could tell it was light out. He wasn't sure how he could tell, but the darkness seemed a little less dense now. Unless it was just a torch two rooms down. But an extra torch might mean more people up and about, and that might mean daytime. He took a deep breath to speak, and said, "Patrick." Then he expelled the rest of the breath in a sigh, exhausted from all that talking.

"Aye, sir?"

Daylight. Patrick knew it, too, for he only called Alex "my lord" when he was certain there would be nobody to hear. "Patrick, are you still praying for me?"

"Every day, sir."

"Pray for yourself?"

"As often, to be sure."

"How long has it been since she was here?"

"I cannot say, I'm afraid. The passage of time is a fluid thing."

Alex certainly knew how malleable time was, and only wished he could manipulate it himself. Stupid faeries. "Think she'll be back soon?"

Patrick shook his head. Alex couldn't see it, but sensed it. Heard it, possibly, just the faintest sound of the priest's neck against the collar of his shirt. Then he said, "You haven't asked about your cousin."

Alex didn't give a damn about the "cousin." He wanted to know about Lindsay. He wanted to be with her. Wherever she was, he wanted to go to her. "What's going on? What is that blasted faerie doing to her?"

"An Reubair?"

"Is she all right? I'll kill him if he's hurt her."

"She doesn't seem hurt. She seems quite well. He appears to be treating her like a guest."

Alex was quieted by that. Reubair was treating Lindsay well. It made him wonder why. It also made him wonder why he and Patrick were still alive. Then he remembered their captors didn't know who they were.

Patrick said as if he'd heard the doubt in Alex's heart, "She loves you more than her life."

"That's not possible. Nobody could."

"You don't think a human being could sacrifice his or her self for another? I happen to think it's entirely possible. Our entire faith is based on it."

"I can't imagine Lindsay doing it."

"Of course she would. And without thinking twice."

"I said I couldn't imagine it. It would be unthinkable for her to sacrifice herself for me, because then I would be alive without her. I don't want her to even want to give herself for me." He began to gasp. Too much speaking.

Patrick said, "Hm," as he considered that. "So . . . you would give yourself for her. Or, at least, you would wish to be killed instead of her."

Alex summoned his breath again and said, "I've always been ready to die, and for less reason. Don't want to go on without her. Especially, I don't want to live knowing there was something I could have done to save her."

"But if she felt the same way about you, you wouldn't respect her wish?"

"No. She's the one who has to live. End of story." He really didn't want to talk about this anymore.

"You're the one who needs to survive now, sir. You're the thing that is keeping her from giving herself up to The Robber. If you give up, so will she."

The image of An Reubair that swarmed into Alex's mind also brought a pain to his gut. Hatred. Anger. They ate at him with fiery agony. He tensed to get up but hadn't the strength for it. He wanted to kill Reubair, and said so as he rolled onto his back on the cold floor. "I'm going to make certain he dies for this."

"Then live so you can."

"I'm not going anywhere."

Patrick sighed. "Good."

* * *

Lindsay sat at table in the Great Hall, wishing the Danann king would be on his way so she and Reubair could go back to taking their meals in private. She hated being on display before Reubair's nobles, pretending all was well and letting everyone who saw her think she was there willingly. She drank her mead to quell the headache that clenched her brain every day now, it seemed. The drink always seemed to soothe the tension, and like the old joke about singles bars, it seemed to make Reubair easier on the eyes.

Sometimes it was a relief to be able to think of him as attractive, for she knew his aim was eventually to take her to bed one way or another. Day after day of that prospect wore on her, and she never knew when he would lose his patience. The drink seemed to make it all better. There were even days when she lounged before a fire, bored and staring into it, and indulged in long, colorful fantasies about him. Ones that left her with damp linens, wanting release and wishing Alex were there and healthy. On the day she'd discovered she wasn't pregnant, there had been a tinge of disappointment she wouldn't need to sleep with Reubair so he would think he was a father, and it made her flush with shame. That day she'd spent hiding in her closet bed, reluctant to even look at him. There was something wrong with her. There had to be, for her to think that way about him.

Today she drank deeply of the mead and felt sunnier for it. When she looked at Reubair, his laughter lifted her heart and his smile warmed it. When he looked at her, there seemed an instant when she thought she might like to be pregnant by him in truth. It went away, but there was no shame. No deep flush of regret for the feeling. She was tired of resisting. It might be nice to surrender to him and have it over with. She ate her meal and glanced over at Reubair frequently. If only this were settled.

Settled . . . if only she could get Alex out of the dungeon and away from this castle.

After supper she went for a walk in the garden, a walled area tucked between the keep and the stables. It wasn't large, but big enough for a bit of exercise that didn't involve being stared at by faerie townsfolk. The spring flora had ventured out, and though there were no hothouses in this castle and therefore no cultured and delicate flowers from the Continent, she strolled down random trails under gnarled pines and oaks covered in moss and dotted with small white and yellow flowers. Less a garden, really, than an enclosed bit of forest. Trees and undergrowth grew thick enough here that one couldn't see the walls of the garden until one came right up on them.

Neither did she see Trefor until she was right up on him.

"Lindsay." He slipped down from his hiding place in the crotch of a huge oak and confronted her.

It startled her, and her heart leapt for fear. She was unarmed, and never felt good about that, so lately she'd been reacting badly to pretty much everything. Reubair let her have a knife only while eating. She'd long given up the idea of fighting him, but wished she had protection from others here. "Trefor. What do you want?"

"To talk."

She looked around but saw nobody. Surely that was why Trefor had chosen this place, for the garden was usually deserted. It was, in fact, the reason she liked walking here. She stood up to him, stiff and as sure of herself as she could manage just then. But it felt false, for the truth of it was she feared him. Unlike nearly everyone else in this century, he was taller than she. As tall as Alex, for he was built like his father. She knew he didn't like her. He was angry with both of them for abandoning him, though it was far from the truth. He just couldn't understand that she had been as helpless as he in the kidnapping. Her heart constricted to a knot, and her hands clenched to fists in anticipation of talking to him. But she bluffed. "Be my guest. Talk."

"Why haven't you tried to get Alex out of here?"

Her face bled to her belly, and she felt nauseated and light-headed. Trefor knew. She opened her mouth for a panicky reply.

Before she could speak, he said, "Don't bother denying it. I saw him in the dungeon. And Patrick. And don't try to tell me you didn't know; Patrick said you've been visiting."

"I told you, I'm being held by a warding spell on the portcullis. I can't get myself out, let alone him."

"And even you know that's not enough to keep you here, because I told you as much. I think I know why you're still here."

She pulled herself up even more erect and looked down her nose at him. "What is it you think?"

"I've been watching you. At dinner. I think it's another type of spell you're under. Reubair has been feeding you something that has you under a love spell."

Lindsay snorted and tilted her head. "Nonsense. I despise Reubair."

"I know. That's what makes your behavior so strange. One moment you're gaping at him like a love-struck teenager, and the next you're looking around for a way out of the room. It took me a while to figure out what was going on, but then I realized it was always at meals. The extreme goo-goo eyes thing always happens at meals, and you level out in the afternoons and evenings. It's something he's done to the food or drink. What does he give you? Do you always eat out of the same dishes? Does his drink come from the same source as yours?"

Lindsay thought back over the past weeks and realized Reubair never drank what she did. His was always wine, and hers the spiced mead. She said, "No."

"And you've been having thoughts you're ashamed of. I can see them on your face when you look at him."

Lindsay nodded. She couldn't deny it.

He sighed. "You know, in a way it's a relief. At first I thought you'd thrown over Alex for that creep."

"I could never. Not even under the strongest spell." Not technically, anyway. Her cheeks heated at the thought she might have surrendered in a weak moment, and she thanked God to have had the strength to resist.

"Which is why Alex is still alive, I expect."

"I risked a lot to save his life."

Trefor shifted his weight in irritation and crossed his arms over his chest. "Not so much. Reubair wouldn't have killed you; he would have killed Alex first. Near as I can tell, you have nothing but him left for Reubair to threaten."

"But at the end of the day, my husband is still alive because I've been hiding him."

"And the question is, now that you know what Reubair is up to concerning yourself, what are you going to do about it?"

Lindsay blinked. What could she do about it? "Stop drinking the mead."

Trefor nodded. "Good start. But you also need to get out of here."

For a moment, Lindsay had a desperate longing to stay. Leaving Reubair seemed impossible, and her heart clenched at the thought of never seeing him again.

"Stop that," said Trefor, peering into her eyes. "He's been using magic on you. He's cast a spell and made you something you're not."

Anger flashed. "You have no idea what I am."

"You're a fighter, Lindsay. I don't know you well, but I know enough to be certain you'd never take this sort of treatment if you hadn't been compromised somehow. I also know you are enough in love with Alex that only a very powerful spell could make you even look at someone else."

For the first time since meeting Trefor, Lindsay looked him in the eye. How did he know these things about her? How was he so sure and how had he put his finger on her so exactly? What had he thought of her this past year of being the son she could never know? Apparently he knew more about her than she'd even wanted him to learn, and it made her feel flattered and vulnerable at the same time. She didn't trust him. He was an adult, raised by someone else, and she didn't understand who he really was. She knew far less about him than he did about her, and she had no reason to believe he gave a damn about her or Alex. Nevertheless, he'd just put his finger on her core.

Trefor pulled in his chin and leaned down to look her in the eye, and she realized she'd been so deep in thought her gaze had wandered to the ground. She raised her head again, and he said, "You need to break the spell."

"How?"

He knew how, but wasn't sure how to tell her succinctly what to do. The training had taken months, and he was still mastering the craft. She had no clue. He said, "Meditate on it. Focus on what it is in you that you want gone, then make an image of it being destroyed."

"Right."

"Seriously. If I were more powerful, and if I thought we could get him to sit still for it, I might try breaking it for you myself. But I'm not, and he wouldn't, so I needn't bother even trying. It would only alert him to our intention, and that would be a bad thing."

"I don't think I can do this." Just then she didn't want to. Like a dieter who knows she shouldn't eat the chocolate, but eats it anyway, she knew she couldn't bring herself to leave Reubair. The knowledge was like a transparency laid over her conviction she also would not abandon Alex. Both were true, and in her heavily influenced mind they were perfectly compatible things.

"You have to. You've got to dig down into yourself and find the strength to break away from him. You've got to do what you know is right."

"I need help."

A shadow crossed Trefor's face, and suddenly she didn't trust him again. There was something going on with him that wasn't quite kosher. No telling what it could be, but right then he'd shifted somehow. "Just do it. Get Alex out of the dungeon and on a horse. Ride with him to the gate. Follow him; don't let him follow you, or the warding spell will reroute you and separate you from him. But if you let him take you to the gate, you'll make it out, and away."

"I can't."

"You must. I can't do it for you. I can't go with you."

"Won't, you mean."

Impatience rose to his eyes. "All right, I won't. Whatever you want to believe. The bottom line on this is that you have to do it yourself. It's up to you. How much does he mean to you?"

For one dizzy second she thought he meant Reubair, but then she realized he was talking about Alex.

Suddenly Lindsay was tired. So tired she wanted to lie down on the grass and sleep right there. Maybe never to wake up. It was all too much for her. Too much trouble. Too much effort. She didn't believe she could succeed at any of this. She rubbed an eyebrow hard with her finger. There was no way she was going to be able to do this thing Trefor wanted. She wasn't strong enough. Tears rose and stung her eyes. Ask her to clobber someone and beat him bloody, and she could manage it. But tell her to control her heart, and she was hopeless.

Trefor crossed his arms again. "Stop that. Stop crying.

It's not you. That's not what you ever do when you've got a problem. You're not a crier, Lindsay. I know you're not."

She wasn't. She'd never been one to break down and weep. But now all she could think of to do was bawl her misfortune. Her head lowered, and she pressed a palm to her eyes.

He took her shoulder, and his fingers dug into it. "I said quit it. Shake that bloody spell. Don't let Reubair get away with this. Take Alex and run. Free your husband and yourself. I know you can do it. You're my mom, and ever since I was a kid I knew you could do anything."

That shocked her into looking at him again. What *had* he thought when he was a boy?

As if reading the question in her mind, he said, "I used to think about you all the time. I pictured a sweet, pretty lady who smiled all the time, but who could make anything happen. I knew you could save me from the people who hurt me. And now that I've met you I see I was wrong. You don't smile much at all, and you wouldn't want to save me from anyone." She blinked hard at his bluntness, and he hurried to continue. "But I still think you can do anything. And you can rescue your husband, because I know you love him more than the world."

Trefor was right. And how he knew that was a mystery to her. But at least he was right. She nodded.

"And you must do it immediately."

She shook her head. "Alex is too ill to travel."

"You can't stay."

"Why not?"

Alex's "Don't argue with me" look crossed Trefor's MacNeil eyes, and a shiver ran up her spine. "Just take my word for it. You don't want to be here after tomorrow."

"And where will you be?"

"Never mind me."

"Trefor—"

"Do it. Take him from the dungeon tonight. Be gone by morning. Take my horses."

"And you'll be along . . . when?"

"When I am able."

"What's going on, Trefor?"

His eyelids lowered with distrust, and so did hers. Suddenly she wasn't sure if anything he'd just told her was true. He said, "Trust me."

"But you won't trust me in return. There's something you're not telling me."

"If you weren't under Reubair's spell, I might. But you've been compromised. I can't trust you so well right now."

"A likely story."

"And I'm sticking to it." He waited for her to acquiesce, and when she didn't, he took a deep breath. "Okay, believe me, or don't. Trust me or not. It's up to you what you would do tonight. Take him out of here, or risk having him murdered before your eyes as soon as Reubair learns he's here."

Lindsay's gut turned sour, for she knew Reubair would do exactly that. Without waiting for a reply, Trefor turned and retreated in the direction of the keep. Lindsay watched him go, and though she also wanted to return to the keep, she continued her walk so she wouldn't look like she was following him.

CHAPTER 16

Alex was standing. Barely, but at least he was on his feet instead of his back, and his belly no longer felt as if his guts would slide out onto the floor if he let go of his wound. The stitches Mary had put in were gone, having been bitten off by Patrick once they were no longer needed. Alex figured he may have been better off without them, since they had probably been the source of his fever and had nearly killed him. As hard as he and Lindsay always struggled to get people to boil things, more often than not they didn't bother, and without Lindsay around to insist, Mary was likely to have spit on the thread to put it through the needle. Basic sanitation was a distant dream, and Alex didn't figure he'd live long enough to die of the plague when it arrived in a few decades.

But for now he was alive, and determined to stay that way as long as he could. He stood in the darkness, one hand leaned heavily against the wall and his feet spaced widely for balance. Somebody had set a torch in the next room, and a dim spill of light came through the barred window in the door. Except for the torches Lindsay brought, it was the first light they'd had in this cell.

He now saw how tiny the room was, barely large enough for the two of them to lie down in. Patrick sat near a corner, leaning against the wall next to the door, elbows on knees. The cold had relented a bit. Though the room couldn't be said to be warm, exactly, neither of them was shivering anymore except when night was deepest and the stone leached warmth.

"How many guards are out there?"

Patrick glanced at the door. "'Tis difficult to know, but I think never more than two. More often, only one."

"A soldier, or just a warm body?"

Patrick grinned at what folks in this century thought of as Alex's "way with words." He replied, "Warm body, as you say. The master of the dungeon is a human and doesn't take his work overly serious. I've never seen him at it, of course, but I believe he sleeps a great deal. Lady Cruachan tells me he's what she calls a 'wanker.' I'm fairly certain I don't need to ask her what that means."

Alex grinned, and the unaccustomed expression felt as if it might crack his face. His skin was dry. Itchy. More than a bath, he wanted some water. Food. The tiniest bit of grease to eat would have been heaven just then.

"Where is Lindsay? When was she last here?"

"It's been some time now. She cannot come every day. When she does, she'll be glad to learn you're standing."

Alex grunted and shifted his weight to take a step. His joints trembled, but he was able to slide one foot forward a few inches. Then he shifted his weight again and moved the other foot. Then he was out of breath and gripped a bulge of stone in the wall. As much as he wanted to run away from this place, he knew he would be hard put to make it to the next room even if the door were wide open. He filled his lungs with the dank air, coughed, and steeled himself for another step. Baby steps. One after another. He had to keep moving so he'd be ready once that door did open. He kept walking, and daydreamed of food.

Trefor sat at supper and fingered his knife, his eye on Dagda at the head table. He'd not committed one way or the other to Morag as to his intention regarding her request. The better to not let her give him away if that was her plan. He watched the king, Morag at his side, lounging in his seat and partaking of the meal, laughing in conversation with his mistress. Morag, for her part, seemed to enjoy his company, and hang whatever Trefor might feel about it. Her pleasure so annoyed him he shifted uncomfortably in his seat. Anger simmered in his gut. Dagda did need killing, just for having his paws all over her.

Once the faerie king was dead, Trefor would rule this place and Morag would be his. *Consort*, she'd said. The prospect was heady. More power and far more wealth than even Alex had dreamed of. And he would be doing a service to the Danann as well as to the Bhrochan, for Nemed was neither. The elf had no claim to these lands; he wasn't even a faerie. He was a king without a people, and therefore no king at all. A nothing. Dog in a manger, and Dagda was a fool for letting him keep this territory. Dagda needed killing.

It would have to be a stabbing. Magic would be useless against such a powerful faerie, even if Trefor had more experience and knowledge under his belt. Dagda would see it coming from too far off. A gun would have been nice to have, but it was too early yet for a firearm portable enough for assassination. Metallurgy wasn't far enough along for him to "invent" a pistol that wouldn't blow up in his hand. Near as he could figure, they were even a few years away from the first enormous and cumbersome cannon.

Poison was a possibility, but hard to pull off, and Trefor wasn't sure what might kill a faerie. It wouldn't do to just make him sick or piss him off. Stabbing was the most common tactic for this, almost a cliché, but Trefor supposed there was a reason it was common. Straightforward, simple, quick, and it could be accomplished by one man without the involvement of kitchen help.

As Trefor watched, Dagda laughed at a particularly funny point made by Morag and kissed her. A big, sloppy kiss, right there among the gathering of faerie knights.

Yeah, Trefor figured he'd be happy to put a knife into Dagda's heart.

All through the midday meal Lindsay thought hard about what Trefor had said. *Love spell.* She refrained from drinking the mead, though she pretended to sip from her goblet. Occasionally she picked up Reubair's wine to ease her thirst, and in that way avoided poisoning herself. She wondered how long it would take for the potion she'd been drinking over the past weeks to lose its power. Today she didn't notice any lessening of it. Her blood still surged when she looked at him.

In a way it was a relief to know the thoughts she'd been having weren't hers, but understanding she was under the influence of Reubair's magic did nothing to lessen the effects of it. When she looked at him, she did her level best to hate him for what he'd done. It was an evil thing. But she still felt the stirring in her belly, and it was stronger than ever. Anymore, all she had to do was think of him and her body responded. The lines of his face, the grace of his lean frame, the timbre of his voice all set her off in the same way Alex's did, but with an edge that was nearly painful. As if the yearning for him was a danger if it would never be satisfied. As if it were doing damage to her heart each day it wasn't.

After eating, Reubair followed her to the bedchamber. Usually he went to his presence chamber for afternoon meetings with members of his court, but today he seemed filled with good cheer and perhaps a bit too much wine. No business at hand today, it seemed. He and Dagda had spent the mealtime flogging a running ribald joke about mistresses and wives, during which Lindsay had maintained an idiot grin and said nothing. She was sure it had appeared she'd thought the ridiculous double entendres funny, and Dagda was led to believe she was there with Reubair by her free will. The thought was so cringeworthy she could hardly eat. But to open her mouth would have invited riposte from Reubair, or worse, and she needed to keep the status quo until she could get Alex out of the dungeon. It would have to be soon, if Trefor was to be believed. Tonight.

Now, in the bedchamber, she eyed her captor as he removed his boots to make himself comfortable. This wasn't good. He never undressed unless he was headed for bed, and the day was far too young for that. She took her cloak from its wall hook to leave, but as she swept it around her he asked her where she was going. There was an edge to his voice she didn't like. She could sense he wasn't going to let her escape, even for the afternoon.

"I wish to take a walk. The garden is prettier than usual these days."

"It's barely summer, and it'll be there tomorrow. And every day until winter, I'll wager." He lounged against a bedpost to regard her.

"I need some air."

"I'm sure you'll find plenty of air in this room. Stay." It

was a command. She was stuck. With a suppressed sigh she returned her cloak to its hook, then went to her closet bed.

"No. Stay with me." Again, the edge in his voice told her something was up and he wasn't going to let her hide. But she went for her sanctum anyway. She had to get away from him.

He pushed away from the post and intercepted her. "I said stay." His fingers on her upper arm dug into her flesh until it hurt. She stared at his hand, then frowned up at him until he loosened his grip. But he didn't let go. She waited to learn what was going on.

The wine shone in his eyes, and she could hear it in his voice, though he spoke more softly now. "Come sit with me. And cheer yourself. I wish your good company."

"You have my company, such as it is. I've nothing better to give you."

"Nonsense. I've seen you far more charming than this." He let go of her arm. "Nevertheless, I'll take what you are willing to bestow. You're not to retreat to your bed so early."

She clasped her hands in front of her. "Fine. Let me know when I'm free to go."

A smile leapt to his face, but it was a cajoling one. "Come, don't be that way."

"I am what I am."

"And I adore that about you."

She blinked. He'd never used any such words to her before, and it touched her. Hard. In a place she'd thought well protected and reserved for Alex. *Adore.* Lindsay reminded herself Reubair had cast a spell over her. A love spell, the faerie equivalent of a roofie, his intention just as surely rape. And now, since she'd not fallen for it, he was attempting a more conventional seduction, the mainstay of human men: lies.

However, her compromised body betrayed her. Her

heart began to pound, and her entire groin seemed to reply. The throbbing was nearly unbearable, and she took a deep breath to calm it. Then she retreated to sit in a chair by the hearth, the farthest she could get from Reubair's bed. Her hands clasped demurely in her lap and her knees pressed together, facing away from him, she turned and leveled a bland gaze at him. Her blood rushed through her, pounding in her ears and in every one of her most sensitive places, but she was determined he wouldn't know it. The corners of her mouth turned up ever so slightly, and she kept complete control over her breathing. He couldn't know what she was feeling.

A big, white grin splashed across his face. "Your eyes have gone dark, my love. You cannot pretend I don't excite you."

Damn. She shut her eyes and wished she could control eye dilation. Her voice was low and careful. "If you think I'm in the habit of throwing my legs open for every man who excites me, you're mad. But then, I do think you're mad, in any case."

He sauntered toward her. "But you admit I have reached you. I've touched you in a private place."

"You've done nothing of the sort."

"That is a lie. I can almost hear your heart from where I stand." He knelt by her chair. "And it beats for me."

"It beats because if it didn't I would die."

"You're a strong woman. I believe there are none stronger in the whole of Ireland, Scotland, or England. I'll wager I could travel all the way to Jerusalem and not find a better wife."

"So long as Alasdair an Dubhar is alive, you won't have any sort of wife in me."

"I'll find him and that will be the end of him."

A laugh burst from her, but it had an edge of hysteria.

"What a charming thing to say! Why, it makes me want to throw off my clothes!"

He sighed in frustration and took her hands in both of his. "I would have you consensually if I could. A divorce would save his life." He bent to kiss her hands in his, and for an instant she considered his words seriously. On the surface it seemed a win-win offer, but then her better sense prevailed.

"Freeing me would save your life." Her words belied her emotions. His lips on her knuckles were tender and sent a charge through her that settled in warm, moist places. It did make her want to throw off her clothes. Her breaths came more quickly than she wished, and there was nothing she could do about it.

Then he drew her to her feet and kissed her mouth, and she couldn't help but respond by opening it. As if she were watching a couple on a movie screen, she observed herself and hated herself for what she was doing. He seemed to dive into her, reaching with his tongue with an eagerness that struck her as nearly pathetic. He wanted her too much, and it made her that much more horrified that she wanted him in return. She accepted him and met his tongue with hers, and the rest of her body tingled with an excitement she wanted to deny but couldn't.

Alex. She focused on Alex. She pictured him finding out about this, and the desire waned enough she was able to break away. She turned her face from Reubair and stared at the floor, unable to look him in the eye, struggling for breath.

"You want me," he said, his voice tight and husky.

"I want to be left alone. I want to go home." Home, to Alex in the dungeon below. She would die with him there, rather than live through this.

"No, you don't. You feel for me."

"I feel revulsion."

"There is no denying that. Nevertheless, you have a desire for me that is plain to see, however perverse you think it. Like the good Christian who lusts after his neighbor's wife. Or ass, whatever the case may be. However wrong you think it, you nevertheless want me."

It was truth, and the empathy it showed in him made inroads on her resolve. A whimper escaped her, and she tensed as he gently removed her headdress and let it drop to the floor. He ran his fingers into her hair, feeling its waves.

"You have glorious hair. So thick, and deep dark. Like fertile earth." His voice went nearly too soft to hear. "Like the scent of you. Dark and earthy. Ready to receive seed."

Excited and repulsed at once, Lindsay closed her eyes against the sight of him. His hands were large and strong. His body warm near her. She could hear each breath he took. He smelled like leather and wool, and a hint of wintergreen. Also ever so faintly of earth. Musty and warm, a burrow among tree roots where life could thrive in safety. He took her face between his palms and kissed her again. The room seemed to spin. She was unable to pull away, but she knew if she didn't, in a few moments she would be with him on the bed and all would be lost.

Alex. She had to think of Alex. If he knew of this, he would rise from the floor of his cell and come after Reubair. Somehow she found the strength to break free again and stepped back. "Alex will kill you."

"Worth the risk." He closed on her again and pressed his lips to her forehead. "Indeed, worth the dying. But remember, he must find me first."

She blurted a panicky laugh. "Your keep is not so large . . ." Her voice trailed off as she realized in a burst of cold sweat what she'd just done. She went very still, hoping he would miss it.

"My keep?" There was a long silence as he searched her

eyes, and Lindsay could almost hear the snap of things coming together in Reubair's head. Her absences. The mystery guests downstairs. He'd only seen Alex once last summer, as an opponent in battle, then the prisoners once on their arrival, but finally Reubair's memory made the connection. Alex wore red and black; why had she mentioned it? He stepped back and held Lindsay at arm's length. His expression clouded, darkening with dangerous rage. "He's here. I can see it in your face." Then a pause, as something else clicked. "It's the real reason your cousin appeared from nowhere." He snorted anger. "It's the reason you've been keeping me out of the dungeon."

She said nothing, and the ache of both wanting Reubair and fearing for Alex was intolerable. She couldn't have spoken even were there something to say to save Alex.

Reubair hauled off and smacked her face. She reeled sideways and fell against the chair behind her. Her head buzzed as she tried to regain her feet, which had tangled in her skirts. He yanked his boots onto his feet and strode from the room.

"Reubair!" Lindsay ran after him to the anteroom and leapt onto his back. He twisted and shook her off, and she was grabbed by the two guardsmen posted outside the chamber. "Reubair, if you kill him you'll never have my goodwill!"

He turned to shout at her, "By all accounts, I'll never have it, in any case. As you know, I'm quite willing to take you by force, and you've made it clear it's the only way I'll have what I want."

"I'll kill myself!"

"You'll try." With that, he turned and continued to the stairwell and downward. Lindsay fought the guardsmen and managed to free herself. She followed Reubair again.

* * *

Trefor stuck with Dagda that afternoon. He wanted to know where the king went, what he did with his days. Reubair, like his counterparts among human nobility, often spent his free time in the chapel, but he was a rarity among the Danann, and Dagda certainly didn't hold with Reubair's religion. Dagda would have other things to do while Reubair prayed.

Today Trefor was disappointed. Dagda hung around the Great Hall and didn't seem to want to go anywhere. Reubair's court gathered around the faerie king in an informal sort of way, pretending an insouciance Trefor knew wasn't possible for these guys. They were, of course, buttering their bread on both sides while their liege was occupied sniffing under the skirts of the Countess Cruachan upstairs. To Trefor it seemed Dagda was also taking advantage of Reubair's absence in chatting up the various faerie knights in residence, feeling out their loyalty and opinions. Trefor lounged in a chair slightly apart from the gathering near the head table and listened in as much as he could. Few paid him much attention, for he was only a minor guest and not of terrible significance in this court, and he summoned *maucht* to aid his invisibility.

The conversation wasn't of much significance, either. Except for the occasional fit of nosiness on the part of Dagda, there wasn't much said that would catch anyone's attention. Every once in a while Dagda would ask a question that struck Trefor as prying into Reubair's life and business. Then, curiosity satisfied, he would talk of other things. Trefor could see that both Dagda and Reubair were right to not trust each other.

Then Dagda stood and announced he would retire to his bedchamber to rest his royal head, and the party broke up. Trefor rose with the cluster, as if he had somewhere else to go, and watched the king gather himself to leave. Morag said to him, just loud enough for Trefor to overhear, "Your Majesty, I must plead a commitment elsewhere."

A shadow of disappointment fell over the king's eyes. Apparently he'd been counting on the company of his mistress during his nap. "You know I don't care to sleep alone."

Duh.

Morag smiled to jolly him out of his pique, and said, "I'll be along as soon as I can."

"I see where I stand in your esteem."

"It would be a lie to say anyone could take precedence over this. Not even you. I know you value my honesty, my liege."

"You're not going to pray, are you? Like that priest's boy upstairs."

"Indeed not. But I might dance a little. Have patience, and I'll do a little for you. I know you enjoy watching me dance, and I promise to come to you an enthusiastic companion."

That brought a smile. "You make me more eager to see you in my chamber."

"I promise the wait will be a small price to pay."

Dagda laughed and kissed her. "Very well. Hurry to me once you've done your obeisance to the goddess. And give her my regards."

Morag grinned, and as she turned away her eyes flitted toward Trefor. A shiver ran through him. Here was an opportunity. The king would be alone. There would be guards, but they could be easily befuddled. No ruler was ever as safe as his protectors believed; it would be a simple matter to redirect Dagda's guard to get past them. That was what made the rules of hospitality so necessary. A visitor was terribly vulnerable to those of his host's household. As Dagda and his guard left the room via the stairwell and Morag left by the door to the outside, Trefor drifted toward the stairwell slowly enough to not catch anyone's attention. He listened to the ascending footsteps, waiting until Dagda had reached the floor where his chamber was before entering the narrow staircase.

He'd gone only a couple of flights when there was a shout from above. It was Lindsay, hollering at Reubair to not kill someone.

Kill who? Then she threatened to kill herself, and Trefor knew. Reubair had found Alex. Horror yawned in Trefor's gut. Reubair was sure to kill both Alex and Lindsay if he found the earl and his priest in the dungeon.

Sounds of hurried footsteps came from above. Lindsay was shouting after them, and Trefor knew it must be Reubair on his way down. His mind flew as he realized his opportunity was improving. All hell was breaking loose, and anything could happen to the king during this sort of confusion. Trefor could easily slip into the king's chambers while the focus of the entire keep was on the commotion headed toward the dungeon.

But it would be at the expense of Lindsay and Alex. His parents. Deirbhile's words returned to him in a cascade that swept his thoughts all sideways. She'd held that family was more important than anything. More important than life. She'd given over the idea of marrying for love, so that her father would prosper. Trefor's mother was the reason he was in the faerie lands to begin with. Sudden shame filled him, that he would let her and his father die so he could assassinate the king.

In an instant he knew what he must do, so surely that he didn't hesitate when Reubair descended and tried to shove him aside in the stairwell. Trefor laid a hand on Reubair's chest in the close quarters and murmured, "The man you want to kill is upstairs." He pictured King Dagda and pushed with the *maucht* he'd nurtured the past hour or so. The energy coming off Reubair was ridiculously easy to redirect. There was so much of it, and it was so out of control, Trefor barely had to touch it to use it. Reubair stopped cold in his tracks, clinging with his fingers to the stone wall, panting with his rage and confusion. His eyes dulled, then brightened again. Trefor repeated the spell. "Upstairs. Dagda is there. Kill him."

Reubair looked upward and made an incoherent noise in his throat. Then he said, "That bastard. I'll kill him," and Trefor knew he meant the king. Reubair turned to run back up the stairs, and Trefor followed.

CHAPTER 17

"Reubair!" Lindsay shouted from the top of the stairwell as she heard steps returning. Cool relief washed
over her. He wasn't going to the dungeon. But then the running stopped at the floor below. The guest chambers. The
king's rooms. She took up her skirts and hurried down.
Where the stairwell opened onto the first anteroom below,
she found Trefor running up. She reached out to grasp his
tunic sleeve, and he stopped.

"What's happened?" she asked.

"You tell me." He panted from the run and looked a bit
walleyed.

"Reubair knows Alex is in the dungeon. He's going to
kill both Alex and Patrick." Panic rose, and she had to
swallow it.

"No, he won't. But you've got to get out of here. All
three of you. Now, and no guff. Take my horses from the
stable, and don't argue."

"How will you get away without a horse?"

In a tone that dripped "duh," he replied, "I'll *steal* one."

She sighed and nodded. *Of course*.

He continued, "I can't hold Reubair for long; once he realizes what's happened and that you've gotten away, he's going to be more pissed than ever. You've got to get Alex and Patrick out of here. Now."

"How will I get them released from the dungeon?" There didn't seem to be any way she could pull off what Trefor was asking.

"Just do it. Shake that bloody spell, and you'll know what to do. Just make sure you don't lead the way to the gate. Ride behind Alex. Let Patrick lead, and you'll make it through. After that, once you're through, you won't have any trouble with the warding."

"Where will you be?"

A shadow crossed his eyes, and that made her want to ask other questions. But he said, "Never mind me. I'll make it out later."

She wasn't sure about that, but it was plain there wasn't time to argue. She nodded and left him in the anteroom to deal with Reubair.

Her skirts tripped her, and at the Great Hall she finally decided enough was enough. These had to go. She took a long dagger from a scabbard hung at the entry with all the other weapons surrendered by knights visiting the keep, and cut the skirt from her overdress, leaving only a tunic-length of it below her belt. Then she cut and ripped the bottom foot or so from her shift so it was knee-length. Legs bare, she now felt unprotected from a sword, but was free of encumbrance that would slow her down and get her killed. She took the dagger with her to the lower levels of the keep.

Panting heavily with excitement, she hurried down the steps. It exhilarated her to be in action. She felt alive in a way she'd only felt in battle. She could die today, but instead of fearing it she accepted it so that the only fear was to fail in rescuing Alex. Alex must live, and that was all she cared about just then. Focus. That was what it took to shake the spell.

At the bottom of the steps, she hurried through the torch-lit chambers and held the dagger just behind her right thigh, out of sight. The guard in the interrogation chamber looked up from scratching himself as she entered. His eyes went wide at sight of her getup, and he pulled his hand from his trews.

"Come for a laugh, aye, Mistress?" He seemed puzzled as he returned his chair to all fours and stood, but there was a glint of hope in his eyes that she could be there for his personal entertainment.

"Open the cell with the priest in it." She pointed with her chin to the heavy, ironclad wooden door.

"What's the matter, my lady? I confess—"

"Now. Just get the keys and open the door."

His eyelids lowered with suspicion. He was dull-witted, but not entirely stupid, and she couldn't hide that something strange was afoot. She didn't have time to hoodwink him. He shook his head. "I'll need to hear from Himself first today, I think."

She raised the dagger, her arm cocked in threat. "Open. The. Door."

"Put the knife down and have someone in authority bring the order for the door to be opened."

Damn. She was going to have to prove to this idiot she meant business. She would have to hurt him. She took a swipe at him with the dagger and caught his chin with the tip of it.

His head jerked backward. Eyes boggling, he stepped back and felt of his wound. Then he looked at the blood on his hand and sputtered. "You cut me!"

"I'll kill you if you don't open the bloody door!"

"You *cut* me!" He couldn't seem to get past his shock at the tiny nick.

"I said open the door."

Finally his focus returned to her, and his expression darkened. "Whore!"

Lindsay sighed and wondered why that was always the first word people thought of when looking to insult her. She raised the dagger again and took a step toward the guard. "Don't make me kill you." She would leave him alone if he would only do as she said.

But, witless as he was, he didn't get that she was more dangerous than he. He hauled off to hit her, and she sidestepped neatly to ram her dagger to the hilt in his gut. He bellowed with a surprise she began to find tedious, and embraced his stomach as soon as her weapon was clear of it. He staggered and retched horribly. The sound nauseated her.

"You bloody idiot! I told you I was going to kill you, and now you've gone and made me do it!" There was a stink of bowel, and with clenched heart Lindsay knew the man would die of the wound, but possibly not soon. He knew it, too, and looked up at her with the horror of that realization. He roared again, with the anger and desperation of his doom, and came at her like a bear. Knowing her action would be a mercy, she stabbed him in the solar plexus and shoved upward, to his heart. Blood gushed over her hand and halfway up her sleeve. The guard cried out again with the pain, but all resistance left him and he collapsed. A moment or two of writhing, and then he was still.

Lindsay stared down at him, disgusted, and told herself the man had been too stupid to live. Then she shook excess blood from her dagger and arm, reached down for the key ring at the guard's belt, and hurried to the cells.

A lex opened his eyes from a doze. A commotion outside the cell brought him around to groggy consciousness. Lindsay, shouting. Threatening to kill someone. He raised his head, and so did Patrick.

"What's going on?"

Patrick listened briefly then said, "The countess is displeased with someone."

Alex had to chuckle. "Woe to him, then."

Patrick chuckled also but sounded weak. There hadn't been anything to eat since yesterday, and no water since the night before.

A key rattled in the lock, and the cell door opened. Light from the torch in the other room fell on them. Alex and Patrick struggled to their feet as Lindsay burst in. "Alex. Get up. Patrick, help me get him up."

"I'm up," said Alex, though he was still trying to make his elbows stop trembling as he pushed off the floor. Patrick and Lindsay each took an arm and lifted him so he stood with feet splayed. Balance wasn't possible; he was barely able to keep from collapsing to the floor. "What's going on?" He squinted at the light.

"We've got to get out of here. Reubair knows you're here, and he wants to kill you."

"Where is he now?"

"Not the faintest. Trefor has done something to keep him at bay." She draped his arm across her shoulders, and indicated to Patrick he should do the same.

Alex peered at Lindsay. "Trefor is really here?" Patrick hadn't merely dreamed it?

"Yes. He came when he learned I was here. But something extraordinary has happened and I don't know what. All I know is that we've got to get his horses from the stables and run."

"Trefor is here?" Alex was agog. Trefor had come.

"*Yes*. Now we must go."

Alex summoned the strength to move his feet and was able to make a semblance of walking. Lindsay and Patrick took most of his weight, for his knees trembled, but the need to get moving gave him strength he wouldn't have suspected.

But then he stopped and looked into Lindsay's face. His wife. "What?" she said. Her voice was characteristically impatient, and suddenly he loved that. He loved everything about her, even that raggedy dress she had on, even with all that blood all over her arms. He kissed her with all his strength. Leaning on Patrick, his arm heavy around Lindsay's shoulders as well, he tasted her mouth and felt of her lips on his. She kissed him in return, her palm pressed against his bearded cheek.

Then she looked into his eyes and said nothing, for there was nothing that needed saying.

They fled the cell and hurried, stumbling, through the rooms of the dungeon. Stairs. Alex's heart fell. A long flight of stairs loomed, and the claustrophobia of burial pressed on him. Stone everywhere, and the only way out was up this nightmare staircase. He gasped for breath and steeled himself for the climb. One step at a time, but hard on each other, for they would die if they couldn't get out in a hurry.

By the time they reached the Great Hall he was completely blown, heaving, nearly vomiting. Every muscle in his body trembled, and sweat dribbled from his hair down his face and neck. Each step was a new challenge, and those challenges came quickly. Lindsay and Patrick hurried him along. No rest. No chance to gather his strength or his wits. They just kept moving. The Great Hall was empty. Strange. There should be knights here; there were always courtiers in a Great Hall. Shouts went up somewhere. Alex couldn't tell where. But he didn't care to puzzle over that. Patrick and Lindsay hefted his weight again, and he leaned as heavily as he dared as they left the Hall and nearly ran across the bailey. Daylight blinded him, and he ducked his head as he struggled to see. Lindsay guided him to the stables, where castle functionaries surely awaited. But the stables were also empty of people. Even more strange, for there should have been men attending to the animals. It seemed everyone in the castle was off somewhere else. Lucky for him, bad for Reubair. Hope brought a little more strength.

Lindsay paused, listening to the hollering in the distance.

"It's got to do with Dagda." She listened more closely, then said, "Something terrible is happening. I hear Trefor and Reubair." She relinquished hold of Alex, whose weight shifted to Patrick. "I've got to—"

"My lady," said Patrick with desperate urgency. "We must go."

Alex wondered who Lindsay wanted to go help: Trefor or Reubair.

"Please, my lady . . ."

"Trefor—"

"He'll be all right. He has God with him."

Lindsay considered that, then without another word took up her place beneath Alex's arm once more. They went down the row of stalls, looking for a likely mount.

"Here," said Lindsay. "These look familiar; they must be Trefor's."

"They're mine," said Alex, gasping for breath required for speech. He recognized his favorite charger, the stallion with the feathered fetlocks. "I rode in on this horse."

"Good. Then we know he's worth stealing. Get on."

Alex reached up to grab a hank of mane and groaned. His body was one huge package of pain. Every joint ached as if he might fall apart like an overcooked goose. The stable building was warm. Alex had nearly forgotten what that was like. He had a mad urge to crawl under a pile of straw to sleep, and would have if Lindsay and Patrick had not demanded he mount. Bareback. Not ordinarily a problem for him, but today he doubted he could cling to a galloping horse by himself. He shook his head. "No. Saddle."

But there was no saddle handy. And no bridle. He would have to control the horse by a lead looped around its head. Patrick was arranging that.

"No saddle," said Lindsay. "Ride behind me. Hang on as best you can." She found a mounting stool and leapt onto the horse. When her shift pulled tight, she ripped the skirt of it up one side to free her legs. Patrick helped Alex to mount behind her, then took another horse for himself. Alex clamped his knees astride his charger's barrel, held Lindsay's waist with one arm, and with the other reached for a fistful of mane. Even having been ill and starved he was heavier than she; he couldn't depend on her to keep him on the horse's back. He braced himself, and Patrick kicked his horse to lead the way.

They burst from the stables at a gallop, and onto the streets of Finias. The curious were gathering at the commotion in the bailey, scurrying across in twos and fives. Some gaped at the escapees, but none thought it prudent to interfere. *No business of mine* seemed to be the attitude. Somebody else's problem. They were all off to see what was going on near the keep. Lindsay, Patrick, and Alex were away, and it seemed they were home free.

No such luck. A guard in the bailey raised an alarm at full voice and ran to the stables. Alex looked behind and saw a scurrying of knights to their horses. The chase was on.

Up ahead, it seemed to Alex there were two views. Like a superimposed photograph, he saw two streets. He blinked. Lindsay shouted to Patrick to slow down. She needed to catch up to him, or she'd be sidetracked by the warding spell. If that happened, she'd lose him and never be able to get out. Patrick waited, and she caught up. They headed for the portcullis again.

The guard there had heard the commotion, and the gate

was on its way down as the two running horses approached. Lindsay cursed like a true knight and kicked the charger to greater speed. "Go, Patrick! Don't let me get ahead of you!" Patrick kicked his mount also, and at a dead run the three of them rushed the exit. As they passed under the lowering gate, Alex and Lindsay dodged one of the spikes at the bottom and plunged through. Patrick's horse stumbled, but recovered, and they were on their way from the castle. The gate rattled the rest of the way to the ground. Shouts from behind came from their pursuers, who commanded the gate be raised for them to pass. There would be a small head start.

Very small.

Trefor rushed into the king's bedchamber and found it empty of people. The bed was turned down, but not slept in, and he figured the king hadn't made it in for his nap. But where had Reubair gone? Trefor turned a circle, puzzled, for he'd been certain there was no exit for Reubair except past him in the stairwell. For one light-headed moment, it seemed he'd magically disappeared. It was a possibility.

A groan from beyond the bed pricked Trefor's ears, and he found a faerie knight lying on the floor, wounded. Reubair had been here, and apparently so had Dagda, for it was one of his guard, the candid fellow who had so willingly chatted with Trefor. He had a badly gashed face and leg, but there wasn't so much blood he wouldn't live. Trefor stepped over the agonized and panicky knight and pulled back a tapestry hung against the far wall of the chamber.

Ah. It covered an opening in the wall. Trefor started into it but hesitated at the pitch darkness. Quickly he returned to the chamber and lifted a candle from a stand on a bedside table, then slipped into the recess behind the tapestry.

Down it went, rough stairs that sometimes gave way to merely sloping stone, and Trefor realized this passage had been built into the mountain of living rock beside the keep. The better to disguise its presence and its destination from people who might want to guess those things.

After a distance of level going, the tunnel ended abruptly. Dead end. Trefor couldn't see a way out, until he lifted his candle over his head and looked up. Rungs embedded in the stone indicated the passage went straight up into darkness. Trefor wondered how far underground he was, and how far from the keep.

With the candle dripping beeswax all over his left hand, he climbed the rungs to find himself up against an iron door, flat and round like a manhole cover. Heavy. He put his shoulder to it, shoved hard, and with a creak of iron and a crunch of grit it gave way. A fine sprinkle of dirt fell on him, into his face, and made him spit. Quickly he shoved again and hinged it away from the hole, and he climbed the rest of the way and out.

He found himself in the garden between the keep and the stables. Well disguised by overgrowth, the tunnel entrance was hard to see even as he stood next to it. When he let the cover fall with a loud clang, it became nearly invisible. A scattering of dead leaves was all it took to make it so. He extinguished the candle and looked around for Reubair.

"Murder!" The shout was Dagda, calling for help. Trefor turned to hear where. "Murder! Assassin!"

"Reubair!" Trefor ran toward Dagda's voice and didn't see anyone until he stumbled upon another faerie knight, this one quite dead, with his sword lying nearby. Reubair had certainly taken Trefor's suggestion seriously. He was out to kill the king.

There was a scuffling noise in a thicket off to Trefor's left, toward the wall of the stables. He went, shouting, "Reubair!" He didn't know whether to yell encouragement or call him off. Minutes ago he had been quite willing to kill Dagda himself, but now he wasn't so sure. Now he wondered if perhaps Morag had given him a push to it. It was something she would do, and he wouldn't necessarily have felt it.

He plunged through a patch of berry shrubs and found Reubair faced off against Dagda, whom he had cornered in the thicket by the wall. The king stood helpless, disarmed, bleeding from defensive wounds and gaping with terror. He held out one hand with palm forward, a gesture of warding, his elbow trembling with the effort of the spell. Reubair was playing with him, enjoying his own power. He laughed and lunged, then held back to keep the king cornered and prolong his game. Blood from slashed forearms dripped from Dagda's fingertips and elbow, and he gasped for breath. His face paled with the bleeding, and as he weakened so did his strength to keep Reubair off. He glanced at Trefor, and the relief showed on his face.

Reubair turned when he realized someone was behind him. In a flash he came at Trefor, who drew his own dagger to defend. He parried Reubair's thrust, then socked him in the mouth. There was no bellow of pain, though his lip split and his teeth went pink with blood. He only shook his head and snorted, blood flying. Trefor attacked again with his knife.

Reubair parried and backed. Trefor followed, slashing over and over, backing him toward the wall that had cornered Dagda until moments before. The king was nursing his wounds, holding closed with one hand one of the deep slashes. The others bled freely. He continued to shout for help.

There was hollering from the bailey, beyond the entrance to the garden. People came running, and among them were knights, some belonging to Reubair and some to Dagda.

"Take him!" cried the king, but the men hesitated, not knowing who to take and only seeing a fair fight in progress.

Dagda's men raised their weapons to Reubair's, and Reubair's to Dagda's, in a standoff.

Reubair lunged at Trefor, who leapt back and parried. Trefor wished mightily for a sword. His dagger wasn't nearly long enough to suit him. But he came back with several quick slashes and sliced through Reubair's shirt sleeve. The silk sagged and ran red. The light of fear came into Reubair's eyes, and it disgusted Trefor. *Coward.* He thought of what the faerie lord had done to his mother, and what he'd tried to do, and wanted to kill him on the spot. He attacked again and caught a forearm. More blood. Trefor felt a surge of satisfaction.

Reubair fell back and cried out, "Yield! I yield!" Fear of Trefor had lost him the fight. He surrendered, his hands up and his head down. Suddenly Reubair looked confused, as if he didn't understand why he was being arrested. He said nothing but went pale and his mouth dropped open. Trefor guessed he'd shaken the push.

"Drop the dagger."

Reubair obeyed and kept his head down. At order from Dagda, the gathered knights took the disarmed Reubair by the arms. Reubair's men stood down, confused. Two of them grabbed Trefor, but Dagda said, "An Reubair has betrayed me. Leave Sir Trefor be."

Reubair hurried to order his men to stand down. Trefor noted the faerie still held command of his troops. Not good. Confused now, and outnumbered at the moment by the king's knights, Reubair's men let Trefor go.

Then Reubair looked over at Trefor with a terrible knowledge in his eyes. Trefor shuddered. Reubair understood what had happened in the stairwell. He was now a steadfast enemy, and the only good thing was that Reubair probably wouldn't live long enough to exact revenge. Trefor watched the king's guard half carry Reubair away from the garden and to his fate of a traitor's death.

Others of the king's men gathered around Dagda to escort him to safety, leaving Trefor in the garden with a scattering of onlookers, wondering what was going to happen next. Trefor wondered whether his mother and father had made it from the castle.

Lindsay, leading the way now, pulled up the charger and slowed to a walk. Riding double, it hadn't taken long for the horse to tire, and they had to slow before it would be completely blown. It was time to get off the beaten track and make their way through the forest. Dodgy, to be sure, because they couldn't go far from it lest they become lost and not find the wall of mist that would take them back to human-occupied Ireland.

The forest darkened, though the sun was still high. She looked behind for something that might look familiar from that angle and was pretty sure they'd come this way en route to the castle. She turned back, took her bearings by the hills around them, and guided her mount into the forest. Ideally, they would find a rocky spot or a shallow burn to hide their tracks and shake their pursuers. Their head start was all too short, and Lindsay hoped against hope Reubair's men would miss the spot where they'd left the forest track.

The blood on her hands was drying now and had passed from sticky to crusty. She tried to wipe the worst of it onto her dress, but it clung to her skin and wouldn't let go. As she rode, she picked flakes and bits from her fingers. She knew from experience it would take a thorough scrubbing to get it from under and around her fingernails.

It was slower going now, moving through underbrush that couldn't help but leave plenty of sign they'd passed. Finally they found a small stream with a rocky bed and followed it down, though they needed to go the other direction. The longer they kept to an unlikely heading, the less likely they would be followed. When the forest finally darkened for lack of day, Lindsay called a stop to rest for the night.

Referring to it as camp would have been overstating by far. They had no food and no way to make a fire even if they'd dared. She'd only found a spot among the trees grassy enough for the horses to graze. Patrick was silent and moved slowly, with very little energy. Alex knelt on the ground, then sat on his heels with his chin nearly to his chest. The paleness of his skin alarmed Lindsay. Dark circles under his eyes made him appear half-dead, and he pressed one arm to his belly, across his wound. It seemed at any second he might collapse entirely to the ground.

She went to Alex and made him pull up his shirt. The wound was an angry red, surrounded by inflamed tissue. But it wasn't as ugly as it had been before. A pocket of pus had collected at one end of the slit, and she made him lie down so she could lance it. He groaned, but obeyed, and she was able to poke a tiny hole to evacuate the pocket. Too bad there wasn't any alcohol. Neither did she know anything about the poultices the women at the castle liked to use. Alex was going to have to heal on his own.

The three of them lay together on the grass to keep as warm as possible while they slept. For Lindsay it was more of a light doze, for she kept one ear out for their pursuers, alert to any fidgeting from the horses. Cold crept in and took hold. As the night wore on, the three shivered and huddled into each other. Lindsay wouldn't have believed it possible to be so cold in Alex's arms, and every so often she felt for the rise and fall of his chest against her back, to know whether he was still breathing. When she slept, she had fitful nightmares of awakening to find herself in his dead embrace.

When the dew fell, Lindsay knew further sleep was hopeless. But Alex was sound asleep, his light snore loud and comforting in the silence of predawn. "Patrick?"

From the other side of Alex the priest replied in a voice
that betrayed he was wide-awake and had been for a while.
"Yes."

"We need to move along."

"We should let him sleep. He needs the rest."

Lindsay sighed and sat up. Her hair was in strings dangling from her head, and her clothes were soaked through.
Every joint in her body was stiff with cold. Though it was
still dark, she gestured to the damp air and said, "We may
be nearer the mists than we think."

"It would be better were we nearer habitation than we
think. I believe it's been more than two days since the earl
and I have eaten."

Lindsay was hungry, too, and had eaten far more recently. They needed to find food. Anything. Now she
wished for dawn, so there would be light for foraging. But
just then there wasn't even a glow on the horizon. To do
anything or go anywhere would get them lost. She ran her
fingers through her hair in a hopeless attempt to organize it
but gave up when it resisted even that gross combing.

She looked down at the shadow on the ground next to
her that was Alex and listened to him breathe. "Such a
wonderful sound," she said.

"What is?"

"Alex breathing."

Patrick's smile was audible. "He lives for you."

"Sometimes I believe that; sometimes I can't."

"I confess, my lady, I've never seen a couple such as
yourselves. Even King Robert, who is a hero to us, never
went after his captured queen the way your husband pursued you when you were taken."

"One wonders if Robert is less loving, or just smarter
than Alex."

That brought a chuckle. "There is that."

A giggle came from a patch of bracken nearby. Lindsay shivered and peered in that direction but saw only varying shadows and droplets of dew in the moonlight clinging to drooping ferns. No movement. No more sound. *Huh.*

Patrick was staring into the woods, as well. He'd heard it. She shivered again and whispered as softly as she could, "What is it?"

The shadow where he was shrugged, and they continued to peer into the darkness. Then there was a rustling. Soft, slight, a lazy movement of bracken leaves that might have been a small animal or a puff of breeze. But there was no breeze and no further rustling. Though they sat and listened until the sun was nearly up and there was plenty of light for travel, the sound never repeated. Nevertheless, it left Lindsay deeply unsettled.

They proceeded more slowly that day, unwilling to rejoin the track and unable to make their way quickly amid the trees. Navigation was a chore, for it meant finding clear spots to take bearings every so often. Guiding by the sun was difficult among the trees, but leaving the forest would have been too risky.

By noon Alex was beginning to sway in his seat. Patrick looked over, a dark, lost look of concern on his face. "He needs something other than water in his belly, or he'll die." Lindsay knew Patrick wasn't far behind. Her own stomach complained, growling an outrage the starving men had bypassed long ago. She kept an eye out for signs of people but found nothing.

Then a shadow flit past in the underbrush. She saw it only from the corner of her eye and wasn't certain she'd seen it at all. She pulled up her horse and stared at the spot and waited. Nothing moved.

Then all the hair on her arms stood on end as she realized what she was looking at. Though nothing moved, and nothing in her vision changed, she made sense out of the lines and shadows amid the bracken. A small face stared out at her, and it had been there the whole while.

Had anyone asked, she would have been tempted to say the face was brown, but really it was only a dark tan. The eyes were also brownish, a light amber color very close to the color of the creature's skin, and the shaggy mop of hair was a tawny color slightly lighter than both. The face was androgynous, and unlike any of the faeries she knew of. The Danann and Bhrochan, even the elfin Nemed, were all the palest of pale, with blossoms of pink in their cheeks. Lindsay had never seen anyone in this century so dark as this. And still. The creature had a stillness that didn't seem natural, particularly for the truly wee folk, who were usually animated in a manic sort of way.

"Hello?"

The face never moved. The eyes blinked; otherwise the face did not move a hair. Patrick stared, also unmoving.

"Who are you?" Lindsay was deeply curious, but what came first to mind was whether or not these folks had food.

Still the face said nothing.

"Can you help us?"

"Who pursues you?" The voice was high and squirrelly, clipped, and with a peculiar rhythm. Like that old television cartoon about singing chipmunks, the vowels were slightly drawn out and each word was separated by a distinct silence. As if Middle English were his or her second language and care was being taken in pronunciation.

Lindsay debated answering the question, wondering where the loyalties of this creature might lie. But then she decided they needed help and would either get it or not, according to the creature's whim. She replied, "An Reubair, lord of Castle Finias. We were his prisoners, and now we seek a way back to the world of humans."

"Humans." The tone expressed a depth of disgust Lindsay

had seen often in the wee folk. "I cannae comprehend why anyone would seek them. Filthy folk. Devious folk. *Dangerous* folk."

"I'm . . ." Lindsay thought better of what she might say, and said instead, "My husband is human." She inclined her head to the rear, where Alex leaned his head against her shoulder in a stupor.

The creature examined him with sharp eyes and said, "So he is. But you're not. You're—"

"Danann. Yes."

"And you flee Himself?"

"Reubair is not a good man."

Harsh, derisive laughter rasped the back of the nymph's throat. An Irish equivalent of "duh."

"My husband, however, is a good man. I wish him to live, and I assure you if he does he would take kindly to it and reward you handsomely."

"Easy enough to say."

"Some good people would help him to live only because it's the right thing to do."

"Are ye disparaging the goodness of my heart?"

"I only remind you of your manners. We are in desperate need of your hospitality, and he will die without it. Minding tradition would save his life. As I said, he's a good man and his life could be of value to you and your people."

" 'Tis certainly of value to you."

"I'm nothing without him."

That brought a grin filled with tiny, sharp, white teeth. "Then, by all means, we must save him to save you, Danann that ye are." The nymph nodded to the left. "Go in that direction, no more than a few paces. Ye'll find what you need there."

"Thank you."

"You'll be well advised to hurry onward once your hunger is satisfied."

"Don't worry, we have no desire to linger in your territory."

Again the creature made a throaty, disparaging noise. "I dinnae care where ye linger, and ye're welcome to dally as long as you like, but for your sake you should move along, for your pursuers are hot on your trail and will find ye here if ye dinnae move along in a hurry."

Lindsay blinked, and a charge of alarm surged through her. "Thank you again. We'll certainly heed the warning."

With that, the face ducked and disappeared. There was a slight rustle of underbrush, then silence.

Lindsay listened for a moment, to hear whether there were others of that kind, but the warning made her want to move on. She urged her horse onward in the direction indicated. Patrick followed.

A few paces, the nymph had said. But a few paces took them to a spot that didn't seem any different from where they'd just been. Thick brush. Prickly gorse, feathery bracken, tiny flowers of yellow and white and a few of purple. Lindsay felt like a fool for believing the creature had meant to help them. "I'm an idiot."

"Are you sure of that?"

She peered at Patrick. "Indeed, I am. Let's move on, before they catch up with us."

But he shook his head and declined to follow. "No. Wait. Think a moment. Do you really believe that creature was lying?"

"I see no food."

"Are you certain?"

"Do you see any?"

He looked around, and his eyes narrowed. Thinking hard. "Nothing I know of. But assume for the moment you weren't lied to. Assume our visitor meant to help. Think the best, then what do you think?"

Lindsay sighed. The best. Assume the nymph was telling

the truth. That would mean there was something edible right here before her. She looked around and saw trees, grass, and flowers. Lots and lots of tiny white flowers in bunches on stalks. They covered the area, it seemed. "What are those?"

Patrick said, "I don't know. I've seen them before, but woodland flora aren't my area of expertise. I was spawned in a town and educated on the Continent."

Lindsay was a modern Londoner and was certain she knew even less than Patrick. She disengaged herself from Alex, who then lay along the back of the charger, and slid down to kneel on the ground next to a spray of the flowers. She picked a stalk and smelled of it. Nothing discernible, so she pinched one of the flowers off and laid it on her tongue. It was bitter, and she spat it out. "It doesn't seem edible at all. Not even to someone as hungry as I am." But then she looked at the ground and wondered. She took her dagger from her belt and plunged it into the ground next to the stalk. The root came up and broke, but she persisted and dug farther down until she found a round, white knob.

Patrick said, a note of amazement in his voice, "Pignut."

"Pig what?"

"Pignut." He slid from his mount to the ground and took the root from her. After wiping the dirt from it, he popped it into his mouth for a taste. Then he nodded and grinned. "Aye. Pignut. I've eaten these, brought to me by parishioners. Come, taste." He gestured that Lindsay should eat the one in her hand. It tasted like the earth it had come from, for there was a bit of it still on the root, but she was hungry enough not to care. It was food. Patrick took her dagger and dug some more while she roused Alex enough to ease him from the horse. The area was thick with the clusters of tiny white flowers. If they hurried, they would be able to gather enough food to get them back to Ireland.

* * *

Alex wandered. So good to be able to walk without pain. To breathe clean air. To be warm again. It was nice here, wherever "here" was. A huge field, high with grass and dotted with oak trees. The scent of growing things under the sun was thick in his nose and filled his head. He seemed alone, but somehow he knew there were people nearby. Lots of people, and he wanted to see them. He looked around, but all he saw was green grass to the horizon. And trees. Not many, but a few.

Then he saw one of those trees move, and realized it wasn't that at all, but a rider on a large horse. As it approached, he saw it was a white horse and the rider a woman. He stood and watched, for he had all day. More than that, he sensed he had all of time at his disposal. While he waited, he enjoyed the feel of sunshine on his skin. He wore nothing but didn't even wonder where his clothes had gone. They were unimportant, and he was enjoying the fresh air and warmth of the sun.

The rider kicked to a gallop at the last hundred yards or so and thundered to a stop before him. Joy filled him that it was Danu. Beautiful Danu, she of the golden hair and shining eyes. But her eyes were lit with anger just then. He'd never seen her angry before and reflected blandly he'd never known she could be that way. "What are you doing here?" she demanded.

An easy smile grew on his face. He liked Danu. Usually. He replied, "Hell if I know. I just got here. Last thing I remember, I was running away from Reubair." There was a dim thought he should not be pleased to have run away, but somehow it didn't matter any more than being naked did.

"Go back."

He looked around. Green grass everywhere, and no indication of which way he'd come. "Okay. Which way?"

"Just go back. You've no business here yet."

"Why not?" He figured he wasn't the one who got

himself here, so someone must think he belonged here. "What is this place?" He liked it, wherever it was, and wasn't too enchanted with the idea of leaving it.

"'Tis the in-between world. A nether place where you dinnae belong. You'll be here long before you are expecting it, but not yet. Not today."

"I kinda like it here."

"Go back, I said."

He sighed. "Okay." He didn't have it in him to argue. Disagreement would ruin this fine day here, and he was enjoying it so. "Will I hurt again?"

The anger bled from her, and her voice filled with regret. "Aye. There's no protecting you from that. Always there will be pain there, for that is the way of things."

That was a disappointment. Then, "What about Lindsay?"

"She's the reason you need to return. She cannae live without you. Not yet, in any case."

That was both good to hear and not. He wanted her to be strong, but wanted her to need him as well. He sighed again. "And Trefor. He was left at the castle. Last we saw him, he was looking to fight Reubair. Something about Dagda, I think. Will he be all right?"

Danu ducked her head to peer into his face. "What?"

"I said he's fighting Reubair. Or was. We've been traveling awhile, I think." He wasn't sure if it had been hours or days. Maybe just minutes.

"He's fighting An Reubair? Or fought him? An Reubair lives, I can feel it."

"Then I hope Trefor got away."

"Och!" Danu's mount danced, sensing she wanted away from there, and she held it steady. "I must find him."

"Reubair?"

But she didn't answer him. She only said, "Return to your wife and the priest. Just close your eyes and think of them. I must go now." Then, without waiting for affirmation or anything else from him, she wheeled her horse and kicked away at a gallop.

Alex watched her go, then took a deep breath and raised his face to the sun. It was nice here. He didn't want to leave. But Lindsay needed him. Danu said Lindsay couldn't live without him. Not yet, anyway. And so he wished to return to the world. He closed his eyes, smiled at the warmth on his skin, then cringed at the cold and pain that followed.

"Alex?" Lindsay shook him. "Alex! Oh, God, let him be alive! *Alex!*"

He gasped and his eyes opened. Lindsay held him and burst into tears. He trembled, but he was breathing. And groaning, muttering something about sunshine in-between somewhere. She made him eat one of the pignuts, and when he realized what it was he wolfed all she had as fast as she could give them to him. She spoke to him in a low voice as he ate.

It was later that day Lindsay, Patrick, and Alex came upon the wall of mist and entered it. They'd evaded their pursuers and soon would be on the coast and headed for home.

CHAPTER 18

Trefor was summoned to the presence chamber.

He'd been in his room gathering himself and his things, ready to leave and make his way back to his men and Alex's who were with Robert in Ireland, but just as he was about to see about his horses—or someone else's if his were gone—a squire attached to Dagda came to his room with a command that he present himself to the king.

"Rats," he muttered to the messenger's back. The faerie squire turned and gawked to see where the rats were, then hurried on, puzzled, when he didn't find any. Trevor strapped on his sword and obeyed the command, though he thought seriously about simply ducking out. He didn't want anything to do with the aftermath of this mess. Especially he didn't want to hang around for Reubair's execution, for though Reubair deserved to die, there was an element of guilt on Trefor's part that he was going to die horribly. Already the castle residents were abuzz with the details of the new method of execution the Danann had picked up from the English king nearly a decade before.

Reubair and those nobles allied with him who had been arrested over the course of the afternoon were to be hung and eviscerated as traitors, their entrails burned before their eyes while still alive. Trefor's stomach turned, and he wanted away from the castle as soon as possible.

But he was stuck. To flee might bring suspicion on himself, and a pack of Dagda's knights on his trail. He found the king in Reubair's presence chamber, and noted it hadn't taken long for him to make himself comfortable. Trefor figured that was the way things were around here; in theory the king owned all the land, so he naturally felt at home everywhere. The room was jammed with courtiers, all of them visitors pledged to Dagda. Reubair's courtiers had either been rounded up or had fled for their lives. The glitter of the king's knights was far beyond even the shine of Reubair's faeries. They parted for Trefor as he entered to approach the dais. Trefor went before the king and knelt, head bowed. "Your Majesty." All eyes were on him, everyone unsmiling, and he didn't know whether he was to be hero or goat.

The king sat in Reubair's chair, lounging in a relaxed manner Trefor figured must be a lie, for he was being stitched up by a faerie seamstress. A large silver bowl filled with pink water stood on the floor at his feet, and the woman hovered over an arm laid across the arm of his chair. Blood dripped onto a puddle on the floor, and the woman's fingers were covered with it. The needle went slowly and carefully in and out of Dagda's skin, and his nostrils flared with each stab. But his voice remained steady and his breaths even.

With a languid gesture, Dagda ordered Trefor to rise. The king seemed fully recovered of his wits after his near assassination, but Trefor didn't imagine it could be so simple. The king would need to appear unruffled whether he was or not, or risk losing the respect of his followers, a vulnerability nobody could afford. Sitting in the chair that earlier in the day had been occupied by Reubair, he seemed to have a core of steel and the calm of a summer's day. He said, however, in a tone of utter sincerity, "I owe my life to you."

Relief flooded Trefor. Hero, not goat. He resisted a smile and said in all seriousness, "I pledged my allegiance to you; it was my duty. Even if it meant taking a bul . . . uh, a bolt . . . Reubair's dagger for you."

"You've proven yourself valuable to me, Sir Trefor. Continue to be valuable, and I will reward you accordingly."

Trefor took a deep breath. Robert sprung to mind. Trefor's hopes had been set on maneuvering himself into the notice of the human king as his father had. It was mental whiplash to realize he'd just done that very thing with the Danann king. Never mind how he felt about faeries, he could no longer deny he was one.

Dagda continued, "Follow the example of An Reubair, however, and you'll find yourself in similar straits. I will not tolerate those who stray from me. Or from Danu."

A frisson of apprehension regarding the goddess skittered up Trefor's spine, but he shook it off and focused on the matter at hand. Then there was Lindsay. For a second or two he wondered whether she would be proud of him, but he told himself it didn't matter.

Another second, and all hell broke loose.

A voice from the door caught the attention of everyone in the room. "Majesty! Majesty, An Reubair has escaped!" The messenger shoved his way through the crowd in a hurry, shouting the whole way. "Reubair has killed his guard and has escaped to the countryside! He's taken all the other prisoners with him as well."

Dagda made no move, but cursed the name of An Reubair and all his descendants to seven generations. "Which direction did he take?"

The breathless messenger said, "He's not disguised his

intent to seek refuge with Nemed. He's gone straight as an arrow to the north."

Dagda looked to Trefor with a bland gaze. "Sir Trefor, it would seem you've another chance to prove yourself, and so soon after gaining my favor."

Trefor's heart sank. He wasn't ready for this, and wouldn't want it if he had been. "I've got no men with me. They're fighting elsewhere." And painfully few, as well.

"Take some of mine." The king pointed out five knights standing nearby and ordered them to bring with them their squires. To Trefor he said, "By my reckoning, that will give you close to thirty men-at-arms to find your fugitive. Lead them well. Go straight to Nemed's lands, and hope Reubair delays himself by attempting to throw you from his trail along the way. He won't, though. I assure you he'll go at speed for as long as his horse holds out."

Nemed. Trefor had heard stories about that guy, none of them pleasant. But he didn't flinch. Couldn't let Dagda see him hesitate. He turned to the king and said, "Aye, Your Majesty. And thank you."

Dagda waved him off, and Trefor left the room with an air of determination he did not feel.

It was no trick to follow Reubair. He made no secret of his destination, and plainly was depending on his head start and speed to elude pursuit. Trefor took his band of faerie knights after him at a dead run, in hopes of overtaking the fugitive.

But after only a few hours' travel, just the other side of a ford that crossed a river unfamiliar to Trefor, a gut instinct made him pull up short and halt his men. They stopped on the track, and Trefor put up a hand to still them. He sniffed the air and found something funky about it he couldn't quite identify. Then he dismounted and felt of the ground. There was no sound, no smell, but there was a miasma in the air. The elf was near; Trefor could sense the evil.

Though he'd never met Nemed, he knew enough about the ancient king to understand the malevolent intent, the anger, the hatred he felt in this place.

"Go back," he said to his knights and remounted. "It's too late. Reubair has found his sanctuary." They turned and signaled the rest of the men to return across the ford.

A whoop and holler went up from inside a stand of trees upslope to the north. Trefor wheeled to find several hundred Danann and human knights thundering down upon them. His mount lunged and reared. His heart leapt to his throat, and he suddenly was certain this was his day to die. But he wheeled his mount, drew his sword, and shouted to his knights to attack, for they were caught against the river and would be shredded in the slow crossing of the ford, with their backs to the enemy. Trefor intended that his men shouldn't be asked to die while fleeing, and if he was doomed, he was going to take Reubair down first. He kicked his mount to a gallop and led the charge.

The onslaught was quick and terrifying, the faerie swords slashing at each other like polished silver fangs. Trefor's company rode into the midst of Reubair's and clashed with a ringing of swords and bellowing of voices. Trefor searched the melee for his enemy and found the tall, blond faerie coming at him. He kicked his mount forward and swung his sword hard. Reubair's rang off his as they passed each other, then whirled for another try. Trefor closed on Reubair and engaged him, trying to unhorse him. He wanted Reubair on the ground, and wanted to pin him to it with his weapon.

But then Reubair broke away and fled to the trees at a gallop. Trefor followed, blindly, like a fool. Anger reddened his vision, and all he could think of was how this guy had compromised and abused his mother. As far as Trefor was concerned, Reubair was a dead man. They blew past trees and leapt bushes of gorse and bracken in their race.

There was a large clearing within the forest, shaggy with new grass and dotted with bare rock. Reubair reined in and wheeled to face Trefor in the center of it. Trefor also reined in, for he saw what stood behind the suddenly bold Reubair.

It was the evil itself. Nemed, he was certain of it. Red eyes glowed from beneath a hooded cloak. His horse was huge and black, a stallion standing as cool as a cat but alert for commands from his master. The miasma was so strong, Trefor could barely breathe, and for a moment he had an urge to wheel and spur his horse in retreat. But he held his ground and faced Nemed and Reubair.

Reubair said, "Fool."

"I'm not the one who just lost all my holdings."

The faerie flushed at that, and his lips pressed together. He spurred his horse and came at Trefor with his sword. Trefor fended, but just barely, and he sidled his horse around to face Reubair. Then another quarter turn to keep Nemed in sight as well. "I'll kill you." Reubair spat the words with all the venom at his command.

"He'll kill me." Trefor indicated Nemed with a toss of his head. "But only after I've cut your throat."

The dull light in Reubair's eyes said he knew what Trefor said was probably true. He wore no armor and wasn't well armed, where Trefor was fully equipped. He blinked sweat from his eyes, then wiped his forehead with his sleeve and said, "I want to know why. Why did you do it? What did you gain by it?"

"Lindsay. You shouldn't have messed with her." He spun his sword in a threatening mulinette.

Now puzzlement deepened. Aristocratic contempt came over Reubair's entire frame, and he straightened in his saddle. "Your cousin? You are about to die, you know. You've given up your life for the sake of someone who not only is just a woman, but isn't even particularly—"

"His mother."

Reubair looked to Nemed. "His what?"

The elf's voice cut through the air in the clearing like a claymore. "Lindsay MacNeil is his mother."

Reubair peered at Trefor, even more baffled. "That's not possible."

"This man was conceived less than two years ago, and born seven centuries from now."

High pique and confusion brought a tone of irritation to Reubair's voice. "Nonsense. You talk like a Bhroch—" Then it clicked, and a light of understanding sparked in his eyes. He said to Trefor, "Ah. A changeling returns to his family and finds it not what it might have been. I see." An ugly grin splashed across his face. Trefor wanted to take Reubair's head and stick it on a spike. The horse between his knees danced with the tension in them as Trefor watched for a chance to charge. The blond faerie continued, his contempt thickening, "Is your mother from the other time as well? Your father? That could explain much."

Trefor's reply was to raise his sword and spur his horse forward. But before his mount could even lunge, Nemed held up a palm and the world froze solid with noise and pain. Trefor screamed, but the sound couldn't leave him. It stuck in his chest and shook his frame so that his bones rattled in agony.

Reubair laughed, a long, loud guffaw. Then with a leisurely flourish, he approached with his sword. One mulinette to the side, and he hauled back to give Trefor the death stroke.

But the sword fell from his gauntleted hand and thudded to the grass below. His arm went limp at his side. He spun, and from the corner of his vision Trefor saw a shining figure astride a white horse. A woman, light of hair and dressed in a gown of ancient style that glowed a pale blue. One hand was poised in a gesture Trefor recognized as warning. A spell was ready, and she threatened to use it. By the trembling of that arm, he could tell she was already spending a great deal of power on the one that had stopped Reubair's sword arm.

"Cease!" she called out.

"Danu, leave this place!" Nemed spoke to her like a disobedient child who just wouldn't follow orders.

"You'll not murder him!" The goddess was grim. Determined to stop this conflict.

"He's mine now. I'll kill him if I like."

"He'll never be yours, Nemed."

"My lands—"

"My blood!" She shouted now at full voice, anger straining it. "My blood, you beast! Leave him be, or I'll make certain you and the entire memory of your race are blotted from human thought."

"You think—"

"It's all you've got, Nemed! Some land and a bit of notoriety. Take it and get away from here. And take your dogs with you. They blight the countryside." She indicated with her chin Reubair, who sat his horse, unable to use either arm so long as she held her spell.

"I've more land than—"

"I said get out! You've taken on more trouble than you know. More trouble than you'll ever truly want, in any case. I know you, Nemed. You're lazy. Too lazy to stand up to what would descend on you, should you kill this boy today."

There was silence as Nemed considered these words. Reubair looked to him, a frown darkening his face, then at Trefor, still gripped by Nemed's spell. Then the agony ceased, and Trefor collapsed over the neck of his horse. Bile tried to rise, but he swallowed hard and held his breath until the need passed. Then he gasped for air and struggled to see straight, through the remaining ache. His body felt as if it had been yanked apart by a giant hand.

Reubair looked to the ground, then at Danu. "My sword?"

"Return for it later. Leave now, and allow Sir Trefor and his surviving men safe passage home."

Reubair gazed at the sword, as if debating the value of attempting to recover it anyway, then at Danu, then took his reins and spurred his horse toward Nemed, past him and on into the trees.

Nemed gazed blandly at Danu for a moment, then without a word followed his vassal.

Trefor pushed himself erect in his saddle to address Danu, but she was gone. He looked around the clearing but found nobody. His stomach heaved again, and this time he vomited onto the ground beside his horse. Then he slipped his sword into the ring on his belt, spat on the ground once more, and returned to his men.

It was nearly morning when the exhausted and decimated company belonging to Dagda stumbled through the portcullis of Castle Finias. They were received at the stable, and the knights went to barracks or keep according to their status with the king. Trefor went directly to the presence chamber, though his greatest desire was to crawl into bed and stay there. He wasn't even hungry. Too tired to eat.

Dagda wasn't there, but the guard on watch had orders to wake him on Trefor's return, and Trefor was immediately escorted to the guest chamber near the top of the keep. There he found the king just risen, rumpled from sleep and wearing only an unbelted silk tunic. The bandages on his arms were dotted with blood. He stood by the washstand, splashing water on his face, and a knight stood by with a towel for drying.

"You failed to capture An Reubair?"

"He gained sanctuary with Nemed, who responded with a force of several hundred." He wasn't going to mention the conversation with Danu and Nemed.

"Casualties?"

"Eight dead, three dying, seven wounded who will live."

Dagda grunted and nodded. "Thirty against hundreds. They're brave men."

"It was a tactical error. I should have sent a scout over the ford. I should have smelled the trap. I was in too much of a hurry to catch up with him."

Dagda considered that for a moment, then nodded. "Perhaps. Then perhaps if you'd dawdled he would have simply gotten away, in any case."

Trefor allowed as that was true.

"Be that as it may," continued Dagda, "I'm moved to reward bravery and loyalty. Other men could learn by your example." He glanced around at the stone walls of the room and added, "Also, I find myself with lands in need of a lord. Lands remote from the place I would center my own life."

The faerie lands? "You wish to confiscate Castle Finias from Nemed?"

A shadow crossed Dagda's eyes. "The elf has shown himself not a good choice to husband this part of my realm. I intend to relieve him of half these lands. That half, including this garrison, I will award to you."

Trefor couldn't help his jaw dropping open, but then he shut it again in a hurry. Then he opened it to say something, but whatever it had been fled his mind and he was left speechless once more. He clapped his mouth shut. Dagda smiled at his discomfort.

"Stop gaping like a trout. If you're to be laird of this realm, you'll need to learn the art of rule."

"Aye, Your Majesty."

"There will be a formal announcement of my decision at supper in the Great Hall this evening. You will preside over the meal as my host. Then, tomorrow, you will commence to organize your garrison and man it with your own household knights. At least a hundred, and as many as two hundred if you've the income for it."

Trefor boggled, for he had never commanded more than fifty of Alex's men and ten of his own. But he said only, "Aye, Your Majesty."

"Now go, claim your bedchamber." He indicated the master's chamber, the only room above his own. "Get some sleep, and I'll see you at board."

Trefor could only say, "Aye, Your Majesty. And thank you."

"Nonsense. I expect a dutiful vassal out of you." His voice carried the threat of what would happen to Trefor if he proved otherwise. Trefor nodded and withdrew.

Tired, hungry, and bowled over by his sudden good fortune, Trefor went to the bedchamber Reubair had once occupied with Trefor's mother. It smelled of Reubair, and he hoped he wasn't detecting Lindsay as well. He noted the closet bed and opened the door of it to see it had been slept in. Good. As he unloaded his weapons onto the table and began to shed his gauntlets, surcoat, and armor, he finally thought about something besides his failure to capture the faerie, and that was to wonder if Lindsay and Alex had made it away from this place. He'd not heard anything, so he figured no news was good news, and the longer it took for Reubair's pursuing faeries to return and discover their master was no longer in residence, the better the chance his parents had made it to human-occupied Ireland.

A knock came on the door, and before he could go to open it a servant entered and bowed low. It was Reubair's human valet. He looked up from his bow, his eyes filled with one question. Trefor answered that question unasked.

"Serve me well and you may stay." He wasn't ready to give a faerie free run of his bedroom yet, and so was glad to have this guy stay on.

The valet bowed quickly again, with a sigh of relief. "Thank you, sir." Then he stood and continued, "A visitor to see you, sir."

"Who is it?"

"The Lady Morag, sir."

Lady. Right. But Trefor only said, "Show her in."

Morag entered, fully clothed and rather ladylike in spite of herself, a smile on her face. In fact, she appeared downright demure in one of the finely made outfits she'd previously worn for Dagda. Her beauty touched him in his most sensitive places, and his heart clenched that she was such a whore.

He said, "All out of magic? Nothing left for popping in and out?"

The enthusiasm in her eyes lost its edge, but she maintained her smile. "I come to present myself formally."

"Why?"

"As I said before, I wish to be your consort. Not to put too fine a point on it."

"Yeah, that's you. Straightforward without fail. Honest as the day is long." The heavy sarcasm was not lost on her, and the smile faltered.

"Do ye not agree I should be by your side?"

"No, I do not agree." He turned to continue making himself comfortable, shrugged his hauberk over his head, and dumped it on the table with a crash of metal links, then added sharply, "Not to put too fine a point on it."

Now Morag's expression was sincere. Anger burned in her eyes. "And why not?"

His weight shifted with irritation, and with a nod he indicated the chamber below the floor. "Does His Majesty know you're here? Am I about to be hauled away as a traitor for banging the king's mistress?"

"As I've said before, we're not married. Dagda cares nothing of who I 'bang,' as you say. 'Tis not as if any child of mine would be his heir."

He eyed her for a moment, then said, " 'Tis not as if you would ever have a child, I think."

"I would have yours."

"And a DNA test, for me to believe it."

She frowned, puzzled, but he waved away the comment rather than explain. He considered shining her with a lie that would salve her pride and make it easier to get her to leave, but a perverse desire to see her suffer made him tell the blunt truth. "I don't trust you, Morag. I haven't trusted you for a long time. I think from the very beginning you've been hustling me—"

"Hustling?"

"Leading me on. Steering me in directions that suit you and your agenda."

"I've guided you in the way you should go. You shouldn't complain. You've gained property. A place in the world."

"Why me? I'm not so powerful."

"Who else but you?"

"I was malleable."

"You were destined."

"You believe that crap?"

"Of course I do. You can see, it has come true, what Brochan said."

"You've lied to me, and told me what you wanted me to hear. You manipulated me so I would commit murder. It's only because I saw what you were doing that I was able to keep from assassinating the king." It still rattled him that he'd nearly done it.

"You were never supposed to kill him."

Trefor blinked, stunned. "Then what was all that about, with the 'He needs killing' stuff?"

She smiled, as if talking to a fool. "You were never destined to kill the Dagda. We all knew that."

"Brochan said I was."

"Brochan said only that your destiny lay with Dagda. He never once said you were to kill him."

Trefor frowned with concentration, thinking back, and

realized she was telling the truth. Brochan had never said anything about killing. "But you did."

"Because I wished you to do it. I still think he needs killing, and you'll regret not doing it. Whether it was your destiny—or still is—is another matter entirely."

"If I'd killed Dagda I wouldn't have been awarded Castle Finias."

"Of course you would. It was your destiny. I told you that. Regardless of what you might have done, or whom you might have killed, the Castle was bound to be yours. And I'll point out that it was not your destiny to murder the king yesterday, and so you did aught but what was in store for you."

"I did what I thought was right."

"It was what you were made for. You wouldnae have had it in you to commit cold-blooded murder."

"I could have told you that." A lie, for even he hadn't known it wasn't in him until the time had come.

Morag gazed at him for a moment, as if assessing his words, then said, "Perhaps. In any case, your destiny was in place and there was naught for you to do but follow it."

Trefor opened his mouth for a denial, but there was no argument to be found. Nothing he'd done contradicted Brochan's prophesy. As far as he could see, the prediction had come true. It was a terrible realization. The universe seemed to close in on him, binding him to a belief he didn't want. If his entire life was already written, then what was the point of living it?

He turned his back on Morag and made like he was examining his new quarters. "So, to reply to your offer, I don't want you here." He picked up a silver candlestick holding a burnt stub of candle and turned it over in his hands. "I said I don't trust you, and I meant that."

"You trust Deirbhile more?"

He gave her a sharp glance. He'd not thought of Deir-

bhile but once since leaving Tiree, but on hearing her name
a warmth surged through him. *Deirbhile*. He'd like to see
her pretty face again.

"Aye," whispered Morag to herself. "He's in love."

"Don't be ridiculous."

"Ridiculous, indeed. She's planning to cuckold her husband; there's a trustworthy wench. One wonders if any of
her children will look like him."

"On the contrary, she said she had no intention of bearing any children but his."

"Easier said than accomplished, and that from one who
knows how to accomplish it."

Trefor shrugged, deeply uncomfortable with the way
this discussion was going. "In any case, she's irrelevant.
She's betrothed, and that's that."

"And you're not man enough to take her from her intended, though she loves him not."

"She can learn to love Wonder Boy."

"Why would she, when she not only believes it impossible, she thinks it a bad idea."

"And why should you care what happens to her? Or to
me, for that matter?"

"Ye dinnae believe I love you?"

"No."

"Then it would be a waste of breath to tell you otherwise, wouldn't it? Nevertheless, I cannae stand here and let
you think you're finished with Herself."

"I thought I was."

"I assure you, you're not."

He considered that for a moment. Fate again? Or did
she simply see something in his demeanor? Then he said,
"Is that your opinion, or is this more of Brochan's bogus
prophesy?"

Now she smiled, a sly look he disliked. "Free will. If
you would persist in believing you control your destiny,

then why do you want to know what Brochan has to say?"

He pressed his lips together. Smart-ass bitch.

She continued, "I suggest you go to her and find out which it is. It'll take aught but a month or two to determine the truth in this. Meanwhile, I'm certain things here will sort themselves out without your assistance."

For a long moment he gazed at her, ideas tumbling in his mind. Was she trying to manipulate him? Of course she was. But which way? Did she want him to go to Deirbhile or stay here? There was no telling.

Then he realized that caring what she wanted him to do was exactly what she wanted him to do. So he stopped. He considered what *he* wanted to do. That was the important thing. And he wanted to go to Tiree. He wanted to see Deirbhile again, while she was still unmarried.

He decided he would leave in the morning.

To Lindsay it was strange to think of Eilean Aonarach as home. During the past several years she had thought of this century as nothing more than the place she was bound to live if she wanted to stay with Alex. But the sight of granite walls clinging to the high cliffs over the castle quay brought a sense of shelter she'd not had since leaving her flat in twenty-first-century London.

Safe within the laird's bedchamber carved into the mountainside, she attended to Alex, who sat in the large, wooden chair by the fire. He was stronger now that he was eating every day. Color had returned to his cheeks, and on his return he had been able to climb the steps from the barbican. Slowly, but under his own steam at least, and that was important progress. Now he lounged by his fire and gazed into it, deep thoughts smoldering in his eyes as Lindsay heated some spiced wine in a pot on the hook over the hearth.

She was afraid to speak. Her thoughts turned with Reubair. What she'd done, what she'd nearly done, what she still felt, to her great shame. Alex could never know. He could know Jenkins had raped her, for that was only her body. But he could never know she'd desired Reubair. Ever. She looked over at her husband, whose gaze into the fire smoldered like the embers there.

"What are you thinking?" she asked.

He glanced at her, then back at the fire, and she wasn't sure he intended to reply. But then he said, "Trefor came."

She nodded. "He did."

"Why would he do that? He wanted to get next to Robert; now he's blown that."

"Are you angry that he reneged on his promise to represent you?"

He shot her a puzzled look. "No, why would I be? He made it possible for us to escape, and he stayed behind. God knows what's happened to him. He should have caught up to us by now. They may have killed him."

"Or not." Lindsay had seen how well Trefor got along with Reubair. Trusting his motives came hard. "If he's alive but not coming here, then where is he? In cahoots with one of the faeries? Nemed?" He was her son, but she'd not raised him. What God, and only God, knew was whether Trefor was to be trusted at the end of the day. And Alex could never know the thing Trefor had seen in her.

"He saved our lives. I think he's proven himself."

"We'll see." Lindsay smoothed the shaggy hair away from Alex's forehead. His eyes closed, tired.

"We'll trust him if he's dead?"

"We'll trust him if he returns to us and takes his place as your knight." God willing, that would never happen.

Alex uttered a noncommittal grunt.

"I suppose it will be a while before you'll be charging off to war again."

Again Alex grunted and stared into the fire.

"You'll need someone to run things around here while you recover."

"I'm not that sick."

"You don't want to overtax yourself."

"I said I'm not that sick, and most of my men are still in Ireland. Without me."

"I could take over command of your knights when they return. You know I can do it. I got us out of Finias. I deserve to be taken seriously."

He looked over at her, then back at the fire again. A long sigh eased from him. "Talk it up around the fire at night. Tell the tale, and make it good. Lie a little; they all do it themselves, and it's expected. If you don't brag, they'll think you have no confidence."

"I know the drill. I've been there."

His gaze turned on her, and it wasn't unsympathetic. "You hid in disguise. You're wearing a skirt now, for which there is no drill in this. You're in unknown territory, and you've got to make it look better than good. You've got to be perfect, or they'll destroy you. Then they'll start on me."

"So, you're saying you'll let me be your second?" She came to kneel between his knees.

"Aye. I know I'll regret it, but I can see you're not going to accept any other answer."

Lindsay kissed him, then smiled, for he was right.